The Spinster's Scandalous Betrothal

A Clean Regency Romance Novel

Emily Barnet

D1739117

Table of Contents

Chapter 1

Belinda sat on a stone bench in the garden of Payton House, listening to the sounds around her. Murmuring voices made a distant backdrop to the sound of bees in the lavender and the tinkling fountain. She breathed deeply, drawing the scent of roses and wet earth into her lungs. The murmured conversation she could hear was coming from the terrace just a few feet away. She listened distantly, shutting her green eyes for a moment at the pain of a headache that stabbed through her temple.

"...and the benches will have to be moved and cleaned. The terrace needs sweeping."

"Yes, my lady."

Belinda tensed as she heard her mother's voice instructing the maids. The pain in her head increased, the sound reminding her that they were cleaning for the evening ball. The whole morning and afternoon had been taken up with preparation, and, when not actually preparing, then they were talking about it and planning it. Belinda ran a hand through her thick honey-blonde hair, rubbing her aching temples.

"Aldrige? Where is Estelle?" Mama called, asking Papa a question.

"She's upstairs, Philipa. I assume that's where she's supposed to be."

Belinda knew her parents were tense, despite their best attempts not to be—their tight, strained voices indicated their mood without their being able to conceal it. Their tension was affecting the entire household. She looked around her, focusing instead on the flowers that grew in the flowerbed behind the hedge.

"I'll need two more of those," she decided, bending down to the lobelias that flowered at the edge of the bed. Their blue color would not keep when they were pressed, she knew that from experience, but still they were so beautiful that she could not resist picking two more.

She added them to her basket, gazing down at her collection. She had made it her intent to press at least one specimen of every spring flower on the estate, and she was getting

3

close to achieving her objective, at least for all the flowers that bloomed in May. She looked down at her basket, her thoughts of her hobby taking her mind off her tension.

"My lady?" the voice of Miss Stirling, one of the housemaids, distracted her.

"What is it?" she called back as the woman rounded the corner, her black uniform in high contrast with the white stone that paved the path, her cheeks flushed and her black hair escaping her cap.

"Your mother was calling for you, my lady," Miss Stirling said. "She's in the ballroom. If you might come soon, my lady?"

"Of course," Belinda replied softly.

She stood up, collecting her basket from where it rested on the bench and walked back towards the house.

The ball for which they had prepared for so much of the day—and for the preceding weeks—was her sister Estelle's debut ball. Belinda gazed at the shadows that were lengthening on the lawn, guessing it to be around five o' clock. The ball would commence in just two hours' time. Her mother had insisted on a larger meal than usual at tea, so that they might be sustained through the evening, but Belinda had barely had an appetite. She was more nervous about the ball than she cared to admit. Her fear was not only for Estelle, who was coming out into society, just turned seventeen. It was for herself. This was her first ball in eight years.

Please, she prayed silently as she neared the terrace, her basket over her arm, her cream-colored dress stained at the hem from the garden. *Please, let Estelle's first ball be wonderful.*

Her own debut in society had been terrible. It had, in fact, been so terrible that, this year, she and her family would not be attending Almack's for Estelle's ball because Belinda could not go there. They were holding the ball at Payton House, the family's estate just two miles from London. Belinda's father was the Earl of Grayleigh, but even he, despite all his influence, could not change matters.

"Belinda! Oh, Belinda. There you are. I'm so glad."

Belinda looked up as her mother called her from the terrace. She was hurrying towards her, evidently concerned, and when she saw her, she slowed down her steps, walking down the path.

4

Mama's soft oval face was tense, but it relaxed as she came to join Belinda.

Belinda studied her face, trying to guess what was troubling her. Her mother's eyes were wide and long lashed, like Belinda's own, except that Mama's were brown. Their soft oval faces were identical in shape, like their mouths, which were generous bows of pink. Belinda's mother had graying honey-brown hair which she wore covered by a fashionable turban-style headdress in deference to her married status, though a few curls escaped to touch her cheek. She looked worried.

"What is it, Mama?" Belinda asked softly as her mother came to join her.

"Estelle is distressed," Mama said gently. "She was getting ready and she's so scared, poor dear. She doesn't want to come out of her chamber. Perhaps you could talk with her?" she asked with a small smile.

"I can try," Belinda answered quietly.

"Thank you, dear." Mama smiled at her, looking up. Belinda was not much taller than average, but her mother was short, as was Estelle. Belinda smiled affectionately.

"I'll try and help her," she repeated gently. "I hope I can."

"Good. The poor girl. Of course, every girl is scared on the eve of her debut ball, so it's quite natural," Mama replied softly.

"That's true," Belinda agreed. She did not tell Mama, but she did wonder if it was her own story that had scared Estelle so.

She wandered into the house, pausing to put her basket of flowers on the table in the entrance. The butler would have it taken to the drawing-room before the flowers wilted. She would check if he placed them in a vase of water before she went to dress.

She reached her sister's room and paused outside the door.

"Estelle?" she called through the wood.

"Please, just go?" Estelle called back. "I don't want to come out. I can't do it, sister. I just can't." Her voice was tight and strained.

"You can, dear," Belinda answered softly. "I promise you can. It will be well." Her voice was low, reassuring.

"I can't do it. I'm scared," Estelle insisted. "And I feel nauseous. I can't go tonight."

5

Belinda took a deep breath, her heart twisting in sympathy. Her own debut had been nothing like this—but then, her own debut had been truly horrible. She pushed aside her thoughts of it and called her sister's name gently through the door.

"Estelle?"

She waited, hearing nothing. As she was about to turn away, thinking of fetching a soothing tea from the kitchen to help her sister with her nausea, she heard Estelle.

"Belinda?" she called nervously. "I want to talk."

Belinda's heart lifted as the door opened. Estelle appeared in the gap, her pale hair, styled in an elaborate style, lit from behind by the candle-lamps, her face white with fear.

"Estelle," Belinda murmured, smiling at her lovingly.

"Belinda. I can't do this," Estelle murmured back, standing back so that Belinda could go into the room. "I'm so scared. It's going to be horrible. What if I make a fool of myself?"

She shut the door behind Belinda. She was close to tears; it was audible in her voice. Belinda took a deep breath.

"Sweet sister," she said gently. "It will all be well. There's nothing you can do wrong. This is your first ball. Everyone will admire you. You will be the most sought-after girl in that room."

Estelle giggled. "Really?"

Belinda nodded, smilingly. Estelle was the image of a lovely young lady on the brink of her debut. Shorter than Belinda, with pale hair that had a slight wave and with their mother's hazel eyes, she had a long, thin face, more like Father's, and a slender, delicate form. She gazed up at Belinda with a mix of surprise and hesitance.

"I promise," Belinda said firmly. "You can do nothing wrong in there. Even if you eat the candlesticks."

Estelle chuckled delightedly. "Imagine if I did!"

Belinda laughed too. "Well, there you are. I don't imagine that you would, and even *that* would not make people think badly of you tonight."

Estelle smiled, then a small frown appeared on her brow. "But, what about when...?"

Belinda tensed. "Yes, I know," she murmured.

She knew that Estelle wanted to ask her about her own debut—about what had happened and what she had done. Belinda swallowed hard at the thought. She'd worn a lovely white gown, much like Estelle's, with her hair set in a beautiful style, and she'd danced with poise. It had not been her fault that she was barred from ever attending Almack's Assembly rooms again. It was Lord Rawlinson.

She shuddered. Even thinking about him made her feel nauseous. He had seemed so polite, so mannerly. But then, when they had been just a few moments alone in the garden, he had tried to force a kiss on her. And when she had refused, when she had evaded him and run back into the hall, he had told everyone that he had done much more than kissed her. He had made up such shocking stories that she had never been able to show her face in high society again, and the lady patrons of Almack's had taken her voucher away.

Having one's voucher confiscated meant that one could not purchase tickets for any of the balls and parties held at Almack's Assembly Rooms. Not being able to attend Almack's was the worst punishment that the Ton could inflict—it ostracized one, barring one from the most important social events.

She had done nothing, and yet she was punished, while he—blessedly—was given a commission in the army by his uncle and set sail to serve the East India Company.

"You are sure it will all be well?" Estelle murmured. Her soft words brought Belinda's thoughts back to the moment.

Belinda sighed. She felt relieved her sister had not pressed her to tell her what happened. Nobody had told Estelle the details, but she knew that her sister was barred from Almack's, because that was why her debut could not be held there.

"Yes, I'm quite sure," Belinda said gently. "I'm very certain that you will be the loveliest debutante this season."

"Oh, sister. You are a dear," she said lovingly. She grinned. "You're the best sister in the world."

The words twisted her heart. "You are too, dear."

Estelle giggled. "Mayhap I'll attend this ball after all," she reflected a little nervously. She reached for Belinda's hand. "And mayhap we shall both have a lovely evening, sister. After all, there will be lots of people. Maybe you will also meet someone who will take your fancy." She grinned at Belinda.

"Mayhap," Belinda said lightly. Estelle did not fully understand the level of disgrace that had been laid on her older

7

sister. She had never been told the whole story, after all. The disgrace was so complete that Belinda could not enter society again. This would be her first ball in years.

Estelle went to the door, her long white dress shimmering in the light. It was pure white silk, the sleeves delicate puffs, the high waistband decorated with silver thread. Estelle had insisted that she wanted no brilliants sewn on the gown—nothing fancy, she had declared, but then she needed nothing fancy, Belinda thought lovingly, to make her shine. Estelle paused in the doorway, turning to Belinda, her loose ringlets framing her face, which was partly cast in shadow in the low candle-light in the room.

"I will go down to Papa," she said gently to Belinda. "When you are ready will you come down too?" She sounded as though she longed for Belinda to join her.

Belinda nodded. "Of course," she said lightly.

She went to her chamber to dress, sure that there would be nobody there for her to meet, and with her stomach tying itself in knots for fear of her first ball for eight long years.

Chapter 2

"I know. I know," Benedict murmured gently as he scratched the black, furry ears of his wolfhound, Rowan. He breathed out deeply. "It's my mood that's making you so worried, old boy."

There was no reason for Rowan to be distressed—the fire burned brightly in the grate even though it was not particularly cold. Rowan had eaten his usual meal that morning, and he had taken a walk about the estate grounds with Benedict twice—first in the morning and then at teatime. Despite that, the huge black hound could not find rest, standing and walking to the fire and then back to his place by Benedict's desk every few minutes. There was only one reason for such distress, and that was that he could sense Benedict was showing discomfort.

"And I have reason, old chap," he told his canine companion with a sigh. The reason was simple—his sister had insisted on attending the coming-out ball of an acquaintance, and that meant that Benedict had to chaperone her.

He hated it.

He shut his dark eyes for a moment, letting his head sink back onto the backrest of the chair. He had not attended any balls the previous Season, and the one before that he had attended only five at his mother's insistence. His fear of being in society was so great that he would have done the same thing this year, except for Nancy's need for a chaperone. Mama could chaperone her, but Benedict did not trust her to keep a good watch over Nancy.

He knew he should be getting ready—it was an hour before the ball. He felt his stomach twist uncomfortably.

His thoughts wandered to his last ball. He'd stayed only as long as necessary and spent most of the evening watching the rest of the guests, not talking to anyone. His mother had berated him, saying that he was not doing what he should as a Duke—which seemed strange, since none of his ducal duties seemed to include dancing or polite chats.

It's not easy, he wanted to shout at his mother. *Not when you are like me.*

He ran a hand down his face. He could feel his firm jaw, his long nose. His face was chiseled, and his jaw square, his eyes dark.

He had never thought that he looked anything less than handsome, but ever since he was a boy his companions at Eton had taunted him mercilessly. More than his appearance, they had mocked his ready temper, which flared with their taunts.

And, he thought sadly, *perhaps they were not wrong. The whole of the* Ton *thinks me a beast.*

He let out a long sigh. Eton was many years ago. He was two-and-thirty years old, and he should forget all that. His mother always said that it was just all childish nonsense. But whenever he had to enter society, the cruel mocking words whispered through his mind, and he could not face anyone. Nonsense, she might call it, but it had left an indelible mark.

"Brother? Benedict!"

Nancy's voice interrupted his thoughts. His hound was already at the door, bounding over to greet his sister as she knocked at the study entrance.

"Brother? Are you there?"

"I am," he called, already standing to open the door, but Nancy pushed it open, her delicate, heart-shaped face appearing in the doorway. She beamed up at him and he felt his heart melt. There were very few beings in the world who made him smile— Rowan was one, Nancy another. They were the only creatures he trusted, with whom he could share his thoughts even a little.

His younger sister crossed the floor and moved to his desk, her long dark hair swaying where it hung loose about her face. He guessed she had been getting ready for the ball, though she still wore her long cream-colored day dress.

"Benedict," she asked softly. "Can I stay a while?"

"With gladness."

She settled into the chair opposite his at his big writing-desk, looking artlessly up at him.

"Will there be a great deal of people there tonight?" she asked, sounding more curious than afraid.

"Mayhap not," he answered levelly. He hoped not. The ball was to be a private ball at a family house, not a coming-out ball at Almack's, which was unusual. Nancy's ball last week had been at Almack's, which had made it hard since all of the *Ton* were there. A private ball might be smaller, more exclusive. He hoped so.

"Mama said to guard myself and not speak to simply

everyone," she told him, a frown creasing her brows. Benedict sighed.

"Mama can be a little too careful sometimes," he told her, but at the same time, he felt himself frown too. His worry had been that his mother would throw Nancy at every eligible man at the ball, and so Nancy reporting on her caution sounded strange. He tilted his head, thoughtful.

"She said that I should be aware of my reputation as a young lady, and the sister of a Duke," Nancy began, and Benedict felt himself tense.

"It's not about..." he was about to say, trying to explain that it wasn't her behavior he was worried about, but the behavior of others, and that she needed not to discipline herself, but simply to take care of herself, when his mother appeared in the doorway. Tall, like Benedict and Nancy, she had a thin, delicate face. Her hair was dark brown, gray strands like silver running through its elaborately styled length. She wore it covered with the briefest of widow's veils, and her dress, in dark navy blue, was likewise a symbol of mourning, though Benedict's father had passed away a decade before. Benedict suspected she had maintained the mourning colors because they suited her, but he would never have said so, since she would likely be offended, and her temper was as quick as his was.

"Nancy! There you are," Mama declared. "I was looking for you everywhere."

"I just wanted to talk to Benedict about the ball. I'm so glad we're going," Nancy gushed. "I can't wait to wear my gown! And Emilia will be there, and Julia, and everyone I know." She smiled brightly. Her manner seemed a little tense to Benedict, who was familiar with her usual moods.

"Good. Good, daughter," Mama said lightly. "I'm pleased. It is right that you should be anticipating the ball. Benedict?" she added, one brow raised as she turned to him.

"What, Mother?" he asked, his back, which was already stiff, stiffening more at her commanding tone.

"It's six o' clock. You should be getting dressed."

"Mother..." Benedict began, about to argue, but he saw her dark eyes harden and decided against it. Nancy would be distressed by it, and he did not wish to upset her. "I need not the time that you ladies need to ready myself," he said instead, trying to lighten his refusal.

"You need time, though...a cravat does not tie itself. And you need to look impeccable. The impressions of others are like the currency of the *Ton*," she reminded him firmly, one manicured brow raised.

"Mother," Benedict objected, but Nancy spoke up brightly.

"I can dress in half an hour, Mama! I checked the hour last time I prepared, and all it took was a little over thirty minutes to get ready."

"A lady needs to take an hour getting ready," their mother said firmly. "Perhaps you were underdressed."

"It was for last week's literary salon!" Nancy said, frowning. "Was I underdressed, Mama?"

"No," his mother had to admit, just as Benedict cleared his throat, ready to divert his mother's attention back onto him before she lost her temper. "No, you were well dressed for Lady Atherly's Salon."

"See? I just dress fast," she said with some pride in her tone.

Benedict smiled, taking Nancy's hand in his across the table. Sometimes she seemed like a little girl, still, and sometimes a young lady. "We're fast dressers," he said firmly, staring at his mother, daring her to comment. She let out a sigh.

"You need to get ready, Nancy," she said firmly. "And you too, Benedict. And I insist that you dance with Lady Penelope, and Lady Gracechurch's daughters, and Lady Hannah." Her voice was hard. She drew herself to her full height, which was quite tall. All the family were tall, and dark-haired, like Benedict himself.

"Mother!" Benedict objected, pushing back his chair as if to stand. He had tried to contain his annoyance, but this was too hard to ignore. "I will dance with whom I please—or I shall not dance. You cannot compel me to do as you wish. I am no longer a child." His voice was firm and level.

"No, you are not," his mother agreed. "And you are the heir of Norendale, which is why I insist that you find a suitable match. It is a matter of the future of Norendale. And you need to take it seriously." Her voice was hard and flinty, her dark eyes holding his gaze angrily.

"That is how I *do* take it," Benedict insisted. "Which is why it seems pointless to have to indulge in hours of chatter at parties."

"That is how society works, son," his mother said tightly. "And you had best learn how to partake in our society."

"Mother..." Benedict was about to argue, but he saw Nancy watching, her eyes frightened, and he took a deep breath. He and his mother had the same temper—one that flared easily and did not cede ground to anybody. If they argued, it would be frightening, and he did not want to scare his young sister. He sighed, distracting himself from his anger with his mother. "I'll race you," he said to Nancy instead. "If you can get ready in half an hour, I bet you a pound that I can do half that time."

"A pound!" Nancy's eyes shone. Benedict saw his mother glare at him in disapproval, but he pushed back his chair, grinning.

"Why not?" he agreed. It was quite a large amount of money for a silly wager, but they could well afford it. The Norendale estate was extremely prosperous. "And how about another wager? I challenge you to see if you can best half an hour."

"Benedict!" his mother said angrily, but Nancy was already running to the door, yelling excitedly that she was going to win that shiny pound coin.

Benedict leaned back at the desk, some of his tension draining from him.

"Now she'll dress too fast and be careless about it," his mother continued. "You need to think sometimes before acting," his mother said tightly.

"And you need to consider Nancy sometimes," Benedict said angrily. "If we argue in front of her, it will ruin her day."

"You were the one who argued," she began, but Benedict stood up and went to the door. Rowan got up and followed him to the door.

"I'll be ready in fifteen minutes," he said stiffly, heading into the corridor. "I'll have the coach readied for us to depart by seven o' clock."

His mother began speaking, but Benedict was already in the hallway, striding down to the kitchen where he sought out the butler. His dog, Rowan, padded soundlessly behind him and walked into the kitchen ahead of him. The staff were mostly wary of Rowan for his considerable size—particularly the outdoor staff— but the kitchen staff, most of all the housekeeper, had come to feel safe with him.

"Rowan! There you are. I have a bone for you," the housekeeper greeted the big dog. "Ah! Your Grace. How may I help you?" she added, seeing Benedict a second later.

Benedict inclined his head. "Thank you, Mrs. Hansford, but I only came to find the butler. Please have the coach ready for seven," he told the butler firmly, who had been sitting having tea at the kitchen table and who had got up as Benedict arrived.

"Yes, Your Grace" the butler replied.

Benedict thanked him and strode upstairs again, his hound following him. He reached his bedroom and looked around, noting that his manservant had already lit the candle-lamps and that his evening jacket, hose, knee-breeches and a clean shirt were hanging on the back of the chair, waiting for him to dress.

He reached for the jacket and then sat down on the bed with a sigh. Rowan settled down on his rug by the fire where he slept and looked up at him confusedly.

"It's all well, old boy," Benedict told him gently. He ran a hand through Rowan's thick hair and gazed at the black velvet knee-breeches that his manservant had laid out. His shoulders stiffened with nerves at the thought of being in public again.

"Nonsense," he told himself firmly, as Rowan whined again, clearly feeling his distress. "I can do this. It's all very simple. It's one ball. How horrid can it be?"

He reached for the fresh shirt and changed out of his old one, gazing down at his chest. Firm, broad and muscled, it seemed, to his eyes, to be just as it ought to be, if not slightly better than most. Yet he had been taunted mercilessly for his bulky build, for his imposing height, and for his ready temper. The boys had dubbed him a "beast", and it had stuck. At every gathering he attended, he heard whispers behind his back.

"Dash it," he growled, and changed into the knee-breeches, knotting them fiercely over the white silk stockings that he wore beneath them. He reached for the velvet jacket, which was black as well, and shrugged into it in a smooth movement. He got away with choosing only black by claiming to be in mourning for his father, though his father had passed away more than a decade ago. Nobody questioned his choice, and that made things simpler. Black suited him, and he felt no need to shift from it. It suited his

14

mood.

He pulled on his boots and strode to the door. Rowan, seeming to understand where Benedict was going, and that he couldn't come too, lifted his head from where he rested on the mat, but did not attempt to follow him.

"Good boy," Benedict said gently, bending to ruffle his ears. Rowan licked his hand and Benedict drew a steadying breath, the gentle, supportive gesture of his hound touching his heart. "Good chap," he said softly, and strode out into the corridor, leaving the door part-open so Rowan could get out if he had to. He had a ball to attend, and, if the sound of light laughter drifting up from the hallway told him anything, he owed his sister a pound.

Chapter 3

The candles at Payton House shone bright golden light onto the polished marble floor of the ballroom. Belinda, standing by the big archways at the back, stared out across the bright expanse, her heart thumping with a mix of pride and nerves. She jumped in surprise as she heard the butler announce the first guests.

"Lord and Lady Arnott, and their daughter, the Honorable Miss Prestwick."

Belinda looked over at the low stairs that led down into the ballroom. Usually, she would be there with the family, lined up to greet the guests, but they had decided to change that rule. She swallowed hard, her cheeks flaming with shame. She had wanted to attend her sister's debut, and Estelle had insisted on it, but to organize things so that Belinda would not be in the public eye was not easy. Once the *Ton* had disgraced a person, there was no way that person could appear in public without that disgrace being discussed, and Estelle's reputation needed no tarnish put on it on the first day she appeared in society.

Belinda stood where she was and gazed out over the ballroom, feeling her heart twist with pain.

"Lord and Lady Westbrooke, and their son, the Honorable Mr. Newbridge."

Belinda watched as a couple walked down the stairs, followed by a young man perhaps four years her junior, his pale clover-honey hair bright in the light. Mama and Papa had stationed themselves near the stairs, so that Estelle could meet the guests informally, without the need for a reception line. Estelle curtseyed to the guests and Belinda grinned to herself, watching the young man bow low. Even from here, she could see the flush in his cheeks. Evidently, Estelle made quite an impression.

"Lord and Lady Atheridge, and their daughter, Lady Julia," the butler announced.

Belinda watched as another group descended the stairs. The young lady was of a similar age to Estelle, dressed in a pastel pink gown. The two young women curtseyed to one another, Lady Julia poised and gracious like Estelle. No smirch hung over their honor— they were free to enjoy themselves.

She swallowed hard again; her throat tight. She did not resent Estelle's happiness—she loved to see her sister's joy, and she wanted to protect her from what had happened to her, at all costs. It was another good reason to hold the ball privately—her parents could be as selective as they liked about the young men on the guest-list. Not that, she thought sadly, one could tell who was going to be bad just by looking at their name or their pedigree.

She let her gaze move around the ballroom and watched the footmen moving silently behind the refreshments table, their dark red livery rather grand against the white backdrop of the ballroom walls.

Her head whipped round again as the butler made another announcement.

"Lord and Lady Lavenham, and their daughter, the Honorable Miss Tate."

"Lila!" Belinda said aloud, pressing her hand to her lips as the delighted sound escaped her. She grinned, watching as her best friend crossed the floor and, after a moment of gazing out over the ballroom, spotted Belinda and walked over to her.

She felt her heart grow warm. Lila was one of the very few friends she had—one of the only people in London who had refused to believe the rumors. Lila had guessed immediately that there was more to the story and lost no time in asking Belinda about it. In a world where only Belinda's own family had shown any care for hearing her side of the story, Lila was a deeply valued friend.

The taint to Lila's own reputation for remaining Belinda's friend was something Lila didn't seem to care about—her parents had already arranged a match for her, and they were somewhat unconventional in any case. Lord and Lady Lavenham were not much part of the Ton either—they were rather eccentric and learned—and any further exclusion counted as a good thing, since they eschewed high society and its foolish whims.

Belinda watched as Lila drifted towards her. She was of average height, her blonde hair arranged in an elaborate coiffure, her dress pale green. She walked across to where Belinda stood, her long oval face breaking into a grin as she saw her.

"Belinda! My dear, dear friend. There you are!" Lila exclaimed, reaching for Belinda and embracing her. Belinda held

17

her tight, smelling the floral scent of her friend's perfume. Their dresses rustled as they stood back.

"Lila," Belinda greeted her warmly, stepping back to look at her. "It's grand to have you here."

Lila smiled. "Look at you! That dress suits you beautifully. Blue is a fine colour on you."

Belinda blushed.

"Thank you," she murmured softly, looking down at her dress. It was a new gown, a pale blue muslin, the waistband darker blue like the ribbons that framed the puff-sleeves. The neckline was a low oval and the long skirt fell from the fashionably high waist to her ankles. Estelle had insisted that Belinda wore her new gown, saying that it suited her so well that she simply had to. Belinda had privately thought it would not matter what she wore, as the *Ton* would ostracize her anyway.

"What do you think of this evening?" Lila asked. They were not too far from one of the two long refreshments tables, and Belinda grinned, noticing that Lila had somehow acquired a glass of lemonade in her one hand without Belinda even noticing her taking it.

"I think it will be a fine evening for Estelle," she commented, reaching for one of the glasses and nodding as the footman on duty poured her the same lemonade.

"Grand," Lila said warmly. "She looks lovely. So young!" she grinned. She was a year younger than Belinda, just four-and-twenty, but they both, it seemed, felt much older than seventeen-year-old Estelle, just entering society.

"She does," Belinda said a little sadly. It felt strange, having her sister already so grown up.

"It looks like it shall be a fine evening," Lila commented, sipping her lemonade. "Good lemonade," she added with a smile. "Your cook does a much better one than the one that they serve in town."

"Good," Belinda said with a chuckle. "I'd be surprised if it was worse."

Lila let out a snort of laughter and they both giggled loudly. A few heads turned and Belinda went white. The scrutiny of the *Ton* frightened her. She stepped instinctively back into the shade of the pillar.

18

"Sorry." Lila looked downcast. "I didn't mean to draw so much attention."

"It is not your fault," Belinda said firmly, making an effort to step out of the shadow of the pillar. "If we cannot laugh at a ball, where then?"

"Quite so," Lila agreed firmly. "How long will the ball proceed?" she asked, changing the topic.

"Four hours," Belinda explained, glancing up at the candles, which were bigger than usual. Most candles would burn for three hours, but her parents had made sure to purchase four-hour ones for this ball, making it last for the longest acceptable length.

"Whew. And that means a lot of standing around and chatting," Lila said with a grin. "And a lot of dances."

"Mm," Belinda agreed. She glanced over to where a quartet of dark-dressed men were setting up their cellos and violins to play later. The ball would feature all the popular dances, including the controversial waltz. It was fashionable, Mama said, and so it had to be included, and Papa would not have gainsaid her in anything. All he wanted was for the evening to be as happy as possible. Belinda had not paid much attention to choosing the music—she was fairly sure she would not dance anyway. After eight years out of society, she doubted even whether anyone at the ball besides Lila still knew her, and she didn't think she would make any new acquaintances—not with the horrible scandal that still clung to her.

The noise in the ballroom increased. The space was getting quite full, the guests starting to arrive in force. There were at least thirty people in the room and another five at the top of the steps, waiting to be announced by Mr. Priester, their butler.

"What do you think about the latest fashion for Whitework embroidery for bonnets and caps?" Lila asked Belinda, distracting her from the arrival of the guests.

"Um...well, it's quite pleasant, I suppose." Belinda did not really have an opinion. She had been out of society and tended not to keep up with fashions. Whitework, she knew, was a design embroidered with white cotton on a white background.

"I like it too," Lila agreed, sounding pleased. "Mama said it's silly, as you can barely see the patterns, but I think it's quite pretty—and it's French, which has to be good," she added with a grin, sipping her lemonade, and lifting one wry eyebrow at Belinda.

19

"Mm," Belinda agreed, not really listening. She was watching the door, where three guests walked down the stairs into the ballroom. The three were striking people—a tall lady, dressed in dark gray, her gray-streaked brown hair in an elaborate chignon, and a young man and woman. The young man was most likely her son, and walked beside her, his head and shoulders rising above the crowd. Like the woman in gray and the younger woman, he was also tall. He wore deep black, his velvet jacket darker than his hair, which also looked black under the pale candlelight. The young lady walked behind them, her black hair arranged in a high bun and her dress one of white muslin, suggesting that she was also new out in society. She looked around the same age as Belinda's sister.

"Who are they?" Belinda asked softly. It was not just their striking appearance which held her interest, but the sudden silence that had descended on the hall. People stared, and some people turned away. More than one lifted their hands, whispering to one another as the group passed them. The three people walked with their heads high, oblivious to the whispers as if they walked behind an invisible shield.

"That's her grace the Duchess of Norendale and her children," Lila explained softly, leaning closer so she could not be overheard. "That's her son. He is now the Duke of Norendale, following the passing of his father several years ago."

"I see," Belinda replied, frowning. "What is..." she murmured, wanting to ask Lila why people were staring at the group, and whispering behind their hands, but Lila's parents, Baron and Baroness Lavenham, had wandered over. Lila's face brightened as she spotted them.

"Come and greet Mama and Papa!" she urged Belinda warmly. "Mama! Papa! Come on," she called as they walked swiftly over. Lady Lavenham smiled fondly at Belinda.

"My dear! How grand to see you."

Belinda greeted them, and got swept up into an embrace by Lady Lavenham, who smelled of rosewater and was wearing a soft gray gown. Her face was much softer than Lila's, a softened oval one.

"Come, my dear," Lady Lavenham murmured. "We were going to take the air on the terrace. Will you come with us?"

"Um...yes," Belinda said in a small voice. She glanced at Lila, who grinned and nodded.

"It's getting stuffy in here already," Lila commented, and before Belinda could object—she had wanted to stay to watch the new arrivals a little longer—she was being guided towards the doors with the Lavenhams.

She turned to glance back at the ballroom, looking for the Duchess and her family. The bright candles lit up the Duke of Norendale, standing at the edge of the room just a few feet away. His stance was straight-backed as if he was enduring the evening rather than enjoying it, his frown long-suffering, and she lifted a brow in surprise. He looked exactly like she must have when she was standing at the back. The tension and discomfort were identical.

His coal-black eyes met hers for a moment. She shivered. Even from the distance of perhaps ten feet away, she could see a brooding, angry glare in his eyes, full of bitterness and rage. She shivered again, instinctively drawing her thin shawl around her. She glanced around, wanting to look away from that hard, brooding gaze. Lord and Lady Lavenham, along with Lila, were out on the terrace—she could just see their heads where they stood beside the rail. She moved to join them, but she was stuck, caught between a group of dowagers and the doors to the garden.

She froze as she recognized one of the ladies, who was looking straight at her. It was Lady Talbot, one of the *Ton's* well-known scandalmongers.

"...and just as I was saying, Amy, it's a disgrace," Lady Talbot stated loudly. "A disgrace!" She repeated the words as if she enjoyed saying them. Belinda felt paralyzed as the woman's piercing eyes held hers.

"Quite so, my dear. Quite so," another lady murmured in agreement.

"She should not have attended. The whiff of scandal around her will cling to her poor sister, young Estelle. She's ruining her chances of advancement."

"Quite so," the other lady agreed again.

Belinda felt tears prick her eyes. They were talking about her!

The group of women had all turned to look towards the ballroom and all seemed to notice her standing there, because, for a moment they fell silent. However, Lady Talbot, who Belinda recognized as particularly cruel, continued loudly.

"A disgrace, I say. If one must behave so shockingly, one should have the grace to exit high society."

"A disgrace. Disgrace!" One of the women who Belinda did not recognize hissed the word. Neither were hiding that they were talking about her.

Belinda glared at them, but she could not stop tears of shame from sliding down her cheeks. She looked around wildly. She had hoped to exit the hall quietly and spend some time with her friends, but to do so, she had to find a way through the group that were tormenting her. She stood where she was, too scared to move.

"You would think," the other woman began again, but then, just as she was about to offer another insult, a low voice interrupted them.

"Hold your tongue," a man growled. "Lest you regret your next words."

Chapter 4

Benedict felt his hand make a fist as the words shot out of his mouth before he could stop them. The two women who had been gossiping stared at him, horrified. The young lady they had mercilessly insulted was rooted in place, her eyes huge as she stared at them.

He reddened, feeling embarrassed by the two older women who were glaring at him in outrage.

"Your words are offensive," he continued, not about to back down, even though displays of temper were one of the things he'd been teased for most mercilessly. "It offends me and all the other ball-goers to hear you insult another guest so rudely."

The two older women stared at him in horror. One of them, the one who had spoken more of the two, hastily dropped a curtsey.

"Your Grace, I meant no offence. Now, if you'll excuse me, I must make my way to the refreshments table. My daughter is waiting there."

Benedict gave her the briefest nod of acknowledgement as she hurried off. The other women began stammering, stepping back as though he threatened her physically.

"I must excuse myself," she stuttered, already moving away swiftly. "I have to take the air."

Benedict watched, grimly amused, as the other women scattered. He felt pleased to have dispersed them. Their words truly were offensive, reminding him all too much of the cruel taunts he had endured while he was away at school. He hated to see anyone bullied, and he would always intervene if he could. He understood the pain all too well. He turned away, thinking of going back to find Nancy. Before he could walk over to his sister, the young woman stammered.

"Your Grace, thank you."

She was looking up at him with a frightened stare.

Benedict cleared his throat, feeling shy. "It was nothing," he began. His heart thumped uncomfortably as her eyes met his. They were very green, and her soft oval face was delicately lovely. The sight of the tears on her cheeks reminded him forcefully of his own pain as a youth.

"Thank you," she whispered again, lowering her eyes as if she, too, felt a little shy. He cleared his throat.

"It was nothing, truly," he said gently, his heart aching with sympathy for her plight. He looked around, not sure what to say. He didn't want to rush off, but at the same time, the awkwardness he felt was making him desperate to run.

She was still gazing up at him, those green eyes holding his. Disarming, they took his breath. She was a lovely woman, her soft face sweet, her full lips a light pink color, her long honey-blonde hair, which was coming a little lose from its chignon, framing her face in a pretty way.

He felt his throat tighten awkwardly and he coughed again, desperate to think of something to say. He still felt the need to flee, but he didn't want to offend the young lady, whose pale green gaze was making his heart pound in a way that it had not in years.

"Benedict!" his mother's voice hissed, making him spin round suddenly. He blinked in surprise at her, stunned that she had managed to cross the ballroom to find him so fast.

"Mother," he objected, cheeks reddening hotly at the thought of the young lady hearing his mother chastise him as if he was ten years old.

"Benedict," his mother began, clearly not even noticing the fact that someone else was nearby. "I insist that you dance with Lady Penelope at once. The first dances are starting now."

Benedict blinked in surprise. There was indeed music playing. He had not noticed anything, so intent was he on his defense of the young lady. He focused on his mother, who was looking at him impatiently, her gaze intense as if she expected him to obey instantly. Annoyance rushed through him, his memories of being tormented at school mingling unpleasantly with the fact that she was bossing him as though he was still of school age.

"I will dance the first dance," he said firmly. "But I will dance with this lady," he added, turning abruptly to the young lady with green eyes. "My lady, will you do me the honour of dancing with me?"

The young woman gazed up at him, shocked and speechless. Benedict swallowed, feeling sudden guilt. He had imposed on her straight after a bad situation, just to evade his mother's

24

commands. He was about to apologize when she spoke, interrupting his thoughts.

"Yes," the young woman said, making him look up, shocked. "Yes, Your Grace." He gaped at her, astonished.

"Thank you," he stammered, heat flooding him as the shame was replaced by relief. He looked over at his mother, trying not to grin as he saw her horrified, angry expression. "I will dance the first dance now."

"I..." his mother began, glaring at him. He tossed a grin over his shoulder at her and bowed low, taking the young lady's hand.

"Shall we make our way over there?"

She nodded. "Um, yes." she managed to say. She was wearing white silk gloves, and her grip was tight on his hand.

He cleared his throat, feeling ashamed again for taking advantage of her distress, and wishing he could think of something to say to make matters more comfortable.

"I believe the first dance is a Polonaise?" he asked.

"Yes. Yes, it seems to be so," the young woman replied, tilting her head to listen to the introductory notes of the music. They were a little late to reach the dance floor, the dance already starting as they slipped through a space that the guests had cleared.

Benedict took her left hand in his right, feeling a little unsure. It was a long time since he had danced a Polonaise. He'd danced at Nancy's ball a week ago, but he'd danced with Nancy, and they had performed a quadrille, which was the only sort of dance he knew well. He glanced dubiously at the young woman, but she looked confident.

"It's not too crowded," she noted as they stepped onto the dance floor.

"Mm," he murmured. He had to focus—he couldn't talk and dance at once, though it seemed she was quite capable of doing so. They glided onto the floor.

He felt impressed as she stepped lightly around, her hand in his. She clearly knew the steps very well. She moved gracefully, her steps light and floating, her head held high and graciously like a rose on a stem.

It was a moment or two before the dance returned to his memory, but then it felt as though his steps matched hers

25

seamlessly and they drifted across the floor. The music was lively, the pace fast, but they stepped together easily.

"Whoops," she whispered under her breath as a couple moved towards them, but they danced neatly past the oncoming people, barely breaking step. He felt her steps match seamlessly to his as they floated across the dance floor.

They moved lightly around the dance floor and Benedict's heart thumped as they stepped in time, her movements matching his effortlessly. He shut his eyes for a moment, overwhelmed by how good it felt. For so many years, he had walked alone, but, just for a second, someone was there with him and held his hand.

He swallowed hard, emotion filling him, and, as he stepped sideways, moving to the edge of the floor, the cadence of the music heralded the closing bars.

The couples around them bowed and curtseyed, applauding one another politely with gloved hands. Benedict bowed low, cheeks flushing as he straightened up and looked down at her. That green-eyed gaze met his, level and unassuming.

"Thank you, Your Grace," she murmured.

"Thank you, my lady," he said in return. He inclined his head. He didn't know what to say. He wanted to thank her by name, but he had suddenly noticed that he had no idea who she was. After sharing such a lovely dance, it felt impossibly crass to ask her name. He felt as though he ought to know. A sound drifted from the corner of the ballroom, making him turn around. The musicians were checking that they were in tune again, indicating their intent to play another dance. He looked back at the lady and saw she was already moving towards the edge of the dance floor, slipping in between the other guests into the crowd.

Dash it, he thought to himself, annoyed, as he walked to the edge of the dance floor and towards the refreshments table. He hadn't even used the opportunity and asked for her name.

There is not much to be gained from asking her for her name, he told himself crossly as he gestured to the footman to pour him a glass of plum cordial. *She was so scared of dancing with me that she isn't likely to do so for another set.*

He thanked the footman and sipped the drink, making a face. It was sweeter than he liked his cordial usually, and he felt sure it was blackcurrant and not plum, which he preferred.

He jumped as someone spoke from behind him.

"You were supposed to dance with Lady Penelope," his mother said crossly, drifting up to the table on his left-hand side.

"And I didn't," Benedict said succinctly, taking another sip of the cordial. It was definitely blackcurrant, he thought sourly, ignoring his mother's angry tone.

"Yes, but you were supposed to," she insisted. "And now I will have to apologise to Lord and Lady Kearney for the slight."

"Mother," Benedict began, wishing she would just leave him in peace. He did not want to lose his temper, and the joy of dancing with the young lady was still fresh. He was about to ask her for some peace and quiet, but as he opened his mouth, Nancy came drifting over. He grinned at her, his soul soaring to see her, but then his heart stopped.

Walking with her, a thin smile on his cruel lips, was Lord Darrow.

He and Benedict had known each other from Eton, and he was the one person Benedict had hoped to avoid at all costs.

Chapter 5

Belinda wandered through the ballroom with the music loud in her ears, not really noticing where she was going. The noise of the guests pressed in like a wall, and it was hard to navigate around the people who stood around her, chatting and laughing. She wove her way between the guests, looking for the doors onto the terrace.

What a strange man, she thought wonderingly. *What a strange way to behave.*

He had asked her to dance confidently, without even introducing himself. When they had danced, he had not proved clumsy or awkward, but he had made no attempt at conversation, not even telling her his name. She knew he was the Duke of Norendale only because Lila had already told her.

The tune of the Polonaise that they had danced played through her mind as she walked. She reached the door sooner than she had expected and stopped, looking around. Her eyes scanned the space swiftly to see if Lady Talbot was still there, but she was not and her grin broadened as she recalled how the Duke had confronted the cruel gossips, defending her. It was the first time anyone had actually lashed out at them to help her. Mama and Papa had tried to diffuse such situations in the past, but they would never directly confront anyone.

She shivered as she walked across the terrace. The evening was cool, and in a passing thought she wished she'd kept her shawl with her rather than handing it to a footman.

"Belinda! There you are!" Lila's voice was loud beside her, causing her to turn abruptly.

"Lila," she murmured, still feeling a little dazed. "You must be cold out here." Her friend also had no shawl, her long opera-gloves the only thing that warmed her. Her brown eyes seemed huge in her slim face, highlighted by the pale-yellow gown that she wore.

"I was inside for a while," Lila told her swiftly. "I saw you. You danced the first dance with the Beast."

"What?" Belinda blinked at her friend, who was gazing at her in concern.

"You danced the first dance with the Beast of Norendale," Lila repeated, a frown creasing her pale brows. "Are you all right?"

"He was quite civil," Belinda replied, a little defensively. "And why would you call him that?"

"Everyone does," Lila answered, sounding defensive too. "The whole of the *Ton* calls him that."

"I don't know why," Belinda replied, frowning. "He isn't brutishly ugly or anything."

"I don't think it's because of how he looks," Lila told her in whispers. "I think it's because of the way he is. Which is why I was worried for you," she added swiftly.

"He was not uncivil to me," Belinda replied, frowning at the thought. If he had such an unpleasant reputation that the Ton called him a "beast", he must usually be much ruder than he was to her.

But then, what sort of reputation must I have? she thought wryly.

"Good. I was worried for you," Lila replied, letting out her breath in a sigh.

"There was no need," Belinda said lightly. Her heart thudded as she recalled the way he had looked at her, his dark eyes—so dark they were almost black—softening for a moment, as if in concern when he rescued her from the gossips by the door.

Mayhap I imagined that concerned gaze, she told herself firmly. *Why would he have looked at me like that?* But then, he had also rescued her when she needed it most. It was confusing. She looked over at Lila, who was smiling.

"Well, you danced beautifully," her friend commented, grinning at her. "I must say, despite all of what people say about him, he seemed a good dance partner."

"It was a pleasant dance," Belinda said carefully. She did not want to share details—the details were still too fresh and too confusing. Like one of her pressed flowers, she wanted time to study it before she put it on display in front of anyone.

"Good," Lila said, grinning. "Oh, look! That's Amelia. What do you think of her ostrich plumes? They are most fashionable."

Belinda smiled as Lady Amelia, the daughter of Viscount Emerton, drifted past with two tall ostrich plumes set in the front of the turban headdress. Amelia looked quite elegant. Belinda was glad that her friend had changed the topic—Lila was lively and lighthearted; two of the things she liked best about her. She did not want to talk about serious things.

"I like them," she murmured, after a moment's thought.

"I thought about a pair for myself, but I don't know if it would suit me," Lila confessed.

"I think you would look most elegant too," Belinda told her, looking thoughtfully at her friend to imagine the ostrich plumes. "And besides, if one likes something, one will wear it confidently. And then it will always look good."

"Yes," Lila replied, nodding. "Yes, you are right there. Confidence suits everyone."

Belinda's thoughts drifted back to the dance with the Duke of Norendale. She felt confident when she danced. That was not unusual—she had always had confidence, which had helped her to weather the scandal without breaking her spirit entirely.

"Look! There's Lady Nancy," Lila commented, gesturing to the door. Belinda looked briefly—she never liked staring at people, knowing all too well how it felt.

"Who is she?" Belinda asked, seeing a tall lady of about Estelle's age with thick black hair arranged in a chignon.

"She is the Duke's sister," Lila explained.

"Oh, yes." She recalled she had seen the tall young woman arrive with the Duke of Norendale and his mother.

"She had her debut ball last week," Lila told her. "All say that she is a very pleasant young lady."

"I'm pleased to hear that," Belinda replied feelingly. It was good that people did not gossip about the sister of the Duke as they evidently did about him. The *Ton* could be so hateful with their words.

"What do they say about him?" she asked Lila, feeling curious despite herself.

Something about the tall, dark-haired man had struck her— perhaps his aloofness, his silence. He was a mystery.

"They say he has a beastly streak—an inhuman temper," she told her, eyes wide and round. "And that he is brutishly strong."

"And quite possibly all of that is entire drivel," she murmured with a small smile.

Lila blinked and then laughed. "It could be," she agreed. "It could well be."

Belinda gazed over to where she thought she saw a head of dark hair. She thought it was the Duke of Norendale and she watched him for a moment, then looked away, chiding herself for her inquisitive nature. She could not stop thinking about the confusing, imposing man.

Stop it, she told herself firmly. She barely knew him—admittedly, their dance had been particularly enjoyable, but still she could not let herself be lost in her memories all evening.

She turned around and gazed at her friend. Lila looked tense, and her lips were darker than they should be, even in the slight candlelight that filtered through the big windows onto the terrace.

"You should go inside," Belinda said swiftly. "You're getting too cold. And me too," she added, realizing that she was almost shivering.

"Yes," Lila agreed swiftly. "Let's go inside."

"Belinda! Belinda!" Estelle drifted over as Belinda crossed the ballroom towards her family. "I had such a lovely dance."

"I'm so glad," Belinda replied softly. Estelle's hazel eyes were glowing, her face bright and her cheeks a little pink.

"He's Lord Westbrooke's son and he asked me to dance the next set with him," Estelle confided, her eyes shining.

"That's lovely," Belinda told her, smiling warmly. "May I meet him?"

"He's over there," Estelle said swiftly. She blushed, her gaze darting to the floor. "He's looking at me," she hissed, her cheeks turning even more crimson, if it were possible.

Belinda grinned to herself. She looked over to where Estelle had indicated and caught sight of a tall youth with pale hair with a reddish tinge to it. She recalled seeing him arrive with his family and how he had blushed as he bowed to Estelle.

"He seems nice," she whispered to Estelle.

"Belinda, shh!" Estelle hissed desperately as the young man made his way over to them.

Belinda curtseyed as the young man bowed to her.

"I am Jeremy Newbridge," he introduced himself politely.

"Belinda Payton, Estelle's sister," Belinda replied softly.

"Very pleasant to make your acquaintance, my lady," Lord Jeremy replied in a cultured tone. His eyes, Belinda noticed, shone like stars as he gazed at Estelle.

Belinda smiled, feeling her worries settle at once.

"I am very pleased to meet you, too."

"Lady Estelle?" Lord Jeremy addressed Estelle politely. "I believe the waltz is starting now."

"Oh! I must hurry," Estelle murmured to Belinda, who nodded, smiling warmly at her younger sister.

"Of course, Estelle. I will wait here while you dance."

It was good to see Estelle so happy and she stood and watched the waltzing people, listening distantly to the beautiful music. Her thoughts were of the Duke of Norendale, and wondering what he was really like.

One thing that must be true of him, she reflected lightly, was that he was confident, like her, if he was even in the ballroom at all. She knew all too well what it felt like to face the rumors of the Ton, and no matter what she thought of him and his abrupt manners, he was strong if he could face their scorn and enjoy his evening.

Chapter 6

"It cannot be ignored," Benedict told his mother loudly. They were sitting at breakfast, the round table covered with a white linen cloth between them.

His mother blinked in surprise, raising an eyebrow. "I did not ignore it. I was very pleased. The man is most influential."

"Mama!" Benedict felt his hand clench into a fist as he struggled not to rage at her. "You are not thinking."

A toast-rack filled with toast stood on the table, along with a teapot, three cups and a basket of croissants. Benedict's vision swam with weariness—he had barely slept. He'd spent all the time between dancing with the unknown lady and waking at home unable to detach his thoughts from Lord Darrow.

That man was no person for Nancy to dance with, or even to have met.

His mind returned to Eton, to when he was eighteen. A group of youths of his own age stood around him, shouting taunts and insults, led by Darrow, who looked at him with a smirk on his slim face.

It had not been Darrow who had thrown the final insult that had made Benedict snap, but it had been him who led the other boys in overpowering Benedict, raining kicks and blows on him, one of which broke his nose. He had lain there, bleeding and dazed, until one of the schoolmasters found them and chased the youths off, but even those bad physical blows had not hurt him as badly as the cruel, taunting words had done.

"On the contrary," his mother said, her intense tone bringing him back to the moment. "You are the one who was thoughtless. You should have a care with whom you associate nowadays. Your sister's reputation may be tainted by your actions also."

"What?" Benedict exclaimed. "What are you talking about, Mama?"

He felt his head throb. Getting angry now made him develop a horrible ache in his head, something, he thought distantly, that had come only now that he was older. He dismissed the thought and focused on his mother.

"You mean you didn't know?" she demanded from her place

opposite.

"Know what?" he asked a little desperately. "Mother, of what do you speak?"

"About her," his mother hissed. "The scandalous girl. The sister of Lady Estelle."

"What sister? Which lady? What scandal?" Benedict demanded. His head was thudding so hard that he could barely see.

His mother put down the teapot and stared at him, raising a brow.

"Lady Estelle. It was her ball we attended," she told him slowly. "You danced with her sister. The scandalous Lady Belinda. And now it'll be a matter of hours before the scandal sheets are full of it. If they are not already," she added sourly. She stood and went to the bell-rope.

"What are you doing?" Benedict inquired, still trying to make sense of what she had told him. He had only danced one dance. Was that Lady Belinda? A glow kindled bright in his heart. Now at least, he knew her name.

"I'm summoning the butler," his mother said lightly. "He will bring us the paper. We'll know soon enough how terrible a stain you've put on Nancy's reputation."

"Mama, please," Benedict murmured, shutting his eyes for a moment. "You are not being reasonable. Please sit down and tell me again. And for Perdition's sake, don't shout," he added, glancing into the hallway. It was cloudy, but he guessed it was already eight o' clock and he did not want Nancy to hear him and their mother arguing.

"I was not shouting," she said lightly.

Benedict stiffened in annoyance. The butler appeared in the doorway and his mother dismissed him when he said the papers had not yet been delivered, but that he would fetch them when they arrived.

"Now," he said, as his mother fell into silence, stirring her tea as if nothing untoward had happened, "please explain to me what you are talking about...?"

"Of course," she said in a pleasant enough tone. "I already have. Lady Belinda, the lady with whom you danced—despite my insistence that you dance with Lady Kearney's daughter—was the

34

topic of scandal a few years ago. She was barred from Almack's for indecent conduct there. Or so the scandal sheets said, at any rate." She shrugged.

"You mean, it might not be true?" Benedict demanded at once. He recalled the faces of the women gossiping, and the pain in the young woman's gaze. He did not believe for an instant that it had been a real scandal. It was probably all malicious stories spread by other women, as such things so often were.

His mother shrugged. "Probably not," she said lightly. "It might be, it might not be. You know how these things are. The point is, though," she added, lifting a finger for emphasis, "that she has a terrible reputation. And nobody in our family can afford to be seen with someone of a terrible reputation. It damages us."

"Mother," Benedict growled, his cheeks reddening. "You know..."

"The papers are here, Your Grace," the butler murmured as he placed the morning newspapers on the sideboard. "Would you like some more tea?"

The Duchess nodded fractionally. "Please," she replied.

Benedict watched as the butler replaced the teapot and went to the door again, his duty carried out. Benedict looked at his mother.

"You have told me your opinion," he said slowly. "But you have not answered my question." He paused, not wanting to speak loudly in case Nancy was in the hallway somewhere.

"I did answer that question," his mother said at once, but he shook his head.

"Not about the scandal," he reminded her. "The earlier one. About the...the fellow Nancy was dancing with last night," he concluded, not able to say the man's name without invoking all his remembered fear and pain.

"I told you," his mother said lightly, selecting some toast from the rack, "that he's a fine prospect."

"You're not serious," Benedict spluttered, almost swallowing a piece of toast the wrong way. He stared at her. She gazed back.

"He has recently inherited the estate after his father's passing," she said lightly. "He is a viscount. I think he's a fine match. Do you agree?"

"Mother! The fellow's a serpent." He paused. "No. No

35

animal is as low as that," he added, glancing at the fireplace where his dog slumbered on the mat. Rowan had been sleeping, but now he was watching Benedict with concern, likely not fond of the sound of raised voices.

"You don't know that," his mother said mildly. Benedict thumped his fist on the table. Rowan sat up, thumping his tail nervously, and Benedict drew a breath.

"How can it be that you think that?" Benedict said angrily.

"Because I know that your opinion of him was formed over a decade ago, when you were both little more than children," his mother said insistingly. Benedict glared at her.

"I was eighteen," he reminded her angrily. "And if we were just children, then tell me why I still have a broken nose?"

His mother raised a brow. "It set remarkably well," she said lightly. "You would never think it had been broken."

"You're intentionally missing the point." Benedict struggled to control his temper. He had been teased for his temper, taunted for it—the fight in which his nose had been broken had been started by boys trying to taunt him into fighting them. "He is a wicked man. He made my school years a torment." He felt his throat tighten, unable to find words. He had lived in fear.

"Your school years. That is nonsense that you must put behind you. You are a grown man. Why are you still fussing about childish squabbles?"

"Squabbles?" Benedict whispered. His throat was too tight to speak. He coughed, and Rowan bounded to his side, making small sounds of distress and nudging his hand. His mind reeled, hearing her use "squabbles" to describe a fight between him and eight other boys, where his nose had been broken and he'd only been rescued from broken ribs because the schoolmaster happened to appear on the scene. "Mother. You don't care, do you?" he managed to say, staring at her in amazement. "You truly care nothing for what happened to me."

His mother raised a brow. "I care that you stop being a fool and allow your sister to advance in society through a fine match."

Benedict felt his heart twist. He had always sensed that his mother didn't really care about him, or Nancy. He was sure she cared only for advancement and what the Ton thought of the family. Now, he knew for sure that he was right. The realization hit him like a fist, and he swallowed hard, rage and sorrow too much for him to put into words.

"Rowan, come," he whispered, pushing back his chair. His mother looked up at him, about to say something, but Benedict turned his back, whistling to his dog.

Rowan bounded after him and he walked briskly to the door, going swiftly into the hallway and then down the stairs to the front door.

"Benedict?" He heard his mother call once, but he ignored her and strode across the hallway. If she had so little care for himself or Nancy, there was no point talking to her about his worries. He would do better to walk and get rid of the worst of his anger.

"Your grace? A letter from Mr. Stewart," the butler informed him at the doorway, but Benedict walked briskly past.

"Put it upstairs in the study, please," he called over his shoulder, striding out of the front door and down the steps into the grounds. Rowan bounded after him.

Benedict walked down the path, not really seeing where he was going, but choosing a direction that led towards the stable. Norendale Manor lay six miles outside London and was surrounded by extensive grounds, the woodland backing onto the property also belonging to the family, as well as much of the surrounding farmland.

Benedict strode through the grounds, following a route that led into the woodlands and up to the stream. Rowan followed him, his long legs breaking into a steady run as Benedict ran with him, the two of them jogging to the stream and then collapsing, exhausted.

Benedict lay on the cool grass for a moment, staring up at the gray sky. Rowan ran up and licked his face and Benedict chuckled, pushing him playfully. The big dog yipped, and Benedict laughed and stood up.

"I'm all right, big chap."

Benedict sighed the words as he sat down heavily on a tree-stump. His lungs burned, his heart racing still after the exertion of running to the stream. He looked up at the sky and took a breath, feeling his muscles twitch and his thoughts calm at the soft sound of birdsong and the light breeze.

"It's not right," he murmured to Rowan, who drank at the stream and then lay down at Benedict's feet, letting out a sigh as he shifted into a comfortable position. Benedict reached down and ruffled the dog's ears, and Rowan looked up at him questioningly, clearly aware of his dark thoughts. Benedict felt his mood lightening as he stared into those beautiful eyes that never judged him.

He stared down at the stream, watching it as it flowed past the bank, trickling in between the rocks and racing down the slight incline towards the distant town of Norendale. He drew in a deep breath.

"I will find a way to counter Mother on this front," he said softly. He had to. Nancy was a dear girl, the sweetest and loveliest creature in his world, besides Rowan. Benedict would have to protect her from Darrow, who was as wicked and cruel as Nancy was kind and beautiful. And he could not trust anyone else to do it—especially not his mother.

He heard Rowan whine, and he bent down and ruffled his dog's ears again. His dark mood was troubling his companion.

As he looked over the landscape, the gray sky low over the bright green trees, all clad in their new leaves, he recalled the pretty young woman with whom he'd shared a dance. The vivid greenness of the landscape was like the grass-green, emerald shade of her eyes. He smiled to himself a little sourly.

"She's probably forgotten," he murmured aloud. "Or she's reeling from the shock of having danced with the infamous Beast of Norendale." He said it with a sad smile.

The young lady he had helped—Lady Belinda, was her name, according to his mother—was sweet and innocent, or so she seemed. She would likely believe the rumors that circulated about him, simply because most people did. She was probably glad he only danced once with her, and he was sure that was the only time he would interact with her.

His thoughts kept on returning, though, to the feeling of dancing with her and he wondered, idly, if she had enjoyed it as much as he had. He knew so little about her.

At least, he thought with a small spark of joy, he had found out that morning what her name was.

That was one good thing about the conversation with his

mother and the difficulties with Darrow and her ambitions.

"Ahoy there!" A voice hailed him, making him spin round abruptly. Clinton—his best friend—was standing by the hedge. Rowan growled low in his throat, but then saw who it was and went over, letting Clinton pat his head.

"You startled me," Benedict growled. He glared up at Clinton, who beamed at him.

"I thought I'd take a ride after breakfast. I didn't expect to find you at the stream. Want to join me on a jaunt up to the village?"

Benedict blinked. He really had to stay and talk to Nancy, but he still had no idea what he was supposed to say—or even if he ought to. His mother was, in some regard, right. Darrow, wicked as he was, did offer good social prospects. A ride might clear his head.

"That sounds like a fine notion," he said to Clinton, who beamed.

"I should think so," his friend agreed, and laughed. Benedict chuckled.

"Come on, then," he said, his spirits lightening. "I need to fetch a jacket and saddle Nightshadow."

"Of course," Clinton said lightly.

"I hope you had breakfast," Benedict grunted as they walked towards the manor, Rowan walking beside Benedict, shoving his hand with his nose to remind Benedict he was there.

"I did," Clinton commented. "And I shall race you to the stream when we are ready. Loser has to walk the rest of the way to the woods."

"Challenge accepted."

Benedict walked back to the house with Clinton, his spirits lifting as they chatted and laughed and teased one another lightly. He had a lot to think about—he needed to decide what to say to Nancy, and the mysterious lady was on his mind—but Clinton had cheered him up considerably and he laughed as he walked to the stables.

Chapter 7

Belinda stood in front of the looking glass, pausing as she rang the bell to summon Gertie, her maid. She had chosen a pale green dress to wear, and she studied her reflection, tilting her head thoughtfully.

Not too bad, she thought with a smile.

The color emphasized the green hue of her eyes and seemed to bring golden highlights out in her hair, framing her soft oval face prettily.

As she rang the bell for her maid, it occurred to her that she had stopped caring for her appearance, wearing practical and comfortable dresses of worn linen, and barely bothering to style her hair. This was the first day she'd taken time to choose something she liked.

She smiled to herself.

Her mind returned to the ball and the feeling of dancing with the unknown gentleman. She felt her lips tug at the edges with a smile. It sounded preposterous and romantic, and it made her laugh.

"I do know his title," she reminded herself aloud, then hurried to the door as Gertie knocked on it.

"Milady?"

"Please come in," she called her, and Gertie entered, her long, thin face bright and her dark eyes lit with a smile.

"Milady! You're up and about early," she commented, going to the dressing table where Belinda was already drawing out the embroidered chair to sit on.

"I couldn't sleep any longer," Belinda said warmly. "It's a sunny, beautiful day."

"Mm. It was cloudy an hour ago," she answered, reaching for a hairbrush and starting to brush out Belinda's long hair.

"Well, now it's bright and sunny," Belinda commented, feeling her spirits lift. She watched her reflection in the mirror as Gertie brushed her hair, the long tresses loose on her shoulders. "Perhaps a chignon today," she suggested, feeling interested in her appearance for the first time in a long while.

"Very good, milady. Perhaps something like I did last night, only not quite as fancy, of course," Gertie suggested, starting to coil up some of her hair as she spoke about it.

"That sounds nice," Belinda agreed, watching distantly as Gertie arranged her curls. She was thinking about the ball again, and the feeling of the Duke of Norendale's hand in her own. He had strong hands, big ones—but then he was very tall, she thought with a smile.

"How about a ribbon to tie it in place?" Gertie suggested, tucking some pins in to hold the hair back. "A green ribbon would be pretty around the back, if you have one."

"I think I do have one," Belinda murmured, opening a drawer and taking out a green silk ribbon, handing it to Gertie over her shoulder.

"That's the very thing," Gertie answered contentedly.

Belinda watched as Gertie completed the hairstyle and then pushed back her chair, feeling her spirits lift. She blinked, suddenly tired as she went over to the door. It had been a long night, she reminded herself—they had held the ball until midnight, and then it had been an hour later when the guests had departed that they could finally return upstairs to sleep.

"Thank you," she called to Gertie as she stepped into the hallway.

"Of course, milady. Enjoy your breakfast."

Belinda walked lightly down the hallway, pausing at the door of the breakfast room. Her parents were already there, the sound of knives and forks clicking on plates suggesting that Papa, at least, was eating his customary breakfast of eggs on toast. Belinda preferred a simple breakfast of pastries, finding eggs a little heavy for so early in the day.

"Belinda!" Mama greeted her as she walked in. "Good morning."

Mama looked tired, gray prints of weariness under her soft hazel eyes. Her long hair—which was the same color as Estelle's, but with gray streaks in it—was arranged in a soft bun, some loose strands framing her face. Papa also looked tired, his skin pale and his eyes weary.

"Good morning, Mama," Belinda replied, drawing out her chair and sitting down. She reached for the porcelain teapot, pouring herself a cup of good, strong tea. The smell of toast and

41

marmalade—to say nothing of the basket of fresh-baked pound cake—all made her stomach twist with hunger.

"Morning, Belinda," Papa greeted her, looking up from his plate. He looked tense, his voice not quite as light as usual, and Belinda frowned.

"Good morning, Papa," she greeted him, reaching for some toast. She wanted to ask him what was wrong, but Mama distracted her.

"I hope you slept well," she asked. Belinda nodded.

"Deeply, Mama," she replied lightly. "I would be surprised if I had not—it was quite demanding, yesterday evening."

"Mm."

Belinda frowned. Both her parents seemed a little odd, and she paused, sipping her tea, wondering what the matter was.

"Good morning," Estelle murmured sleepily, appearing in the doorway. Her pale hair was falling loose from its style, and she wore a white day-dress, a big shawl wrapped around her shoulders suggesting that she was cold despite the sunny day. Belinda grinned as she saw her.

"Good morning, sister," she greeted her warmly.

"Good morning," Mama greeted Estelle as she drew out her seat and slipped into her place. She looked over at Belinda, eyes shining.

"It was a fine ball," she murmured, clearly wanting to discuss it. She had been too tired when they returned upstairs to bed and she and Belinda had exchanged only a few sleepy phrases before they had both collapsed into bed in their respective chambers. Now, despite looking weary, Estelle clearly wanted to talk.

"It was," Mama agreed, reaching across the table for the milk, which was in its little porcelain jug. "I think in many regards most fine."

"Most fine," Papa murmured a little defensively.

Belinda glanced over at him, noticing again that something was troubling him. She sipped her tea, wishing that he could speak out.

"Papa?" she asked, reaching across to take a butter knife. "Is something the matter?"

Her father glanced across the table at Mama and looked uneasily back at her.

42

"Nothing, dear," he said gently, patting her wrist where her hand rested on the tablecloth. He glanced at Mama again. "None of us care what people think, do we?" he asked pointedly.

"No, of course not," Mama replied firmly. Belinda looked at her.

"Mama? What are you talking of?" she asked gently, feeling her heart thud.

"It's the scandal sheets," Mama said, gesturing to the side-table, where the morning newspapers were piled neatly, their rumpled pages suggesting they had just been perused. "It's about the Duke of Norendale."

"What?" Belinda exclaimed, pressing a hand to her lips. "Sorry, Mama. Papa," she inclined her head to her parents, apologizing for the loud noise. "But what is the matter? What about him?"

"He's...well...a controversial man, it appears." Mama let out a small chuckle. She sounded uncomfortable; the laughter somewhat forced. "I take part of the blame. I had no idea. I invited him because of Lady Nancy, his sister, who's a debutante of around your sister's age. I didn't know." She glanced at Papa.

"What is it, Papa?" Belinda asked, heart racing.

"The papers printed a small article about you having danced with him," Papa said, looking at the teapot and then glancing up at her in apology. "It was...not nice."

She felt her heart twist and tears sprang to her eyes.

"Why?" she whispered. She had to be so brave to venture into society, and it was her sister's debut! How could they be so cruel? She took a deep breath, trying not to sob. "What did they say? And what about Estelle?" She glanced over at her sister. Estelle smiled.

"I don't care what they say," she said firmly, her gray eyes a little nervous. "We are good people, and the silly *Ton* doesn't matter, does it, Papa?" Estelle demanded. "They're all reprobates and fools, aren't they?"

Papa grinned, the words his own. "Well, mostly, yes," he admitted.

"Estelle, you're dear," Belinda whispered, her eyes damp with tears. "But what I did..." she felt her heart almost stop. She had brought disgrace to her sister. She could have done damage to her. She knew all too well what it was like to have a tainted reputation, and she did not want her sister to suffer as she had done—the last thing she wished was to share the depths of her disgrace.

"The article said nothing of Estelle," Mama said firmly, making Belinda take a deep breath of relief. "But you must be careful, dear. This man has a dark reputation. Even talking with him might tarnish all of us."

"Me too?" Belinda laughed ironically. "Mama...I'm tarnished enough as it is. I am sure that ten Dukes with a dark reputation will make no difference to my bad name." She looked down sorrowfully.

"No, dear," Mama said, resting her hand on her own. "It is not the same. Associating with a man who has such a scandalous reputation could do you harm too. You must be careful. You're a good person, proper and decent. And he, it appears, is not." She looked at her, round eyed, her mouth forming a small, surprised shape.

"What do they say?" Belinda asked, tired but also curious. Her head hurt suddenly, the shock of it mixing with the pain she always felt about such things.

"Well, they refer to him as a "beast", which cannot be good," Mama said with a sorrowful smile. "They say that he is outcast from the *Ton*, and that he is not to be seen in decent gatherings." She sniffed. "I should have searched a little harder before including him," she added, sounding sad.

"It's not your fault, Mama." Belinda told her insistingly.

"You're a dear girl," Mama said sadly. She squeezed Belinda's hand and Belinda gazed down at her breakfast, feeling worried and confused.

"Come on, dear," Papa said gently. "Mayhap we could go out for tea. You like that."

Belinda swallowed hard. She did not want to visit a tea-house. It was hard enough to show her face in London before the ball—now, with added scandal following the first ball she'd attended, she didn't know how she was going to set foot out of her front door. She took a deep breath.

"I should speak with Mr. Morton about the flowerbeds," she murmured, not wanting to stay in the breakfast room. She needed

44

to get outside where she could think. She wanted to be able to sob, and she didn't want to upset her Papa, who already looked distressed. Estelle was trying to be kind, but she had potentially harmed her, and she couldn't bear it.

She made herself eat some toast—it would not help her to feel less distressed if she was also hungry—and then excused herself, hurrying into the garden.

"It's not fair," she whispered, sitting down on the bench and looking up at the sky, which was still blue, the leaves of the poplar trees fluttering in the breeze that ruffled the grasses around her.

It was cruel, she thought sadly. Cruel and unfair. All she had done was attend one ball, and that just because it was for her dear sister—and she hadn't even asked the Duke to be interested in her. He had just appeared, seemingly from nowhere, and asked her to dance. She grinned a little as the memory cheered her up despite her sadness.

That was very strange, she thought with a small grin.

She sniffed, recalling how she had managed to cause trouble. Lady Talbot had been right—she should not go anywhere with Estelle, lest the taint of her scandalous self was to have its effect on her reputation. She took a deep breath, her heart twisting with guilt.

"Daughter?"

She tensed, not expecting to hear someone, then turned around to see her father, who was standing on the path behind the hedge. He looked over at her, a sad smile on his soft oval face.

"I'm sorry, Papa," she said softly.

"It is not your fault," Papa said gently, walking to the little gate that led into the flower garden and settling down on the edge of the pool around the fountain across from her. "The Ton is ridiculous. What your sister says is absolutely right." He grinned at Belinda, who chuckled.

"A view that you don't share, of course," she teased.

"Absolutely not," Papa added with a grin. "I cannot imagine where she heard those words."

"I'm sorry, Papa," Belinda repeated, feeling sad. "I just can't do anything right."

"Nonsense," her father said gently, folding his hand around her own where it rested on the stone bench. "You do all sorts of

45

things well and beautifully. Like this garden, for a start. You've had it planted so nicely," he added, looking around at where soft white daisies blossomed in the beds, combined with delicate green fronds and tall stands of yellow tulips.

"I did nothing," Belinda said softly. "I like flowers."

"I know," Papa said gently. "You're a fine young lady. Beautiful, talented, knowledgeable, and kind at heart," he told her firmly. "I know that. We all know that. What people think doesn't matter," he added softly. "Some people choose to live for what others think. They wander about as though there are people watching them on every street, judging their every motion." He chuckled, shaking his head at the foolery. "You have never even thought about that. And that's a good thing. You do what your heart tells you. And that's as we all should do. That's where everything that is truly good comes from, after all. The heart knows."

Belinda took a deep breath. She was close to tears, but not with sorrow anymore. Her father's words moved her.

"Thank you, Papa," she whispered.

"Not at all," he said gently, holding her hand. He gazed around them warmly. "Now, come inside, please, and tell your Mama what you think we should do with the western garden beds. I know you have a plan for them, and she'll be pleased to have them planted before we have to attend this wretched party."

Belinda giggled. "You still think I should be there?" she asked, genuinely surprised. They had received an invitation to a garden tea—Estelle was invited as a debutante, but the invitation had been extended to all the Paytons, including herself.

"Of course," Papa said with a grin. "Now, go inside and find your Mama, do. She'll want to know about that garden bed. I'm sure whatever you plan will be the talk of London and better than what Morton might do if we leave him to it on his own."

Belinda giggled. "Oh, Papa," she said softly.

"Go on," he said gently.

Belinda took his hand and squeezed it, her heart filled with gratitude and love, and then turned around and headed in towards the house.

What London thought didn't really matter all that much—or not when she was safe in her beloved garden. All that mattered was Estelle, her Mama and Papa and her beautiful flowers and Papa was right—what was in the heart was all that was important.

She took a breath and tried not to think about the garden party the following week, and who might be attending.

All that mattered for the moment was her beautiful blossoms and her family around her.

Chapter 8

"The coach is here!" Mama called from the hallway. "Estelle? Belinda? Are you dressed?"

Belinda tucked a small daisy into her hair and then turned away from the mirror, her heart thudding and her hands clenching into fists. Standing before the looking glass, all dressed and prepared, she did not think she could face the *Ton* and go to Lady Sinclair's party. Papa had been so kind about the nonsense in the papers, but she still feared entering society more than ever before after the fresh round of gossip they had printed.

"Belinda!" Estelle's cheerful voice drifted in from the hallway. Belinda opened the door. Her sister was dressed in a pale pink gown, her hair in an elaborate chignon, and a big smile on her face. "Belinda? Have you seen my shawl?"

"Is it not in the drawing room?" she asked thoughtfully, and Estelle tilted her head.

"It might be. I'll go and check there. You look pretty," she added, gazing up at Belinda, who wore a white and yellow muslin gown with a square neckline, a modest chemisette tucked into the low neck. Her hair was arranged in a chignon as well, loose curls framing her face and with daisies tucked in here and there instead of pearl-headed pins as she might wear to a ball.

Estelle was watching her with wide eyes, and she could not refuse to go. She could not let her own fears prevent her sister from enjoying the day: she had promised that she would chaperone Estelle. Mama and Papa were all very well, but they tended to position themselves in one place and talk to their friends—Lord and Lady Lavenham, for the most part—which meant that they could not accompany Estelle around the gardens.

"I found my shawl," Estelle called from the drawing-room, and Belinda stepped out into the hallway.

"We'd best be going," Mama said softly, and they hurried downstairs to the entrance, where Papa was waiting. Lady Sinclair also lived just outside London, in a sprawling manor about four miles away from their own.

The coach rattled along for twenty minutes, then slowed down and Belinda tensed, watching as they rolled slowly down a pebbled drive and up to a manor-house. The building was made of gray stone, tall and gracious, with gables and scrollwork adorning the outside. The thing that drew her attention, however, was the grounds. Extensive gardens bordered the manor, which was set amidst vast emerald lawns and tall trees.

"It's beautiful," she murmured as she alighted from the coach. Papa smiled and nodded.

"It is. Though I feel sure that you could do better with the flowers. You and Lady Sinclair will have a lot to talk of, I think." His eyes sparkled with warmth.

"Thank you, Papa," Belinda said, feeling touched. She gazed around, staring up at the tall pine trees, the color a perfect complement for the gray stone of the house.

"Well, let us go in," Mama said, walking slowly over the pebbles of the drive.

They followed her through the front doors, where Belinda and Estelle handed their shawls to the butler. Belinda barely noticed the entrance-way, her heart thudding with nerves as they approached the dining room, where the sound of genteel talk drifted out of the big doors.

Lady Sinclair greeted them at the dining room doors, curtseying low. She was perhaps Mama's age, Belinda guessed, with her black hair—with the lightest touch of gray—styled in elaborate curls which peeked out from under a soft turban headdress in pale yellow. Her gown was likewise yellow. Her face was thin and angular, her eyes a little lighter than her hair, and they sparkled with humor and interest.

"Good afternoon," Belinda greeted her politely.

"Welcome," Lady Sinclair said, sounding deeply sincere. "The rest of the guests are assembling on the lawn," she explained, gesturing them towards big doors at the back of the dining room, which led out onto a terrace and into the grounds below. "Please feel free to join them."

Belinda glanced around the dining room, seeing a few older women sitting at a table there, apparently playing cards. She could not see Lady Talbot or any of her circle there, and she let out a sigh of relief. She followed Mama and Papa into the garden.

"This is nice," Mama exclaimed contentedly, as she walked down the low staircase and onto a stone path which wound around a wide green lawn. Belinda gazed around, looking at the flowerbeds, which hosted lilies, daisies, and tulips. She looked over at the table on the lawn and tensed nervously, seeing Lady Talbot among the guests.

"Look there," Estelle murmured from beside her. "It's a water-garden. Shall we go over there and have a closer look at it?"

Belinda nodded, grateful to go away from the lawn and the table, where Lady Talbot's gaze had turned inexorably to her.

"How beautiful," Estelle breathed, staring out over the pond. It was perhaps six yards long, maybe more, and three yards wide. Belinda stared at it, the beauty of the blue water and the pink lilies calming and alluring, the bank of the pool a mass of lush greenery and framed with tall conifers.

"It is very beautiful," Belinda agreed. In her mind, she recreated the water-garden, only in her version, there were narcissus and irises planted close by, and the bridge was framed with a willow tree, not bordered by tall conifers.

"Shall we go over there?" Estelle asked. Belinda glanced across the bridge, seeing that there were some young people of around Estelle's age there. Clearly Estelle wished to join them.

The moment she had seen Lady Talbot, all Belinda had wanted to do was escape, but Lady Sinclair was calling them from the lawn, and she stiffened, knowing they had to go over there. "In a moment, dear," Belinda said gently. "The others are going to the lawn."

"Mayhap we'll all return and explore after Lady Sinclair has made whatever announcement she needs to make," Estelle agreed, though she sounded a little downcast. Belinda walked with her to the lawn, where Lady Sinclair was waiting to make an announcement.

"Ladies and gentlemen, welcome," their hostess declared. "I do not wish to keep you long, only to mention that there will be lawn games played after tea—battledore and shuttlecock, lawn bowls and throwing hoops, among others."

The announcement was met with high spirited cheers. Belinda looked around and saw Lady Talbot's eyes narrow, and she looked around for an escape.

"Belinda!" Lila's voice drew her attention from the edge of the group by the tea-table, making her heart lift.

"Lila! What a nice surprise," she said with genuine warmth. Lila was wearing a gown in pale green muslin, her hair in a loose bun that was held in place with elaborately twined ribbon. Her smile was warm as she greeted Belinda.

"I am so pleased to see you," Lila said, taking her hands in her own. "Come on...let's find some lemonade and perhaps some sandwiches, if we're allowed to eat anything before the tea arrives."

"Yes," Belinda murmured, feeling her throat tighten at the thought of approaching the table. Lady Talbot was still there, and Mama and Papa were not anywhere nearby, but were deep in conversation with Lady Sinclair and their other friends. She allowed Lila to lead her over to the table, but with a heavy heart. As she neared the table, she spotted Lady Talbot, who likewise saw her.

"Oh! Look," Lady Talbot said loudly as Belinda and Lila approached the table. "I smell scandal coming this way. But look! This time she hasn't got a beast with her."

Belinda felt her blood heat up with a mix of shame and rage and she looked at her toes. She could feel hot tears in her eyes as one of the other women chuckled.

"What a pair that must be, eh? A beast and a girl with a terrible reputation of her own."

More laughter followed, and comments about the Duke of Norendale. Belinda felt her anger rise, blotting out the shame.

"I hope you are just as cruel to all the ladies at your salon, Lady Talbot," she challenged the woman.

"I...I..." Lady Talbot stammered, her eyes widening with shock. "How dare you?"

"I..." Belinda tried to think of something to say, but her courage had deserted her, Lady Talbot's rage almost more frightening than her cruelty had been.

Lila stepped closer. Her brown eyes were dark with anger.

"Lady Belinda is a good woman," she declared. "And, Lady Talbot, you spend far too much time in idle gossip about people about whom you know nothing at all."

Belinda tensed, waiting for the onslaught as the older woman's jaw dropped with indignation.

"How dare you!" Lady Talbot began, "you upstart wretch! I'll show you who to insult..."

51

Lila smiled sweetly at her, interrupting her tide of harsh words.

"My mother knows the lady patrons at Almack's," she said in a voice that had steel running underneath it. "And if you threaten me or my friend, be sure that the whole of the *Ton* will know of it."

She turned her back on the woman and took Belinda by the hand. They moved away. Belinda let out a breath as they moved past.

"Thank you, Lila," she whispered, her hands shaking where she gripped them together, trying to control her emotions.

"What horrid women," Lila answered her, both her cheeks red with high color from her suppressed anger.

"It's my fault," Belinda whispered, barely able to control her tears. "I danced with the Duke of Norendale, and now they have even more horrid things to say about me. I can't bear it," she whispered softly, and she could not stop herself from weeping. The women's words had hit hard, much harder than she would have expected. Following the ball and the horrible articles in the newspaper, it was even more unbearable than before.

"It is nothing like your fault," Lila said firmly as they walked to the water-garden. "You didn't tell those horrid old women to enjoy gossiping about you, did you?" she added.

"No," Belinda said with a sniff. "No, I certainly didn't."

"Exactly. They are just like that. And if they weren't gossiping about you, they'd be tearing someone else to shreds. They are just miserable, cruel old witches."

Belinda giggled, touched by her friend's fierceness in defense of her.

"Do you see? It isn't your fault. Now, let's go and get some tea," Lila said gently.

Belinda shook her head. "I'd prefer to stay here for a minute." Her voice was soft. "I should be chaperoning Estelle," she added sorrowfully. She felt too scared to go out from the safe corner behind the hedge. She didn't want anyone else to stare and be cruel.

"Your mama and papa can keep an eye on her for the moment," Lila said firmly. "You sit here for a bit if you wish. I am going over to the refreshments table. I saw a very handsome officer earlier, and I want to see if he's still out there."

"Lila!" Belinda giggled, shocked surprise making her laugh.

"Well?" Lila asked, grinning.

"Go and see if he's still there," Belinda said warmly. "I'll sit here for a moment and then come and join you. Mayhap Lady Talbot will fall in the pond."

"Mayhap," Lila said with a laugh. "And a big frog will eat her like the troublesome insect that she is."

"A very big frog," Belinda added, giggling.

Lila laughed and went out through the gate and Belinda sat watching from her place on the bench. Sitting there, she could see nobody at all, just hear the distant sounds of laughter and conversation. A butterfly flew past silently, and she watched it, feeling her heart ache.

She had managed to laugh with Lila, but in truth the comments from the women had hurt her deeply. She took a deep breath, steadying herself.

"It's not their opinion that matters," she said firmly. "I matter to myself. The shame belongs to them and not to me."

She recalled what it had felt like, dancing with the infamous Beast of Norendale—she had felt like she was flying. It was a beautiful feeling.

When she remembered that sensation, she felt curious more than afraid and she took another deep breath.

She stood up from the bench, interested to see Lila and the handsome army officer, and interested, too, to see if there was anyone tall and dark and handsome like the Duke of Norendale, who she'd danced with, out there in the garden.

Chapter 9

Benedict surveyed the lawn, his stomach twisting into a knot of anxiety. Since the scandal—or apparent scandal—of his dancing with Lady Belinda, he had been more nervous than ever to go out into society, for fear of the mockery and cruel words that would make him lose his temper. If it weren't for Nancy, he would not have agreed to attend Lady Sinclair's party in the first place.

"Benedict," his mother hissed, as he went to stand in the shade of a tree. "Will you at least attempt to look cheerful? This is supposed to be a party. Lady Kearney and her daughter will be watching you."

Benedict turned a sour gaze on his mother.

"I am only here for Nancy's sake," he said back. "I have no desire to be here. I cannot act cheerful when I have not the slightest inclination to feel it."

"Oh, *Benedict*," his mother sighed in frustration.

She was about to say more, but Benedict turned away and walked briskly down the garden to join Nancy, who was heading towards a group of young people. Young ladies in pastel gowns and young men in velvet jackets stood in the shadow of a tree, and he felt the need to keep watch over Nancy. He tensed, noticing that Lady Penelope was there among the guests.

"...What a charming dress!" Lady Penelope gushed as Nancy joined them. Benedict smiled to himself. Nancy had genuine friends, and he was glad of it. They could protect her at least as well as he might—especially against a threat like Darrow. His own attempts to protect her were proving rather useless, since his mother refused to listen to him in every respect.

Benedict, standing three or four yards away, watched Nancy fondly. She was a dear girl—kind to her peers, courteous and polite. She had a good heart and he tensed as he spotted Lord Darrow: he would recognize that fellow anywhere, even from the back across the garden. He could see a head of sandy hair and a tall, slim frame and he knew it was him at once, his body tensing with remembered fear and his hands making fists.

His mother's words about "squabbles" still hurt, nearly a week later. She truly seemed to believe it was all childish foolery.

He knew better—he knew Darrow was dangerous, and her determination to ignore him was just confusing.

"Benedict! Good afternoon."

Benedict jumped and swore, turning to where his best friend, Clinton, had appeared. Clinton lived not more than four miles away, and he and Benedict had attended Oxford together. Clinton's family was noble—his father was a viscount—but they were famously poor. His mother disapproved the connection, but Benedict was always pleased to see Clinton, even if Clinton startled him and made him feel grumpy.

"You startled me," he growled.

"Sorry," Clinton said, though the grin on his face suggested no such remorse. "I say, old chap—you look moribund."

"Thank you," Benedict said with irony. He turned away, looking sourly out over the garden. "I think I have a reason for it."

"What? That idle nonsense the papers had about you last week?" Clinton chuckled.

"No. Not that," Benedict said swiftly, though, in truth, it had not helped his mood. Being insulted all over London was not pleasant.

"What then?" Clinton asked, lifting a glass. "Dashed good, this lemonade."

"Mm." Benedict looked away, staring out over the garden. Darrow was still at the table, chatting and laughing with someone. He couldn't see who, but he could see the fellow's flippant gestures and he felt rage boil inside him—rage and fear. He knew it was ridiculous—he could have felled the man with a single blow—but somewhere in him, a boy cowered at the sound of Darrow's taunts, and at the chants of the other boys who followed him. He could not see or hear Darrow without remembering.

"I hear there's going to be lawn bowls," Clinton said, his voice level. "I bet I wipe the floor with you."

"What?" Benedict let out an explosive laugh. "Clinton. Please tell me you haven't taken up the pastime of lawn bowls?"

"I did," Clinton said, and Benedict saw his lips tug in a grin, despite his efforts to maintain a straight face. "Yesterday, I did."

Benedict chuckled, shoulders lifting. He turned and looked at Clinton, still chuckling.

"You are unbearable, you know that?" he asked with a grin

he couldn't fail to show.

"I am." Clinton sounded happy with the acknowledgment.

Benedict made a face, raising his brow in mock-disbelief. Clinton laughed.

"You mentioned I seemed worried. It's about Nancy," Benedict explained slowly. The joking and foolery had made it easier to talk. "It's Mother. She's trying to push her into something that I don't approve of." He paused. "It's Darrow," he managed to say, his voice tight in his throat.

"Perdition take him," Clinton growled.

Clinton knew Benedict's story—Benedict had to tell him, since in his first year at Eton, it had affected him strongly, keeping him hiding in his rooms when the other youths were rowing on the canals. When Clinton asked, Benedict had explained why he did not join in, and why his nose was freshly broken. Clinton had understood.

"Mm." He nodded slowly. "That is exactly what I thought."

They stared out over the garden. Ladies and gentlemen stood around on the lawn, glasses of cordial held delicately in their hands, refreshing themselves in the afternoon's heat. Nancy and her friends had moved across the garden to the pond.

"I should go over and join her," he murmured, glancing over at Clinton, who inclined his head.

"Of course, old chap."

They crossed the lawn, walking to the pond.

As he crossed the lawn, he tensed. His mother was standing with Lord and Lady Kearney, not more than three yards away. She spotted him and smiled.

"Benedict! Come here!" she called to him, her voice light and apparently carefree. "Come and talk to Lady Penelope."

Benedict felt his entire body stiffen. It was not Lady Penelope's fault. She was shy and awkward, and he generally found interacting with her extremely difficult, but he could not blame her for that. His mother was to blame for pushing matters.

"Mother," he said tensely, but his mother was already turning to Lady Kearney, who beamed at her.

"My dear, do come and greet Benedict," she asked Lady Kearney.

"Your Grace! Grand to see you," Lady Kearney said,

executing a perfect curtsey. "Penelope will be delighted. There she is on the lawn. Penelope, dear! Come and see who is here."

Benedict glanced over at the pond, feeling desperate. Nancy was there and Lord Darrow had already reached the water's edge. Clinton saw his gaze.

"I'll go and stand with her," he promised.

"Thank you," Benedict murmured. Clinton headed across the lawn, and he whirled round as Penelope wandered over, racking his brain for some reason why he could not stay and talk to her.

"Your Grace," she murmured, her slim face moving into a grin that Benedict thought didn't quite reach her lovely blue eyes. She executed a perfect curtsey, just low enough to show deference to his Dukedom and just deep enough to suit the informal setting. "How delightful to see you here!" Her voice was light and playful and not quite sincere.

Benedict nodded, glancing around awkwardly. "Charmed, my lady," he murmured.

They walked a few paces down the path, neither of them saying anything. Benedict felt as though everyone on the lawn was staring at him. He knew everyone would think he was mannerless and unsociable if he said nothing, but he could not think of anything to say to Lady Penelope, who walked beside him silently, eyes downcast, too shy to speak.

"A fine warm day, is it not?" Benedict asked as they walked down the path, heading towards the front of the house.

"It is," Lady Penelope commented, looking up and then looking down again.

Benedict paused, trying to think of something else to say. He could see the younger guests now, near the pond. Two young men had thrown sticks in, and they were racing them, splashing the water by tossing stones behind them. The young ladies gazed on admiringly.

"Lots of guests today, eh?" Benedict asked, trying to start to talk with her.

"Many guests indeed," she agreed primly, and looked over at the pond. Benedict took a deep breath.

"Do you like tea-parties?" he asked as they rounded the corner of the path, heading towards where he presumed was a rose-arbor, since he could smell the scent of roses and lavender, soft and sweet in the air.

"Yes, I do," Lady Penelope replied.

Benedict took another breath. "Do you like walking?"

"Not particularly," Lady Penelope commented. "My favourite pastime is decorating bonnets. And I like flowers too." She smiled. "And painting still-life."

"Oh." Benedict felt his brow crease into a frown. Nancy had tried painting and arranging flowers, but she preferred riding and even she would have felt out of her depth discussing either of the other topics. Lady Penelope chattered on excitedly.

"I was in Bond Street last week shopping with Mama. Lady Westley went with us, and Lady Gertrude. I found a grand bonnet, and I bought some ribbons for it, and then Lady Gertrude..."

Benedict tried to follow her conversation, but it was full of references to shops, tea-houses, and other places that he almost never went to in London, and much of it was interspersed with gossip about the ladies who had been out shopping at the same time. He had never had the slightest interest in gossip, knowing too well how cruel and false it could be. He tried to make polite comments occasionally.

"And Lady Basingstoke had such a horrid hat!" Lady Penelope giggled. "Why! Whoever would wear a white turban with red acanthus print, decorated with an ostrich feather? The idea!" She giggled loudly.

Benedict drew in another breath. "I thought ostrich feathers were fashionable," he murmured, trying to defend the poor lady a little. Lady Penelope stared at him.

"Not in turbans," she said succinctly.

Benedict swallowed and looked around, trying to find something else to say, to change the topic from her constant degradation of every lady in society. He spotted some ladies standing by the fountain and was grateful that he recognized one of them. He had been introduced to her briefly at Nancy's debut.

"Is that not Lady Gertrude there?" he asked Lady Penelope, and she grinned and nodded, waving at the young lady, who was wearing a pink-and-white muslin dress, her black ringlets framing a long oval face.

"Yes, it is!" Lady Penelope waved at the other young lady, who smiled and waved back.

"We're going to play battledore and shuttlecock after tea," Lady Gertrude called. Lady Penelope grinned.

"Grand!"

"We're one person short," Lady Gertrude added.

Lady Penelope beamed up at him. "Oh, I must go and play!" she declared passionately. "Would you mind if I talked with them, Your Grace?" Her blue eyes were wide as if she implored him to say yes.

"Of course, you must go and plan your game," Benedict said at once. Lady Penelope looked delighted.

"Thank you for the walk, Your Grace" she called, barely glancing over at him as she hurried across the lawn—not running but walking briskly. Benedict smiled to himself and lifted his hand politely in a wave, and then walked across to the lawn where the tea had been served.

He spotted his mother, talking to the Kearneys, but Clinton came over before he could decide if he was going to join her.

"Come on," Clinton repeated, sensing that Benedict wanted to find a seat. "Let's go and sit over there. I have a mind to position myself close to the best food. We have tarts, and cake, and pie, and all sorts of good things up this end. The sandwiches are down there, and, frankly, they are welcome to them." He paused. "I think that..."

Benedict stopped hearing what anyone was saying, because five people had rounded the corner of the hedge and were coming straight towards him. Two of them were older, and three of them were young ladies. One had reddish hair and he didn't recognize her at all, one was blonde, and he knew he had seen her before, and the third, who held all of his attention so that he could look nowhere else, and who was wearing a white-and-yellow dress with little white flowers woven into her soft curls, was Lady Belinda.

He stared into her green eyes and the scene around them faded.

She was here at the party, and she was walking over to him.

Chapter 10

Belinda stared across the table at the Duke of Norendale. She felt her heart stop. She rooted in place, gazing at him, the chatter and bustle fading around her.

"Lady Belinda," he murmured.

"Your Grace." She dropped a brief curtsey, gazing up at him in confusion.

"Come, sweetling," Mama murmured from her left, making her blink, as it brought her back to the moment. "If you sit there, then Estelle can sit next to you, over here."

"Yes, Mama," Belinda murmured, as the meaning sifted through her confused head. She drew out the chair, looking at the Duke as she sat down.

He stared at her as if he, too, was transfixed, and then he seemed to recall where he was because he pulled out his chair and sat down opposite her. Her heart almost stopped.

"There," Mama said from Belinda's left, sounding pleased.

"Sister," Estelle whispered urgently from beside her, making her turn, dreamily, to hear what her sister was saying. "Could you pass me the tea? Please?"

Belinda frowned, wondering at her sister's urgent tone, then nodded in understanding as her gaze focused on the teapot. It was close to Lord Jeremy, the honey-haired young man, and Belinda felt a smile tug at the corner of her lip. Estelle was overcome with shyness—too shy to ask him to pass her the teapot.

She stiffened as she saw that the teapot was too far across the table for her to reach; closer to the Duke.

"Um...Your Grace?" she managed to say, but her voice sounded like a whisper. She could not understand why she was so shy of him. It had to be his fearsome reputation, she told herself firmly. He leaned forward to hear her clearly.

"My lady? May I assist you?"

"Please," Belinda said at once, finding her voice. "The teapot. Might you pass it across to us?"

"Oh. Of course," he reached out for it and lifted it easily, as though it weighed nothing. Belinda reached to take it, her fingers brushing his and an unexpected sensation raced up her nerves and made her heart skip a beat.

"Thank you," she murmured.

"Of course."

Their eyes met and Belinda felt her cheeks flush bright red. His eyes were so striking, the irises so dark she could barely see the difference between them and the pupils. His nose was thin and chiseled, his jaw firm. He was handsome, but there was something about him that made her nervous and uncomfortable.

"Sister?" Estelle whispered from beside Belinda, making her jump with surprise. "Sorry," Estelle added with a giggle, this time speaking a little louder. "Would you like tea too?"

"Oh. Please," Belinda agreed at once, grateful for the distraction. "Thank you."

"No trouble," Estelle said, grinning.

Estelle was looking confusedly at her.

"Sister?" Estelle murmured as she reached for a tart on the tray. "Are you feeling well?"

"Yes. Yes, I'm quite well. Thank you for asking," she added distantly, watching as the Duke of Norendale poured himself some tea. He was watching her, and she did not know what to do, so she swiftly lifted her napkin to her lips, blushing awkwardly. He smiled.

"It's hot today, is it not?" he asked. His eyes sparkled and she felt her throat tighten.

"Um, yes," she managed. "It is. Very hot."

"There is a pleasant breeze, though," he continued, and Belinda nodded a little desperately. Her insides were burning with awkwardness, and she felt her stomach twist with a mix of fear and some strange feeling that felt almost like anticipation.

"Yes. A pleasant breeze," she answered shyly, reaching for her teacup.

"Belinda, dearest?" Mama called her from her right. "I was just telling Lady Lavenham about those beautiful pink flowers you had planted in the arbor. Can you remind me what they are called?"

"Clematis, Mama," Belinda said immediately. When she looked back, the Duke was in conversation with his mother, bending close to her to hear what she was saying. His expression was tense, a vein pulsing near his jaw. Belinda frowned. Something was clearly troubling him. She gazed down at her plate, hoping he did not see her staring.

Estelle called her, making her whip round to her sister on her left.

"What is it?"

Estelle smiled shyly. "I wanted to tell you something," she whispered. "Lord Jeremy asked me to walk with him."

"Oh?" Belinda smiled, feeling joy flood through her. Her smile turned to a frown as she realized that her sister could not risk walking unaccompanied with him. She recalled what had happened to her instantly, concern filling her. "Someone must chaperone you."

"I know," Estelle answered immediately, looking at Belinda a little confusedly. "That is why I told you, sister. You could accompany us. Please?" she added, her tone imploring.

"Of course," Belinda answered, though after her confrontation with Lady Talbot, she did not want to go anywhere without Mama and Papa nearby.

"Good. Thank you," Estelle breathed. Belinda smiled to herself. Her heart melted with Estelle's youthful joy. She had never had the freedom and innocence to feel that way, and she was grateful that her younger sister's life was different to her own.

"Lady Estelle?" A voice called and Belinda looked up, spotting Lord Jeremy across the table. He was staring at her sister, and the shine of his eyes suggested to her that he truly was smitten.

"Lord Jeremy." Estelle's voice sounded like a whisper, as if she had a little trouble forcing it up through a tight throat. Belinda smiled to herself.

"Might you pass me the sandwiches, please?" he asked.

"Oh, of course," Estelle replied, lifting the plate remarkably steadily. He gazed at her raptly.

Belinda grinned, looking down at her plate. They clearly cared for each other already. She reached for her tea, sipping it thoughtfully. As she put it down in the saucer, she tensed. The Duke was watching her across the table, his gaze piercing, his expression unreadable. She put her tea down carefully and her eyes darted to her plate, her cheeks burning.

Lady Sinclair sat six seats away from where she herself was. She heard the lady tap a teaspoon on her cup to get their attention.

"I wished to announce that we may begin playing lawn-games now, if anyone is eager to begin," Lady Sinclair announced in a warm voice.

Three or four youths, clearly tired of sitting and talking politely, stood up almost at once, pushing in their chairs.

"Sister?" Estelle asked, her voice shy and hesitant. "Might we go for a walk?"

"Yes, of course, Estelle," she said swiftly, pushing back her chair. "Come. Let us go for a walk."

The Duke's dark-eyed gaze met hers and she felt her cheeks flush with heat. She could not help wondering what he was thinking.

Chapter 11

Benedict stared out across the lawn to where Lady Belinda walked with her sister, crossing the path and going towards the pond. Her walk was measured and graceful, her motion like a beautiful flower swaying in the sun. He gazed out at her, the brief words he had managed to exchange with her drifting through his mind like petals drifting from the ornamental apple tree beyond.

You're being silly, he told himself firmly. *She's probably half-terrified. You're the Beast of Norendale, remember?*

His mouth moved into a thin, firm line. The rumors pained him even more than usual as he watched her.

"Benedict," his mother said loudly, making him jump.

"Mother," he began, his frustration at her giving him a fright making it hard to focus. "What is it?"

"Nancy and I wish to take a turn about the lawn," his mother said firmly. "We want you to accompany us."

"Of course," Benedict said formally. He was annoyed at the interruption, but he was glad to be able to chaperone Nancy.

"Thank you," his mother murmured, and if she was speaking in irony, it was not blatantly done. Benedict chose to believe she meant her thanks honestly and pushed back his chair.

"I hope you're having a pleasant day," he murmured to Nancy. She was wearing a pale pinkish gown—his mother said it was apricot, but he had no idea—and her long black hair was arranged in a braided bun, decorated with little pink flowers. She smiled shyly at him.

"I am," she said softly. "A very pleasant day." Benedict smiled.

"Good," he said sincerely.

"We shall go that way," his mother said from beside Nancy, and Benedict lifted a shoulder lightly.

He fell into step with his mother, his thoughts straying to Lady Belinda as they neared the path that led to the pond. He relaxed as he walked with Nancy.

Down on the lawn on the left, just a few paces away, Benedict spotted two older women were watching him, one of them raising her fan to her lips as though concealing her words.

Benedict groaned inwardly.

As he rounded the corner of the hedge, he stopped. Standing six or seven yards away, next to an ornamental fountain that he had not noticed before because of the high hedge around the pond, was a tall lady in a long white-and-yellow dress. It was Lady Belinda.

She stared at him, her gaze widening in surprise.

"Lady Belinda."

"Your Grace," she greeted softly.

"Good afternoon again," he managed to say, bowing low. Seeing her took him by surprise and he had not the slightest idea what to say.

"A fine party," she commented lightly.

"Yes," he said at once. "Yes, it is. Most fine." He paused, recalling something important. "My lady," he began slowly. "I wanted to say sorry."

"For what?" Lady Belinda asked, confusedly.

"For having put you in a difficult position at Lady Estelle's ball. I am sorry for the way people wagged their tongues about it."

"You mean about our dance?" Lady Belinda asked, one brow lifting.

"Quite so," he replied.

"It was not your fault. It was as much mine." She sounded sad.

"Not at all," he said at once. "It was not remotely your fault. Besides, these slanderous articles are more than can be tolerated—or should be," he added hotly.

"Quite so," she agreed. "They are too much to be borne. But an unfortunate feature of our current way of life."

"Mm." Benedict sighed.

She smiled and he forgot how to breathe for a moment. She was pleasant to look at usually, but her smile was breathtaking.

As he looked up, he spotted Nancy rounding the pond and his heart stopped. Darrow was with her, and his eyes met Benedict's and held them, a mocking smile spreading across his lips.

Benedict looked at Lady Belinda. She looked back, that soft gaze gentle. She had not noticed the smirk on Darrow's face, evidently.

"Good afternoon," Nancy greeted Belinda smilingly, standing a few paces from them both. She looked at Benedict hesitantly.

"Nancy," he greeted her. He ignored Darrow utterly, choosing not even to look at him. "This is Lady Belinda. Lady Belinda, may I introduce to you my sister, Lady Nancy?"

"I'm pleased to meet you," Lady Belinda murmured.

"We were having a fine walk. Were we not, Lady Nancy?" Darrow commented.

"Yes," Nancy said softly.

Benedict felt his brow rise. He looked at Darrow, trying not to show how he was fighting the urge to hit him. When he beamed like that, all Benedict wanted was to hit him, hard—mayhap break his nose like Benedict's had been broken all those years ago.

"Enjoying the afternoon?" Darrow asked, his eyes sparkling at Benedict. Benedict coughed, his throat tight with fury. He turned to Nancy, about to suggest that he, she, and Lady Belinda go back to the tea-table together, but Nancy was talking to Lady Belinda in a low voice. He and Darrow were alone together.

Benedict scowled.

"Nothing to say?" Darrow taunted.

"It *was* a pleasant afternoon," Benedict managed. "But then you turned up."

Darrow chuckled. "You've not changed," he said spitefully. "Still so unoriginal in your insults. And it seems like you found company on your level." He scoffed.

"I beg your pardon...?" Benedict demanded, fighting to hide how angry he was.

"That one there," Darrow said lightly. "Lady Belinda. She's got a terrible reputation. Just like you. I don't know if you're planning to give yourself an even worse one by associating with her, or what you're thinking. But then, I don't suppose you think before you act."

Benedict felt his hand make a fist and he took a deep breath, knowing that if the fellow did not move on, he would hit him.

He stalked forward, but a hand rested on his arm.

"Brother!" Nancy was at his elbow, looking up at him with a hesitant smile. "Lady Belinda suggested that we play a game of Whist. Do you want to join us?" she asked.

"That would be pleasant," Benedict said, then tensed. If that meant they would play with Darrow, he would rather not. Darrow raised a brow.

"I do not like the game," he said thinly. "I will return to the tea-table."

Benedict let out a sigh of relief.

Nancy giggled. "Come on, Lady Belinda! Let us go and play."

"Yes. That would be a jolly way to spend the afternoon," Belinda replied, smiling.

Benedict felt his heart fill with warmth as he walked with them towards the card-tables, grateful to them both for diverting him from his anger, and eager to play cards.

Chapter 12

Belinda glanced sideways out of the corner of her eye as she neared the lawn. The Duke was behind them, and she could feel her cheeks burning, aware of him walking a few yards away.

Beside her, Lady Nancy smiled brightly at her, then frowned as they approached the place of play. Four tables had been set out on the lawn under the shade of the trees.

"There aren't any unpaired people," Lady Nancy said a little worriedly. "And we need four people for Whist."

Just as Belinda glanced around, looking for a fourth person, she caught sight of a red-haired man, who was waving at them.

"Benedict!" The man called and Belinda realized he was addressing the Duke. "Lady Nancy," he added warmly. "Delighted to see you."

"Pleased to see you here, Lord Clinton," Lady Nancy murmured, dropping a formal curtsey. "Lady Belinda? This is Lord Clinton, a dear friend of my brother's."

"Pleased to meet you," Belinda murmured, dropping a curtsey.

"Charmed, my lady. Excuse my intrusion. I was just on my way to see if anything diverting was happening at the card tables."

"Depends how much diversion you want," Benedict commented lightly.

Lady Nancy chuckled. "We were thinking to play whist," she explained. "But we need a fourth person to join us."

"Well, if that isn't more astonishing than anything else!" Lord Clinton exclaimed with a grin. He bowed to Lady Nancy. "If you would allow me to join in the game, I'd be delighted."

Lady Nancy's eyes sparkled, and she nodded.

Belinda smiled to herself and followed the two of them to the card-table. Beside her, the Duke walked without speaking. She glanced sideways, taking the chance to study him closely. He was handsome, she had to admit, with that long face and square jaw, his nose fine and thin, his cheekbones high.

I wonder if that bump is from a break, she thought to herself, studying his long, fine nose.

She felt herself blush as he looked across and she looked at

68

her toes, not speaking until they were settled at the table.

Lord Clinton reached for a pack of cards that had been set out in the middle of the table for them.

"I'll deal for this round," he said swiftly. He rummaged in his pocket and took something out, then held it out to Lady Nancy. It was two short twigs, held clutched in his fist. "Pick one," he instructed Lady Nancy. She smiled and took one of the two twigs from his hand.

"The one who draws the short stick partners me for this game," Lord Clinton explained, and Nancy giggled as she looked at the twig she held.

"I think this must be the short stick," she told Lord Clinton, holding it out. "For that one cannot be shorter than this."

Lord Clinton laughed and opened his fist. "Right!" he agreed, laughing warmly.

Belinda looked at the Duke nervously. If Lord Clinton and Lady Nancy were playing together, that meant that she and he were playing together also.

Benedict's gaze met hers and held it. She looked away shyly.

"Come on, then," Lord Clinton called, making them both turn and look at him where he stood by the table. "Let's take our places. I'm the dealer. That means you have to shuffle the deck of cards," he added, turning to Benedict, who had sat down on his left.

Belinda, who was sitting opposite Benedict, watched as he raised his brows in surprise when Lord Clinton handed him the pack of cards. He shuffled them with professional ease, riffling them together as if he played cards every day. Belinda looked down at his hands. He had long, elegant fingers and large hands, the nails pared back like a soldier's.

"Well! That's a thorough job," Lord Clinton exclaimed. He took the pack from Lord Benedict, grinning at his friend.

He put them in front of Belinda, who knew the rules of Whist well, though she had not played for years, and knew that she had to cut the deck.

Lord Clinton accepted the cards from her and then started to deal them out, giving them each thirteen cards. As Belinda lifted her hand of cards, Lord Clinton turned over the last remaining card of the pack, which he had kept for himself.

"The leading suit is clubs," he declared. Belinda saw the

Duke smile and she bit her lip, hiding a grin. To judge from the look on his face, that suit favored him well.

She waited while Lord Clinton placed a card. He placed the King of Diamonds.

"Beat that," he challenged Benedict, laughing.

"Pleasurably," the Duke said with a grin, and put down the Ace of Clubs.

They were all silent for a moment and the Duke's eyes sparkled, his expression satisfied. Belinda wanted to smile.

"Damn..." Lord Clinton swore, then reddened. "Apologies, ladies," he said, glancing at Lady Nancy and Belinda. Lady Nancy giggled.

"Apology accepted," she replied warmly, and put down a card on the table. It was the Ten of Clubs. Lord Clinton groaned.

Belinda chuckled and Nancy laughed.

Belinda glanced at her hand. She could not beat the Ace of Clubs, but when the Duke won, then their team would start off on a fine footing.

"There," she replied softly, placing the Eight of Diamonds. Lord Clinton chuckled.

"Well, no question about who won there," he replied, looking at Benedict with a grin. "I should record the scores. First point goes to Benedict and Lady Belinda." He reached for a piece of paper on the desk nearby and scribbled on it with a pencil.

"It's my turn to start, I think," Benedict reminded them smugly. He put down the Ten of Hearts.

"Oh, for..." Lord Clinton blustered. They all laughed.

"I can beat that, brother," Lady Nancy said warmly, and placed the King of Hearts on the table.

Belinda smiled. She had the King of Clubs but hesitated as to whether to use it. After a moment, she put it down. Benedict glanced at her appreciatively. She blushed.

"Oh, blast," Lord Clinton swore, and threw down the Nine of Hearts. They all laughed.

Lord Clinton chalked up a second point for Benedict and her.

"My turn," Nancy declared sweetly. She placed the Queen of Clubs. Benedict made a grunt of apparent pain.

Lady Nancy and Lord Clinton won that round, and then the next one. It was Lord Clinton's turn to begin the next round and he set down the Ten of Diamonds. Benedict played a low card, the Four of Diamonds. Lady Nancy also had a low card. Belinda placed the Eight of Clubs and Benedict grinned.

"This round to Lady Belinda and Benedict," Lord Clinton said warmly, scribbling down the score.

Benedict smiled at her shyly and Belinda smiled back. It felt good to be playing with him. She had never really had a friend— not besides Lila, at any rate, but she had known Lila long before her coming-out ball. Since then, she had never met someone with whom she could indulge in something enjoyable like Whist.

Benedict was gazing down at the table considering. He was following the cards, she guessed—guessing what cards each player might have left. She looked up at him and he smiled warmly. She grinned back.

She considered her own strategy. Lord Clinton must have no high-ranking Diamond cards, as he'd already sworn more than once whenever someone chose Diamonds as the starting suit. She had the Nine of Diamonds, the strongest remaining card of that suit to be played. When it was her turn to choose the starting suit, she placed it boldly.

"Oh, for..." Lord Clinton, sitting beside her, exclaimed loudly. He threw down the Two of Diamonds and they all laughed.

"Another round for Lady Belinda and Benedict," Lord Clinton declared. He did not sound particularly upset about it.

Belinda glanced up, sensing someone was watching her, and noticed the Duke's gaze on her. His expression was gentle, almost fond, and she took a breath, feeling a little confused. He looked down again, apparently studying his cards, and she looked away, cheeks reddening with shyness, her brow furrowing with confusion.

"I can declare a winning team," Lord Clinton announced, when they reached the end of their cards to be played. "With eight rounds won, the winners are Lady Belinda and Benedict." He grinned at the Duke. "And perdition can take you," he added to his friend, who chuckled.

"Thank you, Clinton," he said warmly, as if his friend had complimented him. "It was a grand round of Whist."

"It was. It was," Lord Clinton agreed happily. "We'll win next time, eh, my lady?" he added, beaming at Lady Nancy, who blushed.

"I trust we shall, Lord Clinton," she agreed teasingly.

"Shall we play another round now?" Lord Clinton asked hopefully, but Benedict shook his head.

"No, old chap. I regret it, but no. I must find Mother and ask her if she wishes to return home for the afternoon. And besides, I must stretch my legs," he added, pushing back his chair. Lady Nancy smiled at Belinda and Lord Clinton.

"It was a delightful game," Lady Nancy said softly. "Thank you both. Thank you, brother," she added, turning to Benedict.

"I had a delightful time," he agreed. "I will take a turn about the grounds. Nancy?"

"I'll come too, brother."

Lord Clinton inclined his head swiftly, making Belinda smile to herself. "Me too," he said at once. "Lady Belinda? Will you walk with us a while?"

"I am sorry to say no. I must find my sister," Belinda said a little regretfully. Estelle would be upset, as Belinda had agreed to chaperone her.

"Lady Belinda?" The Duke called as she stepped forward. She tensed, turning. "Thank you," he said softly.

She blushed red and inclined her head politely. "It was a pleasure," she said, coloring further as he bowed.

She watched as they went off across the lawn, and couldn't help thinking that, as well as proving himself a talented card player, that he was also rather handsome.

Nonsense, Belinda, she told herself crossly. *You worked well together. That is all.*

All the same, despite her best attempts to be practical, she could not help thinking that he was a rather fine-looking man as well, if a very odd one who confused her most thoroughly indeed.

Chapter 13

The sound of Rowan snoring on the mat by the fire woke Benedict, as it always did. He lay in bed for a moment, blinking in the early morning light, and then slipped out of bed to the nightstand to rinse his face.

Thoughts of Lady Belinda drifted through his mind as he dabbed his face dry on the flannel: her warm, generous smile, her soft golden hair, her green eyes all played through his mind. He recalled her bright gaze as she placed a winning card, her playful laugh and that astute stare as she watched the other players. She was clearly a sensible, intelligent young woman.

He went to choose a shirt and trousers. He was an early riser—mostly because Rowan was accustomed to taking a morning walk a little after dawn colored the sky.

Lady Belinda's smile drifted into Benedict's thoughts again as he dressed. He swore at himself under his breath.

"Damn it! She's not interested in you, you fool."

She was a decent young lady—whatever the rumor-mongers said—and no decent young lady would be interested in him. He was the Beast of Norendale. His reputation was appalling. He swore again and stood, reaching for his jacket. At the door, Rowan whined, looking up at him with big, black imploring eyes.

Benedict grinned and ruffled Rowan's ears, feeling guilty for his earlier outburst. Rowan was incredibly sensitive to his moods, and any unease in Benedict troubled him. He stroked the dog's head gently and was rewarded with a tongue-lolling grin.

"Come on, old fellow," Benedict said gently as he opened the door. It was a cold day, clouds covering the sky and threatening rain, but Rowan needed to walk, and so Benedict had no choice but to go outdoors too. He'd tried, once, to send Rowan out on his own in the morning, but the big dog would go nowhere without him. Benedict believed it was because he was still scared of being left abandoned, as he had been when Benedict had found him as a puppy. He did not try again to make him go out by himself.

"It's cold out here, old chap," he murmured to Rowan as they went outside. Rowan was clearly untroubled by it, already bounding down the path. This was his favorite time of day. He had the whole garden to himself. The big dog raced along the pathways, heedless of his speed. Many were afraid of him, and Benedict felt that it disconcerted the poor creature, who didn't understand their fear, but only that they recoiled and shouted. It confused the big, friendly dog.

"I know how you feel, old chap," Benedict murmured ruefully. His own size and strength had been targeted, causing the likes of Darrow to see him as a threat and so as a target. Benedict ran a hand through his hair, determined not to let thoughts of Darrow slip into his mind and sour his morning. He would deal with that when he had the chance.

For the moment, he allowed his thoughts to drift to the game of whist again, and his memory of Lady Belinda producing the Ten of Clubs so casually, all the while with a knowing glimmer in her eyes.

She's a fine Whist player, he thought admiringly.

He was still amazed by how easy it had been to partner with her in the whist game. He had never had the experience of being so comfortable with another person—not besides Nancy, and the gap of more than ten years in their ages had meant he was usually more of her protector than her companion.

He frowned, noticing that Rowan had run out of sight. He pursed his lips to whistle, and just then a man walked around the corner.

"I say! A fine morning to you, old fellow!" Clinton's voice exclaimed stridently, making Benedict jump and whirl round crossly to face his friend, who had stopped over by the conifers by the edge of the lawn.

"Clinton! You startled me," Benedict grumbled, then nodded. "A fine morning it is," he agreed. Rowan, hearing the raised voices, bounded back from wherever he had been, running up to Benedict protectively. Benedict ruffled his head, soothing him. "It's all right, old chap," he assured him. He scowled at Clinton. Clinton raised a shoulder in apology.

"Sorry, old fellow," he said sincerely. "I was just taking a stroll. Grand day, this." He looked up at the sky.

"It's a rainy day," Benedict replied evenly.

"It's grand enough." He shrugged. "Couldn't sleep," he added lightly. "Have you had breakfast yet?"

74

"Not yet," Benedict said a little gruffly. He was used to taking his morning walk uninterrupted. It was time for Rowan and himself to enjoy being together, and a chance to work through his thoughts undisturbed before the start of the day.

"Sorry, old chap," Clinton said again. "I need some tea. Care to join me?"

"In a minute," Benedict said testily. "This fellow needs a walk," he added more gently, ruffling Rowan's ears again. Rowan barked, and took off, running to the bushes by the path that led up to the stables. He sat there and waited, looking over at Benedict as if willing him to come over and join him. Benedict took a deep breath. "How do you feel about walking?" he asked Clinton mildly.

"Most fond," Clinton said briskly. "I do like a walk. I like playing cards, too," he added with a grin. Benedict looked at him narrowly, wondering why he raised the subject.

"You seemed like you did not enjoy it much at Whist yesterday."

Clinton chuckled. "I got a horrid hand, old chap. Next time, you can deal. I seem to give myself the worst cards. Maybe I'll have more luck if you deal them." He grinned at Benedict, who grunted.

"You could have played the Jack of Diamonds sooner," he told him. Clinton blinked.

"Were you looking at my cards?" he demanded, laughing. Benedict shook his head.

"I was just following who had what," he said lightly. "I didn't know for sure until you played it."

"Oh! That's a rare talent," Clinton commented. "What did you think of her?"

"What?" Benedict demanded, stopping in his tracks. He stared at Clinton, who chuckled.

"Lady Belinda," he said in a conversational tone. "What did you think of her?"

"Friendly enough," Benedict said gruffly. He felt his one hand clutch at his sleeve, a habit when he was uncomfortable. He made his fingers uncurl and looked at Clinton crossly. "Why do you ask?"

"No reason, old chap," Clinton said mildly. "She just seemed a pleasant sort. That's all."

"Mm." Benedict grunted, glancing over at his friend suspiciously. Had he been watching them? he asked himself shyly.

What had he noticed?

"She played a good hand of Whist," Clinton continued mildly, staring out over the garden. They had reached the stables and Rowan was running ahead, bounding in and out of hedges, his long black tail discernible in the thick mist that still cloaked the estate. The sun might come out later, Benedict thought absently, glancing at the sky.

"Mm," he agreed, frowning. "What do you know of her?" he asked. His throat was tight, and he cleared it gruffly.

"Lady Belinda? Not much," Clinton explained. "I understand she was barred from Almack's a few years ago. I don't know the details, but from what I recall, the story was far from clean-cut."

"Oh?" Benedict asked, raising a brow.

"Mm." Clinton nodded. "I seem to recall a fellow made some allegations about her. Questioned her, um, moral conduct. With himself. Who'd believe that, eh?" He chuckled.

Benedict frowned, not quite grasping his meaning at first and then, as it made sense, he felt anger twist his heart.

"People will say anything," he managed to say. "Probably not a word of truth in it."

"Mm." Clinton nodded. "Quite so. A fine hedge, there," he added, staring out over the garden as they continued down the path. Benedict ignored him.

"I think it more likely that someone was covering up their own misdeeds," Benedict said, feeling his hand clench into a fist. He knew men like that all too well. Darrow was one, if his boasts when they had been at school had even been half-true, and that was one of the reasons he wanted his mother to keep him the greatest possible distance away from Nancy. He felt ill at the thought of what might have befallen Lady Belinda.

"Quite so, old chap," Clinton agreed.

Benedict looked at him confusedly. He had raised the topic of Lady Belinda and now he seemed reluctant to continue talking about her.

"I find it hard to believe ill of her," Benedict said firmly. Clinton nodded.

"As you say, old chap. As you say. But we were both just admiring her whist skills, eh? Just that." He turned away and Benedict felt confused, and then realized his friend was teasing him.

"Inside with you," Benedict grunted. "Let's go and get some tea." He looked around, whistling for Rowan, who took a few moments to appear, then bounded over to Benedict, his feet soaked with morning dew, and jumped up, leaving wet patches on his coat.

Clinton chuckled and Benedict laughed.

"Oh, you..." Benedict laughed, ruffling the dog's hair as Rowan jumped down again. Rowan walked by Benedict's right hand, Clinton on his left, and they all went into the entrance-way, the lamps bright after the darkness of the morning outside.

Benedict shrugged out of his coat, whistling for Rowan, who bounded up the stairs after him. Clinton walked beside him, and they all entered the breakfast room. The table was set with a porcelain tea-service and small breakfast plates, a toast-rack and little dishes of jam and butter set out neatly on the table. Rowan flopped down on the rug, stretching out by the fireplace, and Benedict drew out a chair and sat down, then reached for the teapot.

Benedict poured himself some tea, his thoughts drifting to what Clinton had said. He glanced over at his friend, who was apparently studying the imported porcelain statuettes on the mantel. Benedict frowned.

He felt sure Clinton had noticed something the previous day, and his cheeks burned as he wondered what he had seen.

Chapter 14

"He's going to be here any minute," Estelle hissed to Belinda. "What should I do?"

Belinda grinned to herself. Lord Jeremy and his parents were coming to call on them and Estelle was more than a little anxious. Belinda gestured to the chairs in the drawing room.

"Take a seat, just there," she advised gently. "You look beautiful," she added, and Estelle breathed out nervously.

"Are you sure?"

Belinda laughed. "I'm quite sure. Pink is such a lovely colour for you, sister. You look truly lovely."

"Thank you, sister," Estelle whispered, and settled down in the chair just as the butler appeared in the doorway.

"Lord and Lady Westbrooke, and Lord Jeremy, my ladies."

Estelle stiffened, her eyes big and wide and Belinda smiled to herself. She had never felt like that herself before, but she recognized the feeling all too well—the anticipation, the anxiety. She frowned.

Have I truly never felt that? she asked herself distantly. It was hard to say, since she understood it extremely well.

"Good morning," Lord Westbrooke greeted expansively. "Lady Grayleigh. Lady Belinda. Lady Estelle." He bowed to Mama, Belinda and Estelle; his face wreathed in smiles.

"Good morning," they all greeted softly. Lady Westbrooke came in next, and they all curtseyed. Lord Jeremy bowed, eyes shining up at Estelle.

"Good morning, my lady," he murmured, and Belinda smiled to herself, seeing Estelle's face flush pink at the low greeting.

"Would you all like to move to the tea-table?" Mama asked, gesturing to the table in the corner of the drawing room, where the butler had laid out a pretty porcelain tea-service decorated with paintings of pink and yellow flowers, and some sandwiches and other good things to eat.

"I would be pleased to," Lord Jeremy answered, though his gaze lingered on Estelle. Belinda looked away, hiding her grin. It made her deeply happy to see her sister so joyful.

They all went over to the tea-table to sit down. Belinda

listened with half an ear to the conversations at the table, her mind drifting. Part of her thoughts dwelled on the expected visit of Lila, who had said she would also call for tea, while occasionally thoughts of the Duke of Norendale would drift into her mind, surprising her.

He was prudent and astute—that had been apparent in the way he played cards. He might be a little rash sometimes—the bold way he had played his ace in the first round did suggest a capacity to be extravagant, or impulsive. But all in all, he seemed like a man who thought deeply and said little. She liked that.

Here I am assessing him, she thought, a little confused. What in Perdition's name am I doing that for?

She bit her lip, hiding a grin. It was a strange thing to do, since she barely knew him.

"Pardon me," the butler said from the door, "but Miss Tate has just arrived."

"Oh! Grand," Mama said swiftly. "Please, show her in," she added to the butler, turning to glance at Belinda, who felt a sparkle of happiness lift her thoughtful mood. She turned to the door as Lila appeared, dressed in a white gown with a small blue pattern. She glanced around the room and then saw Belinda and grinned. Belinda grinned back warmly.

"Good morning," Lila greeted the assembled guests, inclining her head politely. "Sorry that I am late. The coach was delayed on the way out of London."

"Oh, you poor dear," Lady Westbrooke murmured kindly. "I understand. The roads are horridly congested at this time of day."

"Yes. Quite so," Lila agreed, giving her a warm smile. She glanced over at Belinda, who had kept a seat empty beside where she was sitting. Lila hurried over and pulled out the chair, sitting down and reaching for the teapot. She sighed breathlessly.

"Heavenly. Here at last," she murmured to Belinda, who giggled.

Conversation at the table had resumed in a lively tone and Belinda glanced over at Estelle, who was watching Jeremy as he related some story about a riding trip. Estelle's eyes were bright, and she seemed as focused on him telling the story as he was on telling it. Belinda felt her heart sparkle with warmth and turned to Lila, who was leaning back, sipping her tea.

"It's a fine morning," Lila commented, glancing at the windows, where the sun shone in brightly. It was a pleasure to have a warm day again after a few rainy, cold ones.

"It is," Belinda agreed. "Should we go for a walk, do you think?"

"A walk would be splendid," Lila agreed. "I've been in London for the last few days and I'm desperate to walk in the countryside. The city can be so stifling. Don't you think so?"

"I do," Belinda agreed. She hardly went to London since she could not attend Almack's and she preferred not to appear in the parks and libraries either; avoiding the cruel gossip. There was nothing she lacked at the estate: she had her flowers, and space for long walks. She was happy.

"Grand. As soon as we've had tea, we must suggest it."

Belinda nodded. She listened briefly to the conversation at the table—Lord Jeremy and Estelle were chatting away happily, as focused as if there was nobody else to talk to. Mama and Lord and Lady Westbrooke were deep in conversation too. Belinda watched for a moment or two, content to sit and not be part of any of the discussions around the table.

"It might be pleasant to take a turn about the grounds," Mama commented, as the group around the table emptied the second teapot and slowly ate the sandwiches. Lady Westbrooke nodded.

"Why! A turn about the grounds would be lovely. You have beautiful gardens here," she added, smiling warmly at Mama.

"You must tell Belinda that," Mama said, glancing at Belinda fondly. "She's in charge of them."

"Oh! How wonderful," Lady Westbrooke said sincerely. "You have a good eye for gardens," she added to Belinda. Belinda smiled.

"Thank you, my lady," she answered, her heart leaping. It was pleasant to be addressed appreciatively and kindly. Her mind returned to the garden-party, where Lady Talbot and her horrid friends had mocked her so cruelly, but she swiftly pushed the memory away and followed the guests to the door, Lila walking beside her to the front garden.

"I left a little early from the garden-party," Lila commented as they went down the path. "I didn't have a chance to ask you how you enjoyed it."

"Well enough," Belinda replied, cheeks reddening at the memory. She didn't know how to explain how she felt about playing cards with the Duke. He was a little frightening, but at the same time, she felt drawn to him and she didn't understand it. They had won the game because they cooperated so well, and that felt strange and pleasant; like he could be a friend.

"I didn't see you. I was playing lawn-bowls," Lila said, rolling her eyes and then grinning. "It was rather fun, actually. Lady Julianne and I and Lord Edgebrook played a game, just as a lark."

"You did?" Belinda asked with a chuckle.

"We did," Lila agreed. "It was actually enjoyable," she repeated with a smile. "But I wondered what you were up to. Did you play battledore and shuttlecock?"

"Oh. No," Belinda replied, cheeks warming. "I didn't. It's a little energetic for me, I'm afraid. No, I played cards."

"You did?" Lila asked, surprised. "I didn't know you liked card games."

"I don't, usually," Belinda answered. "But it was rather diverting. I met some new people—well, I had met the Duke of Norendale before," she corrected, "and..."

"You played cards? With the Duke of *Norendale*?" Lila grinned, her eyes sparkling. "Truly?"

"I did," Belinda said, a little defensive. "Whyever not?"

"No reason," Lila said with a chuckle. "Just that he seems so forbidding. I'm surprised he plays cards. He looks as though he'd find anything jolly a waste of time." She giggled.

Belinda frowned. "He didn't seem that stern," she said slowly. She recalled his big smile as he put the Ace on the pile, his laughter when someone made an amusing comment. "He's actually quite witty," she added thoughtfully. "And he has a sense of fun."

"Truly?" Lila repeated, her eyes wide. She was smiling at Belinda, and her brow quirked thoughtfully.

"What?" Belinda asked, feeling uncomfortable under her scrutiny.

"Nothing," Lila said quickly. "Nothing at all. You said you had planted some new daisies?" she added, and Belinda felt herself frown.

"Yes," she replied, wondering why her friend had changed the subject. She was going to ask her about it, but as they rounded the corner into the rose-garden, where Belinda had organized for some white daisies to be planted—the ones left over from where they planted the front garden-beds—Estelle and Jeremy appeared, accompanied by Lady Westbrooke.

"Oh! Sister," Belinda said with a smile, seeing Estelle blush as she walked up the path with Lord Jeremy. "I'm glad you're here—what do you think of the creeper I chose for that gap there?" she asked, gesturing to a trellis where a fragrant creeper with white blossoms grew. It was an ipomea, its blossoms breathing sweet fragrance onto the morning air.

"I think it's beautiful," Estelle said at once, going to stand by the trellis. "What do you think?"

"I think it's lovely," Lila replied. Lord Jeremy gazed at Estelle.

"Beautiful," he said softly. "Simply beautiful."

Belinda saw Estelle redden, her eyes dropping to her toes, and she bit her lip to stop a big grin flowering on her own face. It was obvious that Lord Jeremy meant Estelle, not the flowering plant.

"I say!" Lila exclaimed as Lady Westbrooke came over. "What do you think of those roses there?"

"Quite lovely," the lady replied, a bemused expression on her face. Belinda felt confused too, then realized Lila was distracting the woman to give Estelle and Lord Jeremy a moment to talk by themselves.

Estelle and Lord Jeremy were deep in conversation, walking a little further down the path. Belinda kept glancing over at them for a moment or two while Lila chattered blithely to Lady Westbrooke about roses, then she let out a relieved breath. Lord Jeremy was certainly no danger. He clearly adored Estelle.

Belinda smiled to herself, turning her attention back to Lady Westbrooke and Lila, who were deep in conversation about the congested roads in London.

"So inconvenient," Lady Westbrooke was exclaiming loudly. Belinda smiled to herself and then noticed Mama and Papa and Lord Westbrooke coming in through the gate. She waved to them cheerily.

"Lord and Lady Grayleigh," Lord Jeremy addressed Mama

and Papa, coming over to join the group by the gate. "I had a request to make." He glanced at his parents shyly. "We had thought to have a picnic in Hyde Park. Might we invite you all to join us? It would be next Monday afternoon."

"Oh!" Mama exclaimed delightedly. "Why! That would be lovely. We would enjoy a picnic, would we not, girls?" she asked Belinda and Estelle. Estelle nodded. Belinda swallowed hard and nodded with as much enthusiasm as she could manage.

"That's a kind invitation," Papa agreed, smiling warmly at Lord Jeremy, who looked down shyly for a moment.

"We will certainly attend," Mama added.

Belinda glanced at Estelle. She was gazing at Lord Jeremy, not looking anywhere else. She felt her stomach twist nervously. Estelle would almost certainly insist that she was there to chaperone her, but she didn't know if she could do it. Being in public was getting more difficult each time she did it. She could not bear the thought of Lady Talbot just happening to be there for the afternoon.

"I don't think I want to attend," she murmured to Lila as they went down the path. "But Estelle wants me to be there."

Lila blinked. "It would be a pity not to. Hyde Park is lovely, especially in the springtime."

"Mm." Belinda nodded. "But I don't wish to bump into Lady Talbot."

Lila chuckled. "It would be a horrid piece of luck if she just happened to be in Hyde Park at exactly teatime on that day," she admitted. "But how likely is it? She's never in the park—or at least, I have never seen her there."

Belinda nodded, though her friend's words were only a little reassuring. "I suppose," she answered slowly.

"It would be very strange," Lila repeated firmly. Belinda took a deep breath.

"I shall have to go," she said. "Besides, it will be good to see Estelle enjoy herself as I am sure she will."

"Yes!" Lila smiled. "It's beautiful, isn't it?" She didn't say what was beautiful, but Belinda knew that she meant Estelle and Lord Jeremy, as she thought the same thing herself.

"Yes," she replied slowly. "Very beautiful."

She and Lila walked silently around the grounds to the arbor, and Belinda found herself lost in thought. She was thinking of Estelle and Lord Jeremy, and of the picnic, and, oddly, she could not help thinking also of the Duke and thinking that it would not be as frightening to attend if he was also to be at the park. His stern, grim presence reassured her, and she would welcome it in the park.

Chapter 15

The study fireplace cast a soft glow over the room, which was mostly in shadow. The quiet, warm space was disturbed by the sound of his mother's voice, shrill and angry.

"I was surprised at you, Benedict. No. I was shocked. And so was Lady Kearney. You have to try harder with winning Lady Penelope's interest."

She glared at Benedict, and he stared at her in disbelief. He struggled to rein in his temper.

"I wouldn't have to try hard at all, Mama," he began hotly, "if you had not contrived this entire plan without asking me! Lady Kearney expects me to court her daughter because you told her I would! You put me in an untenable situation and then blame me for not acting as you wish."

"Shh, Benedict," his mother said crossly. "You'll upset Nancy."

Benedict glared at her. It was the one thing that would always make him hold his tongue. He loved Nancy and he knew it distressed her when he argued with their mother, but at the same time, this was too much for him to be able to keep silent. She could not blame him for not spending time with Lady Penelope, when it was only due to her machinations that her family expected him to.

"Mother, I must tell you," Benedict said in as polite a manner as he could manage. "I do not intend to pursue winning Lady Penelope's hand, and I think she would be quite glad for it. She shows no real interest in me either," he added slowly, realizing as he said it that it was true. With any luck, she was being pushed towards him just as much as he was towards her.

"Benedict! How can you say that?" His mother said angrily. "Have you no thought for the succession? Have you no thought for the future of the estate?"

"Mother," Benedict said quietly, a vein of pure ice running through his words. "Do not attempt to make me budge on this matter. I will not do so. I will not be forced to wed Lady Penelope when neither she nor I wish to do so."

"You are being a fool!" His mother shouted; all attempts at reining in her anger gone. She glared at Benedict, her eyes—as dark as his—black and angry. "Lady Penelope is one of the only society ladies who would think to wed you! You have a terrible reputation, and you have never attempted to correct that. Lady Penelope's parents are interested only because we are a powerful noble house, and Lord Kearney is an earl. You would be fortunate to wed her."

Benedict stared at her, shocked. She had never said that, not directly. His heart ached and he felt his body stiffen at the cruel words as if someone had struck him full in the face. He turned away for a moment.

"I think that is enough," he said quietly. "I think that insult is enough for one day. What think you?" he whispered.

"I only said as I believe," his mother blustered, clearly shocked herself at the level of affront in her words, but Benedict turned away and walked to the door.

"I have to retire to my study," he said, trying not to shout. Inside, he could barely speak with rage and hurt, but he tried not to let her see it. He had learned that showing his feelings was not safe, and—except for rare occasions when his anger was too much to contain—he did not do so. "I have to go over the household accounts before the expenses are paid."

"You could do that tomorrow," his mother objected. "This is an important matter."

"I have heard what you wished to say," Benedict said quietly and before she could argue he turned and walked into the hallway.

"Damn it," he swore, reaching the top of the stairs that led to his study. He leaned back, his eyes shut, one hand making a fist. His mother's words had wounded him. He swallowed hard. Was he really so repellant, so much outcast from society that only families seeking social advancement would even consider him? He felt his throat tighten again, the thought like a physical pain.

He went through to his study, running a hand absently through his thick black hair. It was dark in the study, only the light from the fire in the grate shedding a glow about the room, but he did not pause to light not even a candle. He sat where he was, lost in thought. Rowan, who had been sleeping in the study, came over when he sat down, tail thudding on the floor and a concerned look in his eyes.

"It's all right, old chap," Benedict said, ruffling Rowan's ears as the big hound rested his head on his knee. "It's all right."

A tear slid down Benedict's cheek. He almost never allowed himself to cry, but in that moment, he could not help it. Rowan's care for him could move him where nothing else could. Rowan was the only being in the world, it seemed, who saw any merit in him at all, who wished to spend a second of time with him simply because he liked him.

"That is cruel," he whispered into the unlit space.

As he said it, he recalled that there was someone who looked at him with—if not affection—then also not exactly repellency. An image of Lady Belinda drifted through his mind.

She seems to enjoy my company, or at least tolerate it, he thought slowly. *And I tolerate hers. I do more than tolerate it.*

He felt his heart lighten at the recollection of talking with her in the garden. She was a pleasant woman, amusing and intelligent, and the bright sparkle in her eyes lit his heart. He took a deep breath.

"Even if she doesn't like me," he told Rowan aloud, "she does not hate me either. And that is a beginning."

He glanced out of the window and saw a butterfly drift past, a white one, fluttering up towards the rooftops. His study was on the third floor of the house, so it was quite far away from the safety of the flowerbeds it usually visited. Seeing it made him recall his childhood, briefly. He had rarely been happy—always solitary, always afraid of censure from his father and sometimes from his mother. But on rare occasions in the garden, he had found pleasure in the beauty of the world around him. Butterflies, he recalled, had always seemed a thing of hope to him, a triumph of nature; their very existence as such fragile, beautiful creatures seeming to defy the darkness.

"I wonder," he said aloud, glancing down at Rowan again.

He was in a dark situation—pressure from his mother closing in on him, and his fear for Nancy making him worry almost constantly. But what if he did not have to face those threats alone? Rowan whined, placing his paw on Benedict's lap, and he smiled down at the big dog, ruffling his ears.

"What do you think, eh, boy?" he asked him gently. "What do you think about Lady Belinda?"

The big dog whined, making a big doggy grin as he lolled his tongue, and Benedict smiled to himself. Rowan had never even met Lady Belinda, and yet here he was, asking him about her. But the thought that had drifted into his mind like a butterfly would not shift.

Lady Belinda could be the answer to his problems.

The more he thought about it, the more his plan took shape. She was not exactly embraced by the *Ton* herself—if anything, she was more marginalized than he was. She was likely worried for her younger sister, who had just debuted—in many families, the younger sister's prospects would be curtailed while the elder sister remained in the house. She might be looking for a way out too.

She might be pleased to court a Duke, he thought wryly. *Even a beast.*

He swallowed hard. His mother's words had vexed him, like a blow to a limb that was already weakened. She had taken the last of his strength from him—but then, he thought wryly, she had given him a plan.

He looked up as he heard someone thump on the study door.

"Who is it?" he called, but he had already guessed by the time Clinton called cheerily through the wood.

"It's me. May I come in, or are you busy checking the books?"

"I was about to check them," Benedict called lightly. "But since you're here, I might as well wait. A wait is welcome," he added. He hated checking the accounts.

"I say!" Clinton said, stepping into the room. "It's dashed gloomy, eh? That lamp has already burned down," he added, gesturing to the lamp on the mantel. Benedict nodded.

"I'll light the candles," he replied, standing and holding a candle from the holder in his desk into the fireplace. He lit the remaining candles and the lamps, brightening the room considerably. The sky was overcast outside, the day gloomy, as Clinton said. Clinton smiled, taking a seat at the desk opposite Benedict.

"I suppose you haven't time to go riding?" Clinton asked. "I took a ride over here and I thought we might go up to the river. But if you have to check the books..." he trailed off. Benedict nodded.

"It's a job that needs doing," he replied. His mind wandered to his plan of earlier, and he considered asking Clinton's thoughts on the matter. He cleared his throat. "I had thought to ask your advice," he added slowly.

"On what?" Clinton asked, leaning back in his chair. His angular face was lit by the firelight, his hazel eyes kind. Benedict took a deep breath.

"It's..." he paused; his throat tight. "Mother has been quite firm in expressing her needs for the succession." He let out a breath, sure Clinton would understand. "And I do not wish to do as she requires." He paused. "I had thought...How do you imagine Lady Belinda as Duchess?" he blurted.

"Lady Belinda?" Clinton exclaimed, then paused. "Yes," he said slowly after a long moment. "Yes, I do."

"What?" Benedict demanded. "I need to know what you mean, Clinton. You mean that you think Lady Belinda is a good choice for the duchy?"

"I do," Clinton said at once.

Benedict let out a long sigh. "Well, that's an idea," he commented, trying to sound light. Even he could hear something that sounded like joy in his voice.

Clinton chuckled. "You plan to court her?"

"I will approach the matter with care," Benedict said a little primly. He did not wish Clinton to know all the details, or to be involved in any way. This was his task, and he intended to go about it as carefully as possible. Lady Belinda was clearly a pleasant, gentle-hearted lady, and he did not want to frighten her. He was talked about in the most off-putting terms by the *Ton* and the scandal sheets, and he could not even guess what impression she had of him. If he did not want to scare her off, he had to be careful.

"Well, I think that's grand," Clinton said, sounding happy. He leaned back in his chair, considering Benedict carefully for a moment. After a brief moment, he cleared his throat. "I was wondering if I might ask Nancy for a game of Whist," he said, his eyes moving to the mantel, as though he was nervous. "But we'd need you to join us, of course. And even then, we'd need an extra person." He chuckled.

"I'd be pleased to play a game of Whist with you," Benedict replied, his spirits considerably raised. "But we shall have to wait until we have a fourth person, eh? Or I will play two hands," he added, thinking aloud.

"No." Clinton said firmly. "No. I don't feel the urge to be beaten again."

Benedict laughed. His mood was lifted, but he felt the need to plan. "I'd be pleased to go for a walk with you, even if not for a ride," he suggested slowly. "Rowan needs a run, too, don't you, eh, Rowan?" he asked. Rowan was sleeping on the rug again, but when he heard Benedict, he sat up, alert and ready for a walk.

"That would be most pleasant," Clinton agreed. "I'll walk part of the way with you, but then I think I might ride back," he added, glancing at the window. "I should get back before the worst of the rain."

"Or you could stay for luncheon," Benedict told him firmly. "And stay indoors while Rowan and I take a turn about the grounds. How is that for a possible plan?"

"Most appealing," Clinton said lightly.

Benedict smiled, already pushing back his chair.

"I will see you in around half an hour, then," he replied, glancing at Rowan, who was already heading to the door. He paused. "If you are feeling the need for entertainment, you might look at my accounting books," he added with a grin. "I'd be most obliged if you add them up for me."

"We can bet," Clinton began, "that if I lose the next three games of Whist, I will do your accounting for you." He grinned, his grin bright in the gloomy space. "How does that sound?" he added cheekily.

"I accept," Benedict beamed, and went to the door, pausing for Rowan to bound out ahead of him. He waved to Clinton, who was already heading out into the corridor himself—likely toward the drawing room—and then he hurried downstairs. Rowan bounded with him, and they went out through the front door into the cool, rainy morning.

There was a lot on Benedict's mind, and there was no better time to think about it than out in the garden on a walk with Rowan.

Chapter 16

Belinda looked at herself in the looking glass. She had chosen a white gown for the picnic; a cream-colored muslin with puffed sleeves and the usual high waistline. The fabric fluttered gracefully. Her hair was curled into small ringlets on the sides and drawn up in an elaborate chignon at the back, left undecorated except for two pearl-headed pins. It was a beautiful, fashionable outfit, but also simple, gracious and personal. All the same, her stomach churned, and her head hurt at the thought of venturing out to the picnic.

I can't do it, she thought as she stared at her reflection fearfully. *Lila will not be there; nobody will be there to defend me. What if Lady Talbot is there?*

She felt sick at the thought, a nauseous twist in her insides making it impossible even to think of having a bite to eat before they went. Oddly, as she took a deep breath and went to the door, the Duke's face flashed into her mind. He was always so kind. If he was there, it would help.

She paused in the doorway, feeling strength fill her. She reflected on having confronted Lady Talbot. Having Lila there with her had certainly helped, just as having the Duke of Norendale there had comforted her immensely. All the same, she had faced the cruelty boldly and she could do so again, even if the mere thought of it made her stomach clench and her hands perspire with nerves.

"Belinda? Dearest? The coach is ready. Have you seen Estelle's purse?" Mama called from the hallway.

Belinda stepped out, her heart thudding. "I think it's in the drawing-room, Mama," she replied, trying to ignore her fluttering heartbeat. "That gown suits you well," she added, noticing the pale blue dress her mother wore, a lacy headdress covering her hair modestly.

"Thank you, my dear," Mama commented, smiling at her. "You look as lovely as a painting. You too, my dear," she added as Estelle appeared in the hallway. She was also wearing a muslin day-dress, the fabric patterned with little pink roses. Her hair was curled, and the back was a big braid, coiled into a bun and decorated with little pink flowers.

"Thank you, Mama," Estelle said softly. She looked pale and scared and Belinda smiled to herself. She could imagine how nervous her sister was, and that fact made her feel some protectiveness and confidence.

"Here it is," Mama called, coming out of the drawing room. "Now we can hurry down," she added, passing Estelle her little white drawstring bag. Estelle took it and hurried down the stairs, all of them walking briskly down to the coach.

The drive was long—London was at least an hour away, and then they had to move through the city streets to find Hyde Park. Their coach-driver was unused to the city, and they were all laughing at Papa's funny comments as the coach navigated slowly down the streets. It was mid-afternoon, the avenues and lanes congested with a mix of coaches—private and hired—and horses. People were going to and from the tea-houses and parks, or coming out of clubs and public houses where they spent an extended lunchtime. Belinda watched the streams of people going along the pavements and felt her heart thump.

I wish someone was there who would be friendly, she thought nervously. She wished particularly for the Duke of Norendale to be there, but she could hardly rely on that, since he also lived miles from the city and was highly unlikely to take hours riding in just to walk in the park.

"I reckon we'd be faster walking," Papa said with a grin as the coach rolled slowly forward. "We can race him," he added, tilting his head at the driver. Estelle laughed.

"We're almost there," Mama commented, looking out of the window. "I can see the park from here."

"Hurrah!" Papa exclaimed, making them all chuckle. "I bet we reach the park just at half an hour past three," he added, looking in his pocket where his pocket-watch was secured on its chain.

Belinda smiled to herself, feeling a little calmer. Taking a picnic with her family would hardly be a bad thing, after all.

The coach rolled up outside the iron fence around Hyde Park exactly as the clock chimed, and they were all laughing as they piled out onto the pavement. They walked a few paces to the gate and Belinda felt perspiration trickle down her back. Papa carried the hamper of food that they had brought to contribute—it was traditional to bring dishes to share—and it clanked a little as he walked, the bottles of lemonade and cordial jostling against one another in the small basket as they went.

It was not a hot day—it was not raining, but the sky was dark, and a thin layer of clouds overhung the city. They wandered up the paths, heading to the fountain, where Lord Jeremy's family had said they would wait for them.

"There you are!" Papa called out cheerily. "Good afternoon," he added, greeting Lord and Lady Westbrooke, who bowed and curtseyed and shook hands warmly.

"Grand to see you," Lord Westbrooke greeted them all politely. "We should find a place to sit," he added, casting a glance around the park. "Our butler came down from the townhouse with some picnic-things earlier," he added, gesturing to a basket and rug, which were settled next to the fountain.

"Grand," Mama commented, smiling at them both.

"It is a pleasure to see you," Lord Jeremy said shyly, bowing to Estelle.

"I am pleased to see you," she said softly. Belinda felt her heart twist with joy.

They all fell into step together, heading across the lawn to find a sheltered place to sit. Lord Westbrooke, Lord Jeremy and Papa carried the things, and they set them down on a patch of grass just before a small grove of trees.

"This is jolly," Papa said warmly as they opened the picnic basket, spreading out the contents on the blanket. He selected a bottle of lemonade and Lord Westbrooke passed around some rather fine glasses which their butler had packed. Belinda took one, inclining her head politely, and Papa poured a generous helping of lemonade for everyone.

"Very fine," Jeremy murmured, sipping his own. He was gazing at Estelle, and Estelle blushed and looked down at the picnic rug. Belinda smiled to herself and stared out over the park, giving them some privacy.

People walking along the paths made a colorful tapestry, ladies in pale pastel dresses or vibrant scarlet and green moving past the swathes of bright greenery at a graceful pace. Gentlemen in dark jackets walked with them, their top-hats making them seem tall as they moved at a stately pace along the shade-cooled paths.

Belinda moved her attention back from the people walking to the conversation flowing around her. Lord Westbrooke was talking about something he had read in the newspaper, his voice lower and louder than the burr of conversation between Lady Westbrooke, Mama and the youthful pair who sat closer to them on the rug.

"I say! It was a horrid scandal. How a decent young lady could think to behave in such a way, I have no idea," Lord Westbrooke was saying loudly.

Belinda felt her skin grow hot, her cheeks flaring up. It was not about her that Lord Westbrooke was talking, but about a young debutante who was recently exiled to Ireland by her parents for being with child. Her sympathy was entirely with the young woman, who must have suffered terribly under the withering censure of society. She felt angry. It was a state the young woman had certainly not contrived to be in without a male party involved, and the young man in question had received no censure at all. The burning need to defend the young woman warring with a need to be calm. This was a special outing, and she did not want to spoil it.

"Excuse me a moment," she murmured, standing up. "I saw some pretty flowers over there and I wanted to have a closer look."

"Of course, Belinda, dear," Mama commented lightly. "Don't go too far."

"I won't," Belinda replied, swallowing hard. She could see a patch of white daisies and small pink blooms around the fountain, still in clear sight of the rug. Nobody could think ill of her for wandering off twenty yards from the picnic rug to admire some blooms. She walked as slowly as she could towards the place, trying to find a sense of calm.

Why are people so horrid? she asked herself sadly as she neared the flowers. There was a bench close by and she settled on it, pleased to be out of hearing distance of the conversation. Papa had tried to change the subject, but Lord Westbrooke seemed not to notice his careful effort. Belinda stared at the flowers, feeling her heartbeat slowly return to its normal pace.

Society was cruel—she knew that more than anyone. She glanced about, seeing ladies walk past, one woman laughing lightly, her head thrown back, her black hair in ringlets touching her pale skin. She looked so carefree, and Belinda felt her heart twist. How different it would be if that young lady happened to step even a little out of the rigid confines of society's expectations. She might also be suffering; confined to a rainy, cold house somewhere in exile.

She thought again of the Duke. He knew all too well about society and its cruelty—though he had never told her how he felt, she could sense that he chafed under the censure of the Ton. He had been insulted and ostracized like she had. At least he, of all the people in the city, truly understood.

"But he's not here," she told herself a little sadly, and stared at the fountain. She was here and Lady Talbot was not, and that was the only comfort she had on this cool, cloudy city afternoon.

Chapter 17

"Benedict Chesterton," his mother said tightly, using his surname—something she only did when she was trying to make a point, and something that annoyed him since it was how she would speak to a disobedient child. "Will you please stop scowling on what is supposed to be a cheerful afternoon outing?"

Benedict, who stood at the edge of the park's main path, turned around and glowered at his mother. She had forced him to come on this outing—saying that she required him to chaperone Nancy—but she could not demand that he enjoy it. That was beyond the scope of what anyone could require.

"Mama!" Nancy said brightly. "Look! There is Lady Kearney."

Benedict stopped in his tracks. His mother had told him that this was to be a promenading afternoon for Nancy, so that she might be able to walk and talk with other young debutantes and promising young men in London society. She had dragged him to Hyde Park under the impression that just the three of them would take a walk together, but now Lord and Lady Kearney just happened to be there, along with Lady Penelope, who was standing a little away and looking down, blushing furiously. It seemed too convenient for Mama to have been a coincidence. She beamed at Lady Kearney as if she was expecting her.

He was about to confront his mother, but Lady Kearney had spotted them and was already drifting over, a gracious smile that was impossible to define as either false or sincere spreading across her face.

"Your Graces! How grand to see you. And Lady Nancy. Charmed. Penelope, my dear, come and greet our friends."

Penelope stepped forward, making a graceful curtsey. Benedict tried to rein in his rage, knowing that it was not Lady Penelope's fault that he had been dragged here, or that he strongly suspected his mother had conspired to drag him here under a false impression. She was innocent—as innocent as he was.

"Good afternoon, Lady Penelope," he managed to say, making a graceful bow. He would have lifted his hat, but he never wore one, since it drew attention to his considerable height, which had too often been a target for Darrow and his followers to tease.

"Why, what a lovely afternoon," Lady Penelope said brightly, looking around. "Such fine weather."

"It is fine," Benedict commented, though in fact he felt that the afternoon was rather miserable—not cold, by any means, but not sunny and with a slight breeze tugging at his coat. He looked down at Rowan, who had come forward to see what the fuss was about. Lady Penelope tensed and recoiled and Benedict, sighing, shortened Rowan's leash a little.

"Sit, boy," he said gently. His dog sat by his heel, gazing up at Lady Penelope, his tongue lolling in what Benedict was sure was a friendly grin.

"Um...it's...a fine day for a walk," Lady Penelope commented, shrinking visibly as she took a nervous step back from Rowan. Benedict felt the urge to sigh again in annoyance, but he managed to control it. It was not her fault that she was scared of dogs, he told himself reasonably. It was just remarkably tiresome.

It upset him when people were afraid of Rowan—the dog's big, fearsome appearance reflected nothing of his gentle, tolerant nature, and Benedict felt as though people's fear was as cruel a judgment as the boys had made of him. Like Rowan, Benedict was big and fearsome looking, but it was no true reflection of his personality.

"It is a fine day," he agreed, and turned to his mother, who was—along with Nancy—deep in conversation with Lord and Lady Kearney. Mama saw his gaze and seemed to guess that he wished to get into motion, because she cleared her throat and addressed the group.

"Shall we go and find a nice place to sit?" she asked. "I understand you have brought a basket with you."

"We have," Lady Kearney agreed.

"I must invite you to tea afterwards, then, as our contribution to the picnic," Mama said smoothly. Benedict blinked at her in surprise. She had not been so untruthful as to pack a hamper to bring, but he still felt certain she had meant to meet them here all along.

"How kind," Lady Kearney murmured.

"Most kind," Lady Penelope added, staring up at Benedict. He took a deep breath.

"Shall we go there, Mother?" he suggested, feeling the urge

to move. Walking would at least distract him and make it possible to keep his temper. His mother nodded, seeing the direction in which he had gestured.

"That is a fine idea," she murmured. "We can have our picnic on that grassy lawn."

"Fine! Fine," Lord Kearney agreed brightly. "I will fetch the picnic-hamper. It's there under the tree."

They all walked along the path to where Benedict had indicated. Rowan was clearly restless—he was tugging on the leash and Benedict felt his heart ache in sympathy for his plight. He himself would love to run across the park, far away from these people and their genteel, insincere smiles.

They settled on the lawn and Lord Kearney laid out the picnic rug while Lady Kearney began to unpack the food, assisted by Lady Penelope. Benedict listened as Nancy tried to converse with them, staring broodingly out over the park. It was cloudy and it looked like it might rain, and the weather suited his dark emotions.

"Here! Is not this lovely?" His mother asked lightly, passing Benedict a glass of cordial. It was redcurrant, and he sipped it neutrally.

"Thank you, Mother," he managed to say. He was still furious with her inside, but he had learned to hide his fury and he tried his best to do so, staring out over the park and trying to ignore everyone around him.

"It is a pleasant way to spend an afternoon," Nancy said contentedly, and Benedict beamed. If Nancy was enjoying herself, he could tolerate it. His anger towards his mother was secondary.

"Oh, look!" His mother said loudly, making his eyes widen. "It's the viscount!" She lifted her hand in a wave and Benedict felt his heart stop. Lord Darrow—or whatever he called himself now that he had succeeded to the viscountcy—was there, walking along the path, a top-hat and matching tailcoat in black marking him out against the greenery around them.

He saw Nancy stiffen and he felt his hands turn into fists. He could not bear a second of this. Lord Darrow was walking over, and his stomach twisted in a knot. He saw Lady Penelope stare at him in apparent dismay and he realized that his expression must be frightening, but he could not help it. Darrow's appearance in the park was more than he could face.

"Good afternoon," Lord Darrow greeted them, walking over to the mat. "Your Grace! What a pleasure. And Lady Nancy," he added, turning to Nancy with a bow. "What a delight." He reached out and picked a white flower from somewhere nearby, bowing and passing it to her.

Benedict tensed—the flower he had picked was gypsophila, one that meant purity and innocence in all literary allusions. He saw Nancy's eyes widen and he felt his stomach twist—nothing could be further from Darrow than innocence. He looked away, trying to ignore his anger. Becoming angry would do nothing except upset his sister. And Darrow would seize on any reaction.

"Why, what a grand surprise," his mother said lightly. "Please, come and join us if you have time," she added, beaming up at Darrow warmly.

Darrow grinned and bowed. "Your grace, I would be delighted," he replied, and Benedict tensed. Rowan, feeling his hand tighten on the leash, growled low in his throat, making Lady Penelope shriek.

"Shh, old chap," Benedict said softly, ruffling Rowan's ears in an attempt to calm him. He knew it would not help—Benedict himself was furious and that could not help but communicate itself to his dog, who was fiercely protective of him and would see anything that made him angry as a source of threat.

"He doesn't hurt people," Nancy assured Penelope brightly.

Benedict looked at her gratefully, but he could see Lady Penelope was terrified and pale and he gritted his teeth, a certain amount of understanding warring with absolute annoyance and anger whenever someone cowered away from his beautiful dog.

"Why don't you pour some lemonade for everyone?" Mama asked Nancy, who dutifully began to pour glasses for everyone who had not received any lemonade yet. Benedict looked away, knowing that he would not be able to control his anger as his mother made space for Darrow on the picnic rug. He was seated between his mother and Lord Kearney, but that meant he was opposite Nancy and he smirked at Benedict, who looked away.

I can't do this, he thought wildly. It was more than he could bear, sitting exchanging pleasantries with Lady Penelope and her family if Darrow was there, his eyes mocking and his smile insincere. His mother was clearly utterly fooled by him, and he could not bear to see it.

"Do you like riding?" His mother asked Darrow brightly. Darrow—who Benedict seemed to recall was not a good rider—beamed.

"I love it, Your Grace" he said warmly. "I believe Lady Nancy is a keen rider?"

"Yes! Nancy loves riding. Do you not, my dear?" Mama asked Nancy, who flushed and looked down. Benedict felt his stomach twist. Nancy was a fine horse-rider and he had always been immensely proud of her talent. Somehow Darrow must have heard about her skill and was trying to say the right thing to fool his mother.

"I am fond of riding, yes," Nancy agreed softly. She was always direct and honest, and seeing her barely looking up, so shy she could hardly answer a question, made Benedict angrier than he had ever felt in his life. Even when Darrow and his friends had broken his nose, he had not felt so angry.

"Grand! You must come and try our stables, my lord," his mother said to Darrow, who smiled a big sparkling grin.

"I would be honoured, Your Grace," he replied lightly. "I believe our fine horsewoman might be persuaded to accompany me on a ride? Chaperoned, of course," he added, beaming at Nancy. Nancy looked down.

"Mayhap," she murmured.

"Good! Good," Mama agreed, and Benedict felt himself stand up. Rowan was trying to growl, and it exactly reflected his own mood. He glared at Darrow, unable to hide his loathing, and when he glanced at Lady Penelope, he saw that she was staring up at him fearfully as though he had transformed into some sort of nightmare creature. He took a deep breath.

"I feel a little restless," he said, struggling for composure. "I think I will take a turn about the park."

"Of course, son," his mother managed to say. Perhaps she could see his rage—she had the sense to understand that he needed to walk to contain it, not least because she had the same temper.

"I will return in ten minutes or so," Benedict said tightly. He said that for Nancy, who was gazing up at him with her big eyes full of concern.

"We will start eating then," Mama said lightly. If she was concerned, she was not showing it. Benedict nodded tightly, sketching the closest thing he could to a bow and then turning and striding off. Rowan bounded with him; his energy barely contained as they strode down the path towards the roses.

"You're angry too, old chap," Benedict said softly, bending to pat Rowan. His dog stopped and gazed up at him, his black eyes wide and caring, his tongue lolling. He licked Benedict's hand and Benedict's heart twisted. Of everyone in the world, Rowan clearly cared for him.

"That's better," Benedict murmured as some of the anger drained out. He still felt restless and tense, and he strode on, Rowan bounding along with him as they went down the path, heading for the pond.

A path wound up towards trees and a wide lawn and Benedict strode past, feeling more peaceful with each stride. Rowan was still pacing, tugging on the leash and Benedict loosened his grip, holding the leash—which was two yards long—as far back as he could, to allow the poor dog some freedom. Rowan was not used to walking on a leash, since they almost never used one, and the big dog tugged and pulled strongly, taking all of Benedict's strength to hold him close.

As they walked up the path, Rowan grew more restless, tugging and pulling with all his strength. Benedict leaned back, using his weight to hold him, as, even with his own considerable strength, the massive hound could pull almost more than he could hold.

"Calm down, old chap," Benedict murmured gently, frowning as Rowan pulled and lunged forward. He could see nothing that could reasonably excite Rowan—there were no hares or other creatures to chase in Hyde Park, which was in the middle of the city. He leaned back and his dog seemed to calm, but as they went up the path, which led up the low hillock towards some hedges and a fountain, Rowan took off.

"Stop!" Benedict yelled as the huge dog bounded off, his leash trailing behind him, the loop that Benedict held bounding uselessly over the tussocks of grass. "Rowan! Here!" he demanded, but his big dog clearly had ideas of his own, racing off up the hill.

Benedict whistled as loudly as possible, but Rowan was racing ahead, not with the same relentless pace with which he pursued prey, but with a loping run as if he was running to meet Benedict on one of their walks.

"Rowan!" Benedict yelled, but Rowan ran in between the hedges out of sight.

Benedict, who was not a fast runner, raced as fast as he could up the hillock, gasping as he neared the top, sweating in his shirt and jacket and with perspiration wetting his hair, trying to catch his errant four-legged friend before he scared someone too badly.

Chapter 18

Belinda bent to pick some fragrant pink blossoms where they grew in profusion about the fountain's edge. They were cosmos, one of her favorites, their faint smell just discernible. She sniffed the blooms; the sweet, wild scent calming her nerves.

I should go back, she reminded herself a little sadly. It was one thing to walk to the fountain, but another thing to disappear from view for a few minutes, and she stepped forward towards the fountain. As she moved, she heard a strange sound—a loud panting noise, as if a wild animal ran around the side of the hedge, and she tensed, but burst out laughing as a huge dog, shaggy and playful, gave a delighted grunt and leapt up, placing his big paws on her.

"Look at you!" she said happily, as the big dog jumped down and then jumped up again. His tail was wagging wildly, and he made small sounds of happiness in his throat. "Where do you come from, you big, big chap, you?"

Belinda patted him, not pausing to think whether or not he might be dangerous. As he jumped up again, his now-muddy paws making marks on her white gown, a man burst around the side of the hedge.

"Rowan!" The man yelled, clearly desperate. "Down! *Down,* Rowan."

Belinda shook her head, clearing her throat to explain that she did not mind, that she had no fear of dogs, and she stopped dead.

"Your Grace!" she exclaimed.

"Lady *Belinda*?" Benedict was staring at her in surprise, his dark eyes huge, his jaw dropped.

"It's me," she agreed, then blushed, feeling a little foolish. "What...what are you doing here?" she asked, still stunned to see him. She fidgeted with her gown, feeling a little shy.

"I was walking," he said, running a hand through his hair in apparent nonchalance. "As you see, my dog decided to make his own entertainment. I'm so sorry," he added, his mild expression changing to shock as he saw the paw-prints all over her dress. "I'm truly sorry—he has made such a mess," he added, plainly distressed, but Belinda laughed.

"It is no trouble, truly," she said lightly. "It's far from new. Besides—he's adorable," she added, glancing at the dog, who had flopped down in the shade of the hedge and was panting, his pink tongue lolling out from his teeth in what she could swear was a cheery grin.

"He is," Benedict said, and she saw light glimmer in his dark eyes, a smile of tenderness crossing his face. "But I do apologise. He did make a terrible mess," he repeated apologetically, and she shook her head.

"No. Really, Your Grace Please don't apologise," she said lightly. "He did nothing—just be his big, exuberant self." She grinned at the dog, who seemed to understand because he thumped his tail once on the hard-packed ground.

"Thank you," Benedict said softly. He smiled, a big, relieved grin that lit his stern, chiseled features and made his face, for a moment, a thing of absolute beauty. "You have no idea how much I appreciate that you see it in such a good light."

"Of course," Belinda said lightly, though his big smile was making her heart race and the skin on her hands tingle.

He looked around a little awkwardly, his dark gaze moving to the big dog and then to his toes and up to her face. "I trust you are having a pleasant day?" he asked.

"Yes, Your Grace" she murmured, suddenly wishing that she could tell him how she really felt. "It is pleasant here in the park," she said instead.

"Yes. Not too warm," he replied softly.

"Quite so."

They looked at each other for a moment and Belinda felt that strange flush creep into her cheeks again as his gaze held hers. He looked at her with warmth, and with something unidentifiable that she could almost think might be appreciation or even admiration.

He cleared his throat, almost as if he was shy. "I regret it, but I must return to my family," he said, his head inclining to the left, where she presumed his family were sitting or walking. "Rowan has had enough adventures for one day, I presume," he added, a grin returning to his face again, lighting his eyes.

"I imagine so," Belinda said, laughing.

"I am sorry for your ruined dress," Benedict said again contritely.

"Please, do not trouble yourself," Belinda said lightly.

His gaze held hers and she felt her heartbeat racing again. She held his gaze for a moment or two and then looked away, feeling shy.

"I must go," he said softly, and Belinda nodded. He bowed and she curtseyed, and then he lifted his hand, calling his dog, and the big creature bounded towards him, the leash still trailing.

Benedict bent to lift the leash and then they turned and went down the hillock, back towards the path. Belinda stood and watched, then turned in the other direction, going uphill. She wandered up towards the picnic rug.

As she walked, she found her thoughts straying to Benedict. She turned around, glancing over her shoulder, and she thought she caught sight of a tall man dressed in a black greatcoat, but he was swiftly hidden by the trees, and she might have imagined it.

His smile lingered in her mind, his eyes shining with warmth as he looked at her. She frowned as she tried to understand that look. She had never encountered such a stare before, so gentle, so appreciative. What exactly he meant by that look eluded her.

She approached the picnic rug, and Estelle looked up, eyes wide, a big grin spreading across her slim face.

"Belinda!" she greeted. "There you are. We were just missing you," she said warmly, then frowned. "Are you all right?"

"Yes," Belinda said quickly. "Why do you ask?"

"Did you fall?" Estelle asked gently. "You're covered in mud."

"I, um..." Belinda paused, considering telling a small lie. Saying she had fallen would be much easier than explaining what had happened, but she was honest by nature and so she cleared her throat. "A dog jumped up on me," she explained, and Estelle lifted a hand to her lips in shock.

"Are you all right?" she asked at once. "It didn't hurt you, did it?"

"I am quite all right," Belinda assured her, feeling a little self-conscious. Lord and Lady Westbrooke were both there and, though they seemed kind people, she always felt awkward with people she did not know well, especially if she was being stared at. "He was a friendly dog. He did no harm."

105

"Here," Estelle said kindly, passing her a handkerchief. "Perhaps you can clean the dirt off a little."

"Thank you," Belinda murmured, touched by the gesture. She had tried to wipe some of the mud off the gown but had mainly transferred dirt to her hands without cleaning much off the gown.

"You can have a napkin instead?" Mama offered, passing her a linen napkin from their picnic basket. Belinda shook her head, dabbing at the dirt with Estelle's handkerchief instead.

"We thought to walk over to the pond after the meal," Lord Jeremy informed Belinda brightly.

"I'd be happy to," Belinda agreed a little absently, accepting a plate from Mama that held some smoked chicken and a slice of fresh bread. "Thank you," she added to Mama, who just smiled.

As she sat eating the delicious food, Belinda found her mind wandering to the conversation with the Duke repeatedly. She recalled his surprise at seeing her, and his gallant bow, his low voice and his grin. He was a most unusual gentleman. When they had played whist together, she had thought him amusing and intelligent, but still gruff and cold as his fearsome reputation suggested. But in that instant, when he had smiled so brightly, he had seemed gentle and kind.

"That flower over there," Estelle asked, pointing across the park at some bright pink blooms. "What is that? It's very pretty."

"Is it not a hydrangea?" Belinda asked, giving it a slightly absent glance.

"Oh. Yes, I believe you must be right," Estelle replied, then turned towards Lord Jeremy, who was saying something that Belinda couldn't quite hear.

She stared out over the park, her thoughts wandering back to the Duke and his dog again. She found herself wondering what they were doing, and she pushed the thought away, a little annoyed with herself for her continued thoughts of him.

He was a strange man, she reminded herself, but she could not help also thinking that he was a rather pleasant one; someone she was pleased to know.

Chapter 19

The scent of lavender wafted up from the table where Belinda worked. She had shut the windows in the drawing room and requested the butler to move the table slightly so that any draft from the door would not disturb her flower collection. Pressed flowers were so light, and she did not want the slightest gust of wind to blow away any of her precious blooms.

She bent over carefully, her gaze narrow with concentration, scraping a stray lock of tawny gold hair out of her eye lest it obscure her focus. On the table, carefully pressed between layers of tissue paper, her collection of spring flowers was set out in order of how long each had been pressed. She reached for the tulip she had pressed weeks ago, opening up the paper, and staring at the vibrant yellow that was still just visible on the flower. It was as thin as the paper and she touched it in wonder, her thoughts drifting to the garden and the patch near the wall to the water-garden where tulips grew in profusion.

She smiled to herself. From the garden at Payton Manor, her mind wandered too easily to the park and to the meeting with the Duke just a few hours before, yesterday afternoon. She recalled explaining to her family whose dog exactly it had been who had dirtied her gown. None of them had asked until they were in the coach, then Papa inquired if he should report the dog's owner to the Watch for neglecting to hold back his dog.

"No, Papa," Belinda said speedily. "There's no need. No harm was done, and besides, I know the owner," she added, looking down at her feet for a moment, feeling shy.

"You do?"

"Yes. It was the Duke of Norendale's dog."

"Rhe Duke of Norendale?" Papa frowned uncertainly. "Who is that?"

"You remember, Aldrige," Mama stated indulgently. "The fellow at Estelle's debut. The big, tall one. He danced with Belinda."

"The one the newspapers mentioned? Oh!" Papa nodded, his frown clearing. "Big man, dark hair. I remember. He has a dog?"

"He seems to," Belinda explained, looking up from her

contemplation of the coach floor. "It's a very big dog."

"Oh? Then I am very pleased you were not hurt," Mama said quickly.

"He really is a very nice dog," Belinda supplied.

"Fellow should be more careful," Papa grumbled, but Mama shot him a look and he fell silent. Belinda looked out of the window, a little confused. Perhaps Mama was just worried about Papa arguing with the Duke and that was why she changed the subject. The Duke was not scary at all, though, not like people said.

But then, there is no reason to think anyone is like the Ton *says*, she reminded herself.

A slight breeze blew in from somewhere and she frowned, the rustling paper on the table making her thoughts return to the moment. She stood to close the window, then sat to reach for another flower, using tweezers to lift it from the paper carefully. As she placed it down gently on a page in her collection, she heard Mama in the hallway.

"Belinda? Are you busy?"

"A little, Mama," Belinda answered, turning to face the door, where Mama peered around, a frown of concern on her soft oval face. "I had thought to work on my flowers today."

Mama came over to the desk, looking down. "They look very fine!" she declared, looking down at the paper. "Our garden boasts flowers as fine as the flowers in Hyde Park."

"Yes," Belinda agreed and giggled. "But I didn't get to pick any of those for my collection."

"No," Mama answered, her eyes soft as she looked at Belinda. "You were somewhat abruptly—but not unpleasantly—disturbed."

"Rowan is a lovely dog, truly he is." She spoke defensively.

"You know his name?" Mama asked, a soft smile playing about her lips.

"I do," Belinda replied, frowning. "The Duke said it several times. Is that odd?" she asked, feeling a little annoyed at Mama for that glint in her eyes as if she knew something.

"No. Not at all," Mama replied warmly. "He sounds a pleasant gentleman."

"He is," Belinda said firmly. She hoped her mother did not believe the things that high society said about him. "He is a pleasant man."

"I believe you," Mama said, making Belinda frown.

"You do?"

"Yes, of course," Mama said, her eyes sparkling. "You looked very happy when you joined us at the picnic-rug after meeting him."

"Mama!" Belinda giggled, but she saw her mother's smile widen and she could not help but match it with a big grin. "Yes, I suppose I was, rather," she replied shyly, looking down. Her cheeks flamed and delicious warmth filled her inside.

"I'm glad," Mama replied, then tilted her head to the side. "I wanted to ask if you might have a look at the *Ladies' Gazette* with me," she started. "I wanted to choose a dress style, and there are some lovely color illustrations in there. I thought I might take one to Mrs. Hensley when we go next week to have a new dress made..." She trailed off when the butler appeared in the doorway.

"Lady Grayleigh," the butler addressed her formally. "Lady Belinda. I apologise for the interruption, but a gentleman has arrived. He was asking after Lady Belinda."

"A gentleman?" Belinda's heart thudded fretfully. She looked at Mama, who inclined her head to the butler.

"Who is it?" Mama asked. "Did he give his name?"

"Yes, my lady," the butler replied swiftly. "He is the Duke of Norendale."

Belinda stared at her mother, her heart thumping wildly in her chest. Her jaw dropped for a moment, shocked surprise overcoming her. She looked around swiftly, seeing the flowers carefully laid out all over the big drawing room table. What if he wanted tea? They would have to use the other table. She had chosen a green muslin gown, the color very pale and the style simple. It was nonetheless one of her favorite dresses and she glanced in the mirror hastily, checking that her hair was not in too much disarray.

"Shall we ask him to step in?" Mama asked Belinda. She nodded swiftly.

Mama smiled. "Please show the Duke to the drawing room."

"Yes, my lady."

Belinda looked around, feeling flustered, and she could not help wondering at her own reaction. Why was she so startled, so nervous, but happy as well? It made little sense.

"If it..." Mama began to say, but the butler appeared at that moment and Belinda's gaze hastened to the door, where he stood. The Duke was just behind him.

"The Duke of Norendale, my ladies."

"Thank you," Mama replied, and the butler stood aside from the doorway to allow the Duke in. Belinda lifted her hands to her mouth in a gasp. In his right hand, the Duke held a magnificent bouquet of flowers. They were a mix of pink flowers—roses, tulips and sprays of gypsophila. He bowed solemnly.

"My lady," he murmured, addressing her first. "Lady Grayleigh," he added to Mama. "I thank you for allowing me to call. I have these to give to Lady Belinda, if I may," he added, holding out the bouquet to Belinda. "I wished to give you some flowers to replace those that my errant companion trampled so carelessly."

Belinda stared at him in surprise. Then, swiftly, she composed herself and reached out to take the bouquet, which he held out to her politely.

"They are beautiful," she murmured, lifting the bouquet up to her nose. The scent of roses was exquisite, the pink tulips providing their own subtler, wilder scent. The gypsophila was delicate among the bigger, pale pink blooms. The bunch was magnificent, bound with a pink satin ribbon; clearly the product of a master florist. It was large, the stalks at the base forming a bunch an inch across.

"I am glad you like them," he said softly. He looked down for a moment and Belinda could swear that he was shy. She felt herself smile.

"They are beautiful. Truly beautiful," she replied, gazing at the flowers. They truly were beautiful, and even as she looked at them, she was thinking that she would like to press some. Not just because they were beautiful specimens, but because—well, because they were special. Her heart sang and she turned to face him. "I will ring to ask for a vase of water," she informed him, turning to the bell-rope. Belinda held the bouquet in her right hand firmly, trying to ring the bell with her left, which felt strange, but she did not want to put the beautiful flowers down even for an instant. She listened as Mama, who was standing opposite him, conversed with the Duke in a soft voice.

"Thank you for coming to visit us," Mama said politely. "I can send for Lord Grayleigh and Estelle, and we can have some tea, perhaps?" she asked, glancing at the smaller table over by the fireplace where the tea-set could be placed at a pinch.

"I would be pleased to see Lord Grayleigh," the Duke said at once. "If it is not an imposition, I would be glad to take tea with you all."

"It is certainly not an imposition!" Mama chuckled. "I'll ask the butler to send for them." She glanced around, clearly wondering where they could set out the tea-things.

The butler appeared in the doorway and Belinda spoke first, feeling a little guilty at their multiple requests.

"Could you please bring a vase for these flowers?"

He nodded, his lips lifting in a small, warm smile. "Assuredly, Lady Belinda."

"And please fetch Lord Grayleigh and Lady Estelle to come and take tea?" Mama asked. "And bring the tea-set up. And some cake and Madeira loaf."

"Yes, my lady."

Belinda let her glance move to the Duke, who was looking over at the windows, seeming a little nervous. She felt the urge to help him calm down.

"Did you have a pleasant ride?" she asked him. She was not sure where he resided—his estate was not too far from theirs, and she couldn't really imagine him in a London townhouse.

He smiled, his eyes warming. "I did. It is a good day for riding. Not hot, not cold."

"Good," she replied. She gazed up at him, warmth flooding through her as she stared into his eyes. They were, she reflected, very unusual—so dark they were almost black. She had noticed those unusual eyes the first day she met him at the ball.

"Ah! Estelle. Aldrige." Mama called, interrupting their conversation for a moment. "There you are. We have a visitor."

"Your Grace," Papa greeted, bowing low.

Estelle curtseyed. She looked a little nervous and Belinda smiled to herself. She had been a little afraid of him too when she first met him. Oddly, she was no longer nervous of him.

"Come and sit," Mama said, gesturing the Duke to the chairs by the fireplace. "We can have the tea put there."

They all went to sit by the fire and the tea arrived. Belinda felt her cheeks heat up as she walked over to the table. The Duke was staring at her. She looked at the window, her entire body burning with heat as he gazed at her. She sat down on the chair across from him, which was the only chair open for her to sit in. She looked at the tea-tray for a moment, feeling too shy to look up.

"You must have had a pleasant ride this morning," Papa said affably. Benedict inclined his head.

"Yes, I did," he said in the low, resonant voice that Belinda had come to recognize. "Very pleasant indeed."

The conversation flowed around the table, moving to the weather in London—they all thought it was too hot in the city, where the stone buildings warmed up and there was no breeze to cool them.

"I trust the weather will be good for Lady Westbrooke's ball next week," Mama commented.

"Lady Westbrooke?" Benedict frowned. "I believe I am going to attend that ball too. As a chaperone to my sister," he added, his mouth tilting in a wry way.

Belinda felt her heart almost stop. She gazed at him in surprise. He would be there! Her soul soared. She realized she was staring and looked down shyly.

When she looked up, Estelle looked at her, eyes bright.

"There is your pressed flower collection!" she commented, looking at the table. "You must show the Duke the blooms. They are so beautiful."

Belinda went pink. She glanced at Mama, thinking that perhaps it was improper somehow to go across the room alone with the Duke, but her mother inclined her head instantly.

"Yes, Belinda. That is a fine idea."

"Your Grace?" Belinda murmured, feeling desperately self-conscious. "Would you like to see my collection?"

He nodded gravely, as though he was making an important decision. "I would be pleased to," he answered her.

Belinda pushed back her chair, her heart thudding, her breath tight. She had not ever thought she'd be showing her collection of flowers to anyone, never mind a man who confused and intrigued her. She went over to the table.

"Here it is," she tried, but her throat was so tight that her voice was a croak. She cleared her throat and tried again. "This is my collection. I'm sorting them now. These ones are ready to be put in the book," she added, gesturing to the tulips she had pressed first.

"Most pretty," the Duke murmured. Belinda felt warm inside.

"Thank you. I think they turned out well, too," she managed to say. Discussing the flowers made it easier to talk. "I was impressed that the red ones held their colour."

"Is that unusual?" he asked seeming quite interested.

"Usually, red flowers do not hold their colour very well," she began. "Yellow flowers hold their colour well, and some pink ones."

"What are those?" he asked, pointing to another paper that she had opened.

"Those are lilacs. They are tricky to press. Trickiest of all are the very wet blossoms, though...they tear so easily, or they can become spoiled with mildew."

"I see."

They chatted about flowers, and Belinda was surprised at how many of them he knew. She recalled the cosmos at the park and smiled.

"How is your dog?" she asked him warmly.

He smiled, his eyes softening. "He is well," he answered. "Not too happy that I rode off today. But my sister will take him for a walk. He loves her too."

"That's good," Belinda replied. "How many years has he?"

Benedict frowned. "I think three. He was still quite small when I found him."

"Where did you find him?" Belinda asked at once.

"In the woods," Benedict said, his eyes filling with sadness. "He was tiny. And so thin! I don't think he'd eaten anything for a couple of days at least."

"Poor fellow! What happened?" Belinda asked, her hand to her lips, feeling shocked.

"I never did find out. I suspected someone's wolfhound had pups, and they could not keep them. He might have been the weakest of the litter. Whoever left him there, I hope something bad happens to them." His face was set in angry lines.

Belinda nodded. "Me, too."

He smiled. "I'm glad," he replied. "He's a dear, dear creature. I think he rather liked you, too." His smile broadened and his gaze, which had been staring into the past, moved to hers.

"He's a beautiful dog," Belinda said warmly. "It's horrid that someone left him out like that." She felt shocked—he was just a small, defenseless baby, after all.

"They are the ones who robbed themselves," Benedict replied slowly. "They did not get to have the dearest, most loyal friend anyone could ever have." His gaze softened as he spoke of his beloved hound.

"I imagine he must be," Belinda replied gently. His care for his dog touched her heart.

"He is. And very protective. And sometimes quite cheeky, as you saw." He chuckled.

Belinda laughed warmly. "That might just be true," she agreed fondly.

He smiled, his gaze warm where he stared into her eyes, and she blushed.

"Would you like some cake?" Mama called, interrupting the silence in which they locked gazes, and Belinda nodded and stood, feeling confused by the warmth and tenderness she saw and felt when she stared into the eyes of the feared Beast of Norendale.

Chapter 20

Benedict patted his horse, Nightshadow, as he walked past the stall.

"Give him plenty of bran mash," he told the groom, Harry. "And brush him well. He deserves a treat."

"Yes, Your Grace," Harry called cheerfully, already carrying the saddle and bridle to the tack-room from where Benedict had hung them on the fence.

Benedict thanked him and strolled up the path towards the house, his mind filled with recollections of Lady Belinda. Thinking about her made him smile. Her beautiful gaze, her sweet smile. Spending even a few minutes with her—just her—was like a gift, one that soothed his soul and calmed him deep within.

"Your Grace" the butler called, hurrying down the steps. "There you are! Your mother was looking for you."

"Oh." Benedict felt his entire posture stiffen. He had been out for perhaps five hours in total—he'd ridden to the village to purchase the flowers, then ridden to Payton Manor with the bouquet in his saddlebag. He was often out for hours at a time—what could possibly be so urgent? he asked himself. "Well, I'm here now," he added a little crossly.

"She is in the drawing room, Your Grace," the butler said lightly.

"Thank you," Benedict replied. He felt a little annoyed—there was surely no cause to go sending the butler out to fetch him? He went slowly up the stairs, determined not to let his mother unsettle him. As he neared the top of the staircase, she stepped into the hallway.

"Benedict! There you are," she said firmly. "I was looking everywhere. It's a few hours before it starts."

"Before what starts, Mama?" Benedict asked with a frown. He reached for his pocket-watch, which showed that it was around midday.

"Before dinner," Mama answered parsimoniously. "And you will have to get ready at four at the latest," she added, looking at him. Benedict felt his fingers close around the edge of his sleeve, a habit when he was confused or discomforted.

"What exactly for, Mama?" he asked, feeling uncomfortable.

"Dinner, of course," his mother replied. "I think that a new black jacket would do admirably. You know, you might try another colour, though. Mayhap blue. Everyone is so used to seeing you in black, and..."

"Mama," Benedict interrupted her. "Will you please tell me what I should prepare for?" he asked, trying his best not to get angry.

"For dinner tonight. Lord and Lady Kearney will be coming. And Lady Penelope as well. And Lord Rathgate will also be here. I must remind the cook we will need fresh bread..." she trailed off as Benedict stiffened.

"You invited Lord Rathgate? Here?" his voice was shrill.

"Yes, of course," his mother said with apparent disinterest. "He must have dinner here with us. He and Nancy are courting now."

"*What*?" Benedict demanded, his hand making a fist. "Mother. I warn you..."

"And I warn you," his mother countered, and this time her voice was dark with rage; the black eyes that she shared with him full of anger. "You will not get in my way with this."

"I most certainly will," Benedict said softly. His anger was too much for shouting. It choked him.

"You have no idea how hard I have worked to ensure a good match for you and Nancy!" His mother raged. "And all you can do is try and counter my every attempt. It is too much."

"No, Mother," Benedict said bitterly. "Lord Darrow is too much. Or whatever he calls himself now. He is dangerous. And as for the Kearneys..." he began, but she interrupted.

"Lady Penelope is a pleasant girl, if a little tedious. She is well-bred and well-thought-of, and she is a fine match. You're lucky any woman is willing to be associated with you. The reputation you have..."

"Which is not my doing! Damn it!" Benedict yelled. This time, he could not contain himself. His mother flinched and he stepped back, suddenly exhausted.

"You..." his mother began, but Benedict interrupted.

"I apologise," he said tightly. "I misspoke. But Mother, I must warn you that you go too far in this. Nancy and I are not prize livestock that you can sell to whoever pays more."

"It's not like that," his mother said instantly, her expression offended. But Benedict cleared his throat.

"You know that is *exactly* what it's like," he said stiffly. "You care nothing for what she thinks, or what I think. You care nothing for our hearts and minds."

"That is not true," his mother countered, but Benedict shook his head.

"I will attend this horrid dinner of yours," he stated, knowing that when she had made up her mind, there was nothing he could do to change it. The invitations had been issued and the guests— along with the horrible Darrow—would turn up anyway. "But I will not do it again. And nor will you do this to Nancy again."

His mother glared. "You let me decide..." she began, but Benedict could not let her continue.

"I think it is time that Nancy and I decided something for ourselves," he said firmly. He turned around and went to the stairs, but his mother called out after him.

"You're selfish, Benedict!" she shouted. "Selfish and impulsive. Think about how advantageously these matches will work for you. And do you not care a whit for Norendale? We need heirs, and soon."

Benedict ignored her, letting her voice fade as he rounded the stairs and strode out into the garden. He walked a few paces then turned and went back, ascending the stairs quickly to search for Nancy. She was in her chamber, and Rowan was with her, clearly smuggled in since their mother did not really approve of Rowan being in either of their chambers, but she could not prevent Benedict.

"Nancy! Rowan!" Benedict greeted, his anger turning to laughter as the big dog leapt up, licking his chin, his paws on Benedict's chest. "Good afternoon, old chap. Easy, boy," he added. Rowan was whining, his tail thrashing and dangerously close to knocking Nancy's evening-clothes off the chair where the maid had placed them.

"Good afternoon, brother," Nancy said with a smile. Her black eyes searched his. "Did you have a pleasant ride?"

"I did," Benedict replied. He had told Nancy that he might call in on Lady Belinda, hesitant to say more, but yet not wanting to conceal anything from her.

"Good," Nancy answered, her gaze still holding his curiously.

"Has he had his walk?" Benedict asked, ruffling Rowan's head where the big dog bounded around him with unbridled excitement.

"I took him around the grounds," Nancy replied. "He ran a lot." She chuckled as the large hound wandered over and licked her hand. "He's a fine boy."

"He is," Benedict agreed, patting Rowan on his long furry back. "I'll take him out again after luncheon. He needs a good run."

"If we have any time at all after luncheon," Nancy said gloomily.

Benedict nodded. "If that," he agreed.

The afternoon went past surprisingly slowly, each moment agony for Benedict, who was dreading the arrival of Darrow. At six o' clock he was dressed in his best jacket and trousers—both black, despite his mother's distaste. He wore a simple cravat around the high-necked collar of his shirt and his black hair gleamed.

"There you are," Mama murmured. "We'd best go and meet our guests."

"Are they already here?" Benedict asked, feeling his stomach twist.

"Lord Kearney's just arrived," Mama commented, gesturing to the long gravel drive. "Their landau is drawing up outside."

"They're exactly on time," he commented lightly, his stomach twisting. Lady Penelope was harmless but dull and uninteresting and, he suspected, a little overly interested in titles and wealth.

"Good evening!" Mama said brightly, curtseying as Lord and Lady Kearney came up the steps. Nancy curtsied and Benedict bowed. His gaze moved to Lady Penelope, who was wearing a white evening gown, the filmy muslin falling from a blue satin waistband, her pale curls decorated with a blue ribbon and pearl-headed pins.

"Good evening," he greeted her.

She smiled, her gaze darting coyly up and then away. Benedict sighed inwardly.

"Shall we all go in?"

"Yes, Your Grace, let's go inside," Lady Kearney replied,

118

following his mother indoors. "I cannot wait to taste the syllabub you promised."

Benedict walked slowly in with Nancy, noticing that she was oddly quiet. He tensed as Mama halted in the doorway of the dining room.

"We must go and welcome our other guest," Mama commented, and Benedict felt as though he could not move, fear and dislike holding him in place.

You're being silly, he reminded himself angrily. What can anyone do to you now? All the same, he felt like the persecuted youth he had been when Darrow and his friends had made his time at school unbearable.

"Good evening," Darrow smiled smoothly as he bowed to the duchess. He bowed to Nancy and raised her hand to his lips. Benedict felt his hand clench into a fist, and he glared at Darrow, who laughed.

"Ever the protective brother," he teased. "Do be careful of your bad temper."

Benedict turned away. He wanted so badly to throw the fellow down the stairs that he knew that if he had to look at him once more, he would do something he would wish he hadn't. He walked into the hallway and walked briskly to the dining room.

"You must know the Viscount?" Mama asked Lord and Lady Kearney, who beamed.

"Ah, yes! Yes. We saw each other recently. At the garden party," Lord Kearney added, shaking Darrow's hand.

Lady Kearney said something polite, but Benedict didn't hear the words. All he could see was Darrow smirking at him.

"This is pleasant," his mother said brightly. Benedict, who was opposite her at the table, could see she was quite tense. "Let's all sit down, shall we? And I'll ring the bell for the first course to be served."

The soup arrived, a delicious, steaming bowl of pea soup, and Benedict wished he could enjoy it, but he felt so tense that his stomach was heaving nauseously. He poured some water and drank, determined to keep a level head. On his left, beside Nancy, Darrow chuckled.

"Water, eh?" he asked. He reached for his wineglass, gesturing for the butler to come and pour him a glass of Burgundy.

119

Benedict looked away. He was not going to let the fellow provoke him. He had to do something about him. He would talk to Clinton and perhaps they could come up with a plan to stop his mother and her awful matchmaking for Nancy.

"Did I tell you about the time I was in a storm aboard the *Seafarer*?" Darrow asked.

Benedict saw his mother's eyes brighten and he looked away, angry and bitter. She was entirely beguiled by him. Benedict was not sure, but he'd be willing to bet Darrow had never been to sea.

He tried to eat some of his soup and ignored everyone around him.

"Benedict," his mother interrupted his thoughts. "Did you tell Lady Penelope about the fabric and ribbons at the market in Norendale?"

"I didn't," Benedict began, about to try and think of something to say to Lady Penelope, ideally something that would divert her interest to another topic, perhaps one that he would find easier to discuss. As he racked his brains, desperate to think of something, the door opened.

"Ah. The next course," his mother began, but before she could say anything, a black, hairy form appeared and Rowan bounded across the room, running straight for Benedict.

"Easy, boy," Benedict began, laughing as the big dog bounded towards him. As he neared Benedict, Lady Penelope, who was seated on his right, let out a scream.

"Help! Help!"

Rowan, confused by the noise, diverted his course towards her and stopped at her chair. He reached out, pawing at her leg, clearly worried about her.

"Help!" Penelope screamed, pushing back her chair, and running towards the balcony doors. "Help! Keep it away! Filthy beast," she spat, her eyes filled with disdain.

"Just a..." Benedict began, fury filling him to see her attitude to Rowan. He was no more a beast than Benedict himself was, and he was Benedict's dearest friend.

"He won't hurt you," Nancy called. "Stop running. He'll chase you if you run."

Benedict was already on his feet, and he grabbed Rowan's

120

black leather collar, dragging him back from where he ran at Lady Penelope.

"Easy, boy. Easy," Benedict said to Rowan gently, ruffling his ears. Rowan was grinning, clearly waiting for Lady Penelope to do whatever the next step was in this fascinating new game.

"Come here, dear. Come here," Lady Kearney soothed, putting an arm around Lady Penelope's shoulders, who had begun to sob noisily.

Benedict looked away. Rowan was calm, staring at Lady Penelope in confusion, clearly utterly unsure of why she was making such a strange noise. Benedict led him to the door and took him upstairs, ignoring the fact that he was doubtless needed downstairs.

"She was scared for nothing," he said to Rowan, who was settling down on his blanket by the bed in Benedict's room. "You just pawed at her leg," he added, patting the dog's big shaggy head.

As Benedict went to the door, he could not help recalling Lady Belinda's reaction when Rowan raced up and jumped up on her. She had laughed, that delightful, bright laughter that stole his soul and warmed his heart. He smiled at the memory. She had not screamed, running away and sobbing. She had ruffled Rowan's ears and said he was beautiful.

Benedict took a long sigh. He had to go back down to dinner, but his mother had helped him to make up his mind and he would be seeing Lady Belinda very soon, at the ball. He frowned, heading to the door, and wondering absently if he should wear his new shirt and cravat. The thought made him smile and his mood lifted. He was looking forward to it.

Chapter 21

The light of a half-dozen chandeliers laden with four-hour candles poured over the large ballroom. Benedict, standing near to the back of the large room at Westbrooke Manor, with its polished marble floor, blinked and looked around. The heat was stifling already, the guests standing close, chatting and laughing. Nancy and his mother stood a few yards away and Benedict tugged at his cravat, feeling hot—and not just because of the proximity of so many people. He was sweating with a mix of tension and excitement.

Somewhere in the ballroom, Lady Belinda was waiting.

He cast his gaze around, spotting a woman with golden curls near the front of the room. He narrowed his eyes, but when the woman turned around, he noticed that it was not Lady Belinda, but someone he did not recognize. He looked away, a little annoyed at himself.

Where is she? he asked himself.

He gazed out over the ballroom and this time he spotted two ladies—one with pale curls, and another with darker blonde hair. They were near the refreshments table on the left, and when the woman turned around, he recognized her immediately and his heart leapt.

"Excuse me," he murmured to Nancy and his mother, but they were chatting to Lady Sinclair, who was also in attendance, and they did not hear him. He walked towards the front of the room, striding briskly, but just as the musicians started to tune up, when he was perhaps eight yards away from Lady Belinda, a hand clamped onto his wrist.

"Benedict," his mother's voice hissed in his ear, making him whirl round with disbelief and rage. "You need to go and dance with Lady Penelope. I insist."

"Mother," Benedict whispered, his cheeks burning, his hand making a fist with anger. "You cannot command me to do anything."

"I can," his mother whispered back. "You will dance with Lady Penelope, or I will fetch her here myself and make you do it."

"You wouldn't..." he began, but he knew his mother. She

was perfectly capable of doing exactly that—she had practically done it already at the garden-party when she made him walk with Lady Penelope.

His mother just looked at him. He sighed.

"One dance, Mother," he said firmly. "One dance. And no more."

His mother inclined her head. "I'm sure you will dance more than one with her. She's a good dancer."

Benedict glared at her. He could barely exchange a sentence with Lady Penelope, who was more interested in gossip than anything else, and besides, the way she reacted to Rowan showed him a side of her character he disliked.

"The quadrille is starting," Mama hissed. "Go! Now."

Benedict walked stiffly over to Lord and Lady Kearney, and bowed to Lady Penelope, who was wearing a white gown, her pale blonde curls arranged in ringlets decorated with a circlet of white satin.

"My lady?" he asked simply, holding out his hand.

"Oh! Of course, Your Grace," Lady Penelope replied politely. "We need two more people for the quadrille. Lady Amelia is also dancing. There she is. Let us join in with her."

Benedict nodded, letting himself be swept up into the group. As Lady Penelope had said, the quadrille required four people, two couples walking around one another, linking hands, and stepping in time with the music. It was a particularly formal, stately dance. It was one he enjoyed, because the steps were easy to learn, but it required concentration and that meant that one could remain aloof if one chose.

They all walked onto the dance floor together. Benedict took Lady Penelope's right hand, while Lady Amelia linked hands with Lady Penelope on her left. Her partner, to whom Benedict had swiftly been introduced but whose name he hadn't retained at all, stood on Lady Amelia's left-hand side.

The music started up, slow and serious. They stepped forward and back, then forward again and then he and Lady Penelope were hand-in-hand briefly, moving sideways three steps. Lady Amelia and the lord whose name he didn't recall chatted away as they danced, but he could not think of a word to say to Lady Penelope, who clung to his hands and stared up at him, her blue eyes impossible to interpret.

They joined hands with Amelia again and then they all joined hands in the grand chain.

The dance seemed to last for ages and Benedict focused as hard as he could, since it had been a long time since he danced a quadrille. He blushed, feeling a little awkward for the fact that he was a little behind in his steps every now and again.

"Thank you, my lady," he murmured as the music reached its conclusion and he bowed low to Penelope. She curtseyed deeply.

The other dancers were applauding each other and the efforts of the group, and Benedict stepped off the dance floor with, holding Lady Penelope by the silk-gloved hand.

"That was a fine dance," Lady Penelope said, but even she did not sound as though she really meant it and Benedict could not be cross with that. He knew he had danced a little clumsily and he looked over at the doors to the terrace, trying hard to think of something to say, but no topic of conversation came to mind. He spotted Nancy by the table and his anger boiled to see that his mother was with her and that Lord Darrow was chatting to them. He felt his hand make a fist as Lord Darrow led Nancy towards the dance floor.

"Your Grace?" Lady Penelope gazed up at him. She looked confused and Benedict realized he must have looked fearsome.

"Sorry," he murmured lightly. "My thoughts were on other topics."

"Yes, your grace." Her voice was empty of emotion of any sort.

He said nothing, trying to school his face to neutrality even though he was raging inside at the thought of Nancy dancing with Darrow. He was so false, so untrustworthy. He could not understand his mother. She could surely see it?

Lady Penelope shifted from one foot to the other and Benedict shut his eyes, wishing some sort of inspiration for a topic of conversation would come, but he could think only of Darrow and Nancy, and nothing sprang to mind. He fidgeted with his sleeve-cuff, trying to think of something to say. They were standing side-by-side, without speaking, and it felt very awkward.

"Your Grace," Lady Penelope murmured after what felt like eternity, but must have been two minutes at the most. "I think I can see Lady Julianne there. And Lady Gertrude."

"Mm?" Benedict widened his eyes, gazing out across the ballroom. He could see many young ladies, and it didn't really matter if he could see them or not, he realized, because Lady Penelope was looking at him a bit expectantly. "What is it?" he asked swiftly. "You want to go over there and talk to them?" he inquired mildly as a thought occurred to him. She seemed to be as discomforted in his company as he was around her. She was eager to escape, it seemed.

"Yes, Your Grace." She inclined her head in confirmation.

"Oh. Well, then, by all means," Benedict said, not impolitely. He felt grateful that at least she had been as uncomfortable as he.

"Mayhap we will see each other at the refreshments table," she murmured politely, and Benedict could see in her expressionless face that she didn't really want that, any more than he himself. He inclined his head.

"Quite so," he agreed mildly.

She curtseyed and hurried off, and Benedict sighed. How unsurprising, that his mother was forcing her into things as much as she was forcing him. He glanced about the room, determined to find Lady Belinda. He could not spot her, but he could see Nancy and Lord Darrow talking. The dance—it was a waltz—had just concluded. Darrow's posture was overbearing, his form blocking Nancy's exit from the dance floor. Nancy looked uncertain.

Benedict swore inwardly and strode towards them, but Darrow must have seen him coming because he bowed low to Nancy. He turned to the refreshments table and Nancy smiled at Benedict, looking relieved. Benedict walked briskly over, but his mother—who, he noticed, had been standing at the refreshments table just two yards away—stepped forward first.

"Benedict!" she said smoothly. "Should you not be talking to Lady Penelope? There are more dances in just a few minutes."

Benedict scowled at her. "I think Lady Penelope has no more interest in dancing with me than I do with her," he began, but at that moment, Darrow appeared, two glasses in one hand, one in the other.

"Your wine, Your Grace," he murmured to the duchess, passing her one of the glasses. "And cordial for you, my lady," he added, passing the other to Nancy. The third wineglass he kept for himself. He turned a mocking smile on Benedict, as if daring him to confront him.

"That is kind," the duchess murmured. Benedict felt his stomach twist nauseously.

"Excuse me," he said quickly. He could not stand there a second longer without challenging the man to a fight, and he knew that to do so would upset Nancy. It would also cause a scandal—dueling was illegal, and fisticuffs would be ignoble—and he did not want to harm his sister by causing rumors to fly either.

He walked briskly across the room, aware of Darrow's gaze following him, and stormed out through the doors onto the terrace. The cool air surrounded him, and he leaned on the rail, staring out onto the dark-shadowed garden. At least there was peace and calm outdoors.

On the terrace, he leaned against the railing and stared down into the garden below. There was laughter and chatter all around him, but nobody came to disturb him, and for that he was grateful. He stared down at the garden and tried to find calm. He longed to go into the ballroom and find Lady Belinda, but he was practically shaking with rage, and he wanted to calm down first.

He would walk into the ballroom and sweep her into the dance as soon as he felt calm again. His mother could fuss and flap as much as she liked. His mind was made up and she could do nothing about it. He took another deep breath and let himself imagine dancing with Lady Belinda and the thought made him feel better. Soon, he would go in again and find her.

Chapter 22

The glow of the chandeliers was bright where Belinda stared out at the ballroom. Beside her, Estelle laid a hand on her shoulder, the touch of her silk-gloved fingers cold against Belinda's skin. She turned around.

"Belinda," Estelle whispered. "I need to...um...go. Could you come with me?"

Belinda, taking her sister's meaning from her slightly embarrassed glance, nodded immediately.

"Of course," she agreed. She looked around, searching for a door that led into the main house. There was always a privy available for guests to relieve themselves, since most balls were at least three hours long and it would be unreasonable to expect that they would last the entire evening without doing so.

"Thank you." Estelle smiled at Belinda, who inclined her head, spotting a door where a footman in dark livery stood. The noise of the ballroom was loud around them—the music and chatter. She had to raise her voice so that her sister could hear her over the sounds.

"There's a door. I'm sure he must know where we need to go," she added.

"Of course."

They walked over to the door and the footman guided them to a doorway a few feet along a corridor that was well lit with lamps bracketed to the walls. Estelle knocked at the door, and when nobody answered, she slipped inside.

"I'll be just a minute," she called to Belinda, who nodded.

"I'll wait right here," she promised.

She stood at the door, staring out at the corridor. It was not nearly as noisy, though the sound of the music drifted out even to here and she tapped her foot, listening to the quadrille. She narrowed her eyes as the lamp-flames flickered and she saw someone coming along the hallway. Another guest, desperate for the privy, she guessed. She smiled to herself. The form of a woman hurried along the hallway and Belinda tensed as the woman got closer.

"Ah! If it isn't the princess of scandal," Lady Talbot hissed.

"At least I am a princess," Belinda said dryly. She looked up at the woman's gaunt face and black-dark eyes, daring her to insult her. She made her back stiff, feeling scared but not letting it show.

The older woman's gaze narrowed. "Defiant!" She exclaimed. "I don't know how you dare to be. You shouldn't even show your face in society."

"At least I don't spend my evening insulting defenseless people," Belinda challenged. She was shaking, and she clasped her hands at her sides, fighting not to run away from this bully who had made her life miserable.

The Duke, she thought in her heart. I wish you were here.

"How dare you!" Lady Talbot hissed. "I try only to defend my own reputation and that of my relatives. Your presence sullies all of us here. All of the decent young women."

Belinda stiffened, her stomach twisting nauseatingly. She did not think she could stand another second. She had managed to defy her, but one more word from her and she would start weeping. Lady Talbot's words were like blows, and each one made her feel worthless and stupid.

"You..." She whispered. She could not think of any way to turn the comment, and she stood straight and proud, trying to ignore it, but Lady Talbot glared at her.

"You are an insult to your family."

"How dare you?" Belinda hissed. She was very close to tears now, and she bit her lip, fighting to hold them back. She looked down at the floor, humiliated and hurt.

The door of the privy burst open, and Estelle appeared. She glared at Lady Talbot and took Belinda's hand.

"Come on," she said in a loud voice. "Let's go back to the hall. I'm sorry you had to wait outside with that there."

Belinda smiled seeming exhausted. She could barely find the energy to conceal how terrible she felt. She bit her lip, fighting not to cry.

"Let's go," she said softly.

Estelle walked with her, her hand in hers, and when they reached the ballroom, she turned to her caringly.

"Belinda? Are you quite well?"

"I want..." Belinda whispered, fighting the weight of weeping. "I want to go outside. Just a moment."

"I'll come too," Estelle offered firmly.

"No. I'll just be a moment," Belinda insisted. "I just need a little time."

"Of course," Estelle agreed, her hazel eyes soft with understanding.

Belinda nodded, thanking her without speaking because Estelle's kindness was bringing her closer to tears. She turned away and hurried though the ballroom, the tears glistening in her eyes. She could barely see.

"Excuse me," she murmured, walking blindly to the doorway. She could feel cool night air and smell moisture where the light breeze blew in and she walked forward, heading out through the door onto the terrace.

The terrace was far from empty, with men and women standing and conversing here and there, their voices muted, the sound of their laughter bright in the half-shadow. She breathed in, smelling pomade and the scent of dew, and walked over to the railing. There was a gap at the end of the terrace of perhaps five yards where nobody stood.

She leaned on the rail and stared out into the garden. The lawn was utterly black, the sky dark blue. The shadows of the trees were black ink-lines against the dark sapphire shade of the night sky. She gazed out over the darkened garden, breathing in the scent of dew and listening for the sound of crickets.

"Please," she whispered to the empty night sky. "Please make her stop bullying me."

Lady Talbot had been tormenting her for years and she could not stand it a moment longer. In spite of her defiance, she felt so defenseless, so helpless. She needed someone to help her.

She took a deep breath, trying not to cry. It would be obvious if she cried, and she didn't want to let anyone see. She could feel tears and she looked up, holding her breath.

"My lady. May I be of assistance?"

She looked down, blinking in surprised disbelief.

"Your Grace?"

He smiled. "It is me, yes." He beamed at her. "I thought I saw you come outside." He paused, frowning. "Are you all right?"

She nodded, taking a deep breath. "Yes," she whispered. "Yes."

129

He gazed into her eyes, his frown deepening. "No, you aren't," he said gently. "You've been crying. What ever happened?"

Belinda took a deep breath. His words were so gentle, his black eyes so full of concern it made her heart melt. His voice was low and deep and when she stood with him at the edge of the garden, she felt utterly and completely safe.

"It's Lady Talbot. Mayhap you recall her: She was at Estelle's ball. You intervened on my behalf with her." She gazed up at him, not sure he even remembered the evening, despite how meaningful it had been for her.

"We danced together afterwards," he said, lips lifting in a grin.

"Yes."

He chuckled. "And then all of London heard of it."

"Yes."

They both laughed. Here, in the darkness, with him to talk to, it was possible to take humor from all that had happened.

"What did she say?" he asked gently.

"It doesn't matter," Belinda said swiftly, feeling her tears threaten to fall. "She just...she said...she called me a disgrace. A stain. A shame."

She heard the Duke let out a low growl. "How dare she?" he whispered.

Belinda smiled up at him, feeling the ache in her heart mend a little at the sight of his rage. "She dared easily enough," she said a little sadly. "Because there's no reason for her not to say it. I have a terrible reputation."

"One you did not make by yourself, I think," Benedict said firmly.

Belinda nodded. "It was..." she sniffed, and now she really was crying. She had never discussed the incident with anyone outside her own family. Lila was the only other person who knew her side of the story, and she had not needed to tell her because her mother had done so already. "It was a man. He told lies. Wicked lies about me." She sobbed, wishing she had her little drawstring purse with her, with a handkerchief.

"Here." She felt him lift her hand and he fumbled with his other hand in his pocket, producing his handkerchief from his coat.

"Use this."

"Thank you," Belinda murmured. She dabbed it to her face.

"Better?" he asked gently.

"Better." She smiled up at him, her heart aching.

"This lying fellow?" Benedict pressed when she had stopped sobbing. "Is he still in London?"

"No," Belinda admitted. "He was sent to India with his regiment."

"Good," he growled.

Belinda giggled.

"Well, I hope something bad happened to him," he demurred.

Belinda smiled. "You are kind," she said softly.

He shook his head. "No," he said gently. He gazed into her eyes. "No. You are one of the dearest and best people I have met in this world. A truly good soul. That is worth fighting for."

Belinda took a deep breath. She gazed up at him, her heart thudding in her chest, slow and deep. He looked back. His dark eyes were steady on hers and she could see how focused they were on her. She felt her body shiver and she drew a deep breath, heart racing.

"Thank you."

Benedict took a deep breath, shutting his eyes. "You don't need to thank me," he said softly. "I have you to thank. You have shown me a great deal. Your strength, your gentleness, your endurance. And I have also learned that, just sometimes, being angry isn't wrong."

Belinda frowned, a confused smile on her lips. "Isn't always?" she asked gently.

He sighed. "I have a temper," he said slowly. He was looking at his boots now, his voice distant as if he was recounting someone else's story. "And when I was young, the other boys at Eton delighted in it. They thought it was funny to taunt me, to bait me, like hounds set to bait a bear. It was cruel." He took a deep breath.

"That's horrid," Belinda whispered. She gazed up at him. He was so quiet, so self-contained. She would never have thought he had suffered even a little.

"I was not good at hiding my rage," he said slowly. "And the taunts got worse. The boys broke my nose," he added, running a

131

hand down his face. Belinda frowned, noticing a slight bump about three-quarters of the way along its length. She recalled noticing it when she met him first and nodded in understanding. "They likely cracked a few other bones too, but the nose was the worst," he added, his mouth a thin, amused line.

"That's terrible," Belinda said softly. "What happened?"

"A group of them tormented me a little too hard," he explained. "And when I retaliated with fists, they all attacked me."

Belinda pressed her hand to her lips, shocked at the image of the poor youth being set upon by a group of other youths. He was unusually tall, and well-built, but even such a strong man would not help but beaten down by a large group of other men.

"My mother never believed me," he said softly. "I think nobody did. Not even my tutors. And so, nothing was ever done." He paused. "At least when I got to Oxford, none of those cruel, bullying boys went with me." He smiled wryly.

Belinda felt herself relax. "Good," she murmured.

He sighed. "But this epithet of "beast" was their fault. It stuck, and they spread it through society so that it followed me everywhere."

"That's not fair," Belinda murmured.

"I think what happened to you was even more unfair," he said gently.

"Mayhap," she admitted softly.

He looked into her eyes. "Certainly. And I know there was no truth in it. None whatsoever." His voice was serious and low, the sound thrumming through her, tingling on her skin.

She swallowed hard. "No more than there was in the story of your being beastly."

"Maybe there's just a *little* truth in it," he said, his lips lifting gently. "I did fight back quite hard." She chuckled. "Good."

He grinned and they stood silently for a moment.

"It's hard, though," he murmured. "To ignore it, I mean."

Belinda inclined her head. "It is," she agreed. "But shame is a strange thing. You don't have to believe it or accept it. To make someone ashamed is, in itself, despicable. The shame belongs to them. Not to you."

He breathed out, a long, ragged sigh. When he looked up at

her again, his dark eyes seemed clearer somehow.

"Thank you," he murmured.

"Of course."

They looked at each other, his gaze warm on hers. She felt her heart melting as she stared into his eyes. She had never felt so close to anyone before. He understood her, for she had never heard any other story that was as close to her own. She smiled up at him, shy and uncertain, and he smiled back.

"If you would allow me," he said softly. "I have a suggestion. I have been thinking about it for a long time. Since I saw you in the park."

"And Rowan jumped on me?"

"Yes," he said with a chuckle. "Yes. Then. Or maybe a little before."

"What is it?" Belinda asked, feeling curious.

He took a deep breath. "I want to speak to your father," he said softly. "If I may. I want to ask for...for your hand."

"What?" Belinda blurted. She stared up at him. In her chest, her heart felt as though it was growing, melting, shining. "Sorry, Your Grace. You mean...you mean..."

"I want to wed you, Lady Belinda," he said softly. "I think we would go well together. I thought so since we played cards together. You are intelligent and sensitive. You understand like no other. I think it would be right. Besides, it would offer you protection from the *Ton's* gossip. And it would throw my mother off her pursuit of a match for me." He blushed furiously. It was one thing to think of such a thing, but another saying it.

She looked up at him, a small frown creasing her brow. "You really mean it?" she asked softly.

"Of course," he breathed. "Of course, I do."

She stared at him, her heart racing. It was not just the promise of protection, the assurance that the Ton would, eventually, have to forget the scandal. It was the fact that it was him. He was funny, warm, friendly, and sweet.

It's just convenient for him, she reminded herself firmly. And it is very convenient for you.

"Well, then," she said, struggling to stifle her own feelings and be practical. "Well, I accept. But I must ask one thing."

"Of course," Benedict said at once.

"I must ask that we have a few weeks of courtship first. So that we are, well, friends, before we..." She felt her cheeks go bright red. "Before we wed."

"Of course," he said at once. "But you mean it?" he asked, sounding incredulous.

"Yes. Yes, certainly." she said, smiling at him. He looked down at her, his black eyes warm.

Gently, he took her hand and wrapped it between his. Her fingers were gloved, but she shivered at his touch, feeling his warm, strong hands close around hers, which were cold.

"Thank you," he said softly.

"No need to thank me," she said briskly. His touch was sending thrills of feeling through her body, but he would not want to hear that, she thought firmly. This was practical for him, as it had to be for her.

"You're getting cold," he said gently. "I think it's time we went   indoors." She nodded and kept holding his hand and they walked back into the ballroom. She felt brave walking with him, confident that nobody would think to hurt either of them when they stood side by side. They walked into the bright lights and loudness of the ballroom.

Chapter 23

Benedict walked into the ballroom with Lady Belinda holding his hand. He could feel her warm fingers tight around his even through the silk of the elbow-length opera-gloves that she wore. He stared out over the crowded room, the loud chatter of the guests washing into him like a wave. He would normally have flinched at the sound—gatherings always troubled him—but he ignored it, Lady Belinda's words in his mind.

The shame belongs to them, he reminded himself strongly. *Not to you.*

"The music is rather lively," Lady Belinda commented, a wry smile tilting her lips.

"It seems to be a waltz. Would you honour me with another dance?"

Lady Belinda beamed. "Certainly."

Benedict felt dazzled, her big grin lighting him up. He took her hand and walked to the dance floor, feeling like he floated.

As they reached the dance floor, he spotted Nancy and Darrow. Nancy beamed at him, lifting a white-gloved hand in a wave. Darrow scowled, but Benedict ignored him. He did not care what he thought. He didn't care about what anyone thought. He was with Lady Belinda, and he was having an enchanted evening.

The opening refrain was moving into the body of the waltz and Benedict bowed low. Lady Belinda curtseyed and gazed up at him from under her eyelids. The striking green of her eyes and the sultry glance she gave him made his heart race.

The music started and he placed his hand very demurely on her back, just below her shoulder-blade, the other hand in her own.

He stepped forward and she stepped gracefully back.

They moved smoothly around the floor. Benedict shut his eyes for a moment, then opened them, not sure if what was happening was real or if it was simply a dream from the first dance they had danced. She moved so lightly, so gracefully.

"This is a pleasant tune," she murmured as they moved around the corner.

"Nancy would know who wrote it, I think," Benedict said

with a smile. "She knows all those things."

"She seems a lovely girl," Lady Belinda commented warmly.

"She is."

They stepped neatly around the corner and then waltzed down the length of the floor. Her soft skirt brushed his ankles as she whirled and Benedict swallowed hard, his cheeks flushed, his heart racing. She was so beautiful. He could smell the scent of her hair—lavender and roses, he thought. She smiled at him, and his heart stopped for a moment. Her eyes were bright in the light of the candles, her smile a flash of brilliance.

They whirled down the short side of the dance floor and then reached the corner, and Benedict blinked in surprise as the music shifted cadence, sounding as though it was concluding.

The couples around them were applauding one another's efforts, their gloves muting the sound, and Benedict bowed low, feeling dazed.

"Thank you," he murmured, as Lady Belinda made a low curtsey.

"Thank you," she said softly.

Benedict gazed at her wonderingly. It had felt as though they danced forever, but then it also felt as though the waltz had been much shorter than usual. He felt a little confused and he blinked as he walked towards the refreshments table with Lady Belinda. Her gloved hand rested on his arm, and they drifted through between the guests.

He reached the table and turned to Lady Belinda. He raised a brow inquiringly.

"Lemonade, please," Lady Belinda said swiftly.

"Lemonade for the lady, and a blackcurrant cordial for me...if that is blackcurrant," he added to the footman working behind the table. The man inclined his head.

"It is, Your Grace," he murmured.

Benedict took the drinks and handed the lemonade to Lady Belinda. As he did so, he noticed two women whispering to each other behind their fans, clearly watching them. Across the hallway, a man whispered something to a woman and both their eyes darted towards Benedict. He ignored it.

Let them talk, he thought calmly. I care nothing for their slanderous words.

He glanced at Lady Belinda, but she was ignoring the whisperers too, if she had even noticed them. He smiled warmly.

"Would you like to move somewhere quieter?" he asked her. The area close to the refreshments table was particularly noisy, the queue of people waiting for drinks seeming louder than the other people in the room.

Lady Belinda nodded. "I would like to," she said softly. "But I must find my sister soon."

"Of course," Benedict nodded, impressed by her dedication. "I must too," he added, scanning the ballroom for a glimpse of Nancy.

They stood and talked for a moment or two, Benedict barely following her words, so intent was he on staring into her eyes.

"I must go," he said when they had settled into silence. "Nancy must be somewhere in here."

"Of course, Your Grace," Lady Belinda murmured, looking up at him with those beautiful green eyes. "I will try to find Estelle as well. I hope to speak some more with you."

"Of course," he said swiftly. It was only as she wandered off, slipping between the guests, that he realized she had wanted to speak with him.

Of course she does. She likes you, you fool, he reminded himself.

He wandered off across the ballroom, looking for Nancy.

"Benedict!" His mother hissed as he rounded the corner of a pillar. He jumped. Here at the far end of the ballroom, where the musicians were situated, it was too loud for many people to stand. He had gone there to take advantage of the view out over the ballroom. He had not expected his mother to grab his wrist.

"Mother," he hissed back, feeling angry. "What on earth is it?"

"Outside. Now," she said firmly.

Benedict felt his jaw loosen in shock. He was not ten years old—how could she think to order him about like that? But before he could argue the point, she grabbed his wrist again and he had to fight to control his rage.

"I'll go with you," he said firmly. "But if you ever grab my wrist like that again, I will cease to listen to you at all."

His mother's eyes narrowed for a moment, but she nodded.

She let go and he walked beside her to the door.

Outside, there were still many people on the terrace and Benedict followed his mother as she wove her way to the end of it and then down into the garden. He looked around, feeling angry.

"Mother! How can you leave Nancy in the ballroom unchaperoned?" he demanded.

"She's with her friend Amelia," Mama said quite calmly. "Amelia's parents will keep an eye on both of them. I need to talk with you," she added, her voice angry again.

"About what?" Benedict demanded. If it was about Lady Penelope, he was going to struggle to keep his temper even more.

"You cannot think I did not notice with whom you danced? Or with whom you were conversing so intently just a moment ago?"

"Mother..." Benedict felt his throat tighten. He was so angry he could barely speak.

"She's scandalous, Benedict! They say she gave herself to a man on the night of her debut! There can be no woman more scandalous than her in the whole of London!"

Benedict felt his hand make a fist. He did not know what his face did, but he saw his mother step back and he realized that his infamous rage was showing on his face. He drew a breath, his words a hiss.

"The man who claimed that—who boasted that, no doubt—was lying. Lady Belinda has said so and I take her word for it. The man in question? Where is he now? Did he stand by her and promise to defend her and the baby, should there have been one?"

"Well...well...no," Mama stammered, and Benedict nodded.

"Exactly! What sort of a monster would boast such a thing to the *Ton* and then let the poor woman be torn apart by the gossips, without even staying in town to see if he had a child? Surely, we are not going to believe the word of such a fellow?"

"Well," his mother noted, and Benedict saw that she was considering his words, but then she hastily pushed them away. "That is not the point at issue!" She was almost as angry as he was, her dark eyes like jet. "The point is that her reputation is terrible, and you are a Duke! You should have more care for the name of your ancestors."

"I am a Duke," he hissed. "And my reputation is as tarnished as hers. What harm can it do?"

"Benedict!" His mother exclaimed. "You must think of your family."

"I have been thinking of my family," Benedict said firmly. "But I must also think of what is meaningful to me. And I will court Lady Belinda whether you wish it or not. She is in many ways an ideal duchess. I will call on her when I can, and you will do nothing to stop me. Or change my mind."

"Benedict!" His mother's exclamation was shocked. Benedict turned away.

He walked back into the ballroom, his heart twisting with the unpleasantness of having to confront his mother, but his soul feeling lighter at the thought of seeking out Lady Belinda.

Chapter 24

Belinda walked lightly down the hallway to the breakfast room, her soft white-and-yellow muslin day dress lifting on the morning air as she hurried, light-footed, to breakfast. She grinned, her soul soaring. She had not felt so carefree for years and she stepped into the breakfast room, a big grin on her lips.

"Good morning, Belinda," her mother greeted her warmly. She was wearing a pale blue day-dress, her hair in a simple chignon. Papa sat to her left, buttering a slice of toast. He looked up warmly as she drew back her chair.

"Ah! Good morning, daughter," he said warmly. "You rose early after such a long ball."

"I couldn't sleep," Belinda said, her soul as light and bright as the sunshine that poured in through the easterly windows. "I simply had to rise."

"Good, good," her father said absently, reaching for the marmalade in a little bowl beside the tea things. He looked up, fixing her with a hazel-eyed gaze not unlike her own. "Are you quite sure about this, daughter?" he added firmly. Belinda nodded. She had mentioned to her father privately, when they returned, that the Duke of Norendale might come to ask for her hand.

"You don't have to, you know," Mama said firmly.

"I want to, Mama," Belinda said in a definite tone. She was surprised by how true that was. She had woken feeling wonderful, and she knew it was because of the Duke. Not necessarily because he was handsome and romantic...In her deepest heart, she thought he was both, but she would not let herself admit it. This arrangement was practical, it was convenient, and it would serve her well. That was almost certainly what he was thinking too.

"Well, then," her mother said gently. "That is another matter. I am glad."

"Mama, I..." Belinda began, trying to explain that she liked him.

"Good morning," Estelle said from the doorway, making them all turn around abruptly. "Did I do something wrong?" she added when they all stared at her.

"No! No, sweetling," Papa said with a laugh. "Not at all.

Come and sit down."

"Did you have a good rest?" Mama asked gently as Estelle pulled out her chair beside Belinda. Estelle flopped into it, dark prints of weariness under her eyes.

"I did. It was so late when we returned home," she added, stifling a yawn.

Belinda smiled to herself. In a few minutes, she knew Estelle would revive and be far livelier than all four of them put together. She reached for some toast, though she was feeling far too excited to eat. And far too tense.

"Did you sleep well?" Estelle asked Belinda.

Belinda nodded slowly. She had lain awake for some time, her mind reeling with all that the Duke had said. But then she had fallen abruptly to sleep and slept deeply for hours, waking refreshed.

"Good," Estelle murmured. She reached for a croissant and bit into it. Belinda chuckled to herself. At seventeen, she had not had nearly as healthy an appetite as Estelle, but then Estelle took after their father, all slender angles and long limbs.

The conversation at the table turned to other matters, and Belinda stirred her tea, her thoughts drifting. She recalled the Duke, his dark eyes luminous in the light of the candles, and her heart thudded in her chest.

"Sorry to disturb," the butler called from the doorway, making Belinda turn around abruptly. "But there is a visitor."

"What manner of visitor?" Mama asked, but Belinda's heart was already thumping. She glanced at the clock on the mantel. It was nine o' clock already. It was the Duke—somehow, she just knew.

"He is the Duke of Norendale, my lady," the butler said. "Should I show him in?"

"Show him upstairs to the drawing room," Papa said swiftly. "We will greet him in a moment."

"The Duke of Norendale?" Estelle asked, a frown creasing her fine brows. "What is he doing here?"

"He has something to tell your papa," Mama said swiftly, and Belinda felt her throat tighten. She walked out of the room without even being aware that she was walking.

When she reached the drawing room, Papa was already

seated, and she went to take a seat. Estelle and Belinda settled on the chaise longue together, Mama sitting opposite them on a floral-patterned wingback. The butler appeared in the doorway.

"The Duke of Norendale, my lord. My ladies," he announced.

Belinda looked up at the Duke, who wore his customary black jacket. He was staring straight at her, a tender expression on his face. Her heart almost stopped.

He's just doing this for convenience, she reminded herself. But her heart was racing, and she could barely breathe.

"Lord Grayleigh," the Duke greeted Papa formally, inclining his head in a bow. "Lady Grayleigh," he added, bowing low to Mama. "Lady Belinda and Lady Estelle." He bowed to them in turn and Belinda felt her heart flip.

"Welcome, Your Grace," Papa said, gesturing to a chair. "Sit down, if you will."

"Thank you," he replied. He settled himself rather stiffly on a wingback chair at the end of the table and Belinda tilted her head, studying him—he seemed tense.

Nonsense, she told herself firmly. Why would a Duke be tense about such a thing?

She looked down at the table.

"Please bring some tea for our guest," Mama called to the butler, who bowed and withdrew. They all looked at each other.

"It's a fine day," Estelle commented brightly, making conversation. "Sunny and fine."

Benedict grinned, his dark eyes brightening. "Most fine," he agreed.

That relaxed matters somewhat, and conversation flowed around the table. Tea was brought, and Mama led the chatter as they drank. After a few moments, Benedict cleared his throat.

"I would like to speak with Lord Grayleigh a moment, if I may," he said formally. His voice was tight, and Belinda felt her lips lift. He really was tense.

"Of course," Papa said at once. "Let us make our way to my study."

The two men went out of the room together and shut the door behind them. Estelle gaped at Belinda.

"He is...he isn't..."

Belinda laughed aloud, seeing the shock on her sister's face, her big hazel eyes wide with surprise.

"He is," she said softly. "It's just convenient for him, and for me, so we thought we had to. Nothing romantic..." she began, though her cheeks were flushing bright red, and Estelle gaped.

"You mean he asked you? You said yes?" Her mouth formed into a big smile.

"Yes. I did."

"Belinda!" Estelle whooped. "That's wonderful! That's grand. I'm so happy. You are happy, aren't you?" Estelle demanded, looking concernedly into her face.

"Yes, Estelle," Belinda said softly. She felt a deep contentment, a deep warmth flowing through her. "Yes, I am happy."

"Good."

Mama smiled. "That is very good, yes," she agreed.

They all seemed a little tense and Belinda sat straight and nervous, waiting for Papa and the Duke to return. In a minute or two, the door opened.

Papa beamed at Belinda, who went pink.

"I am very happy to consent," he told Belinda firmly. Belinda swallowed hard.

"Thank you, Papa," she murmured. She gazed up at the Duke. His dark eyes were a mystery. She felt at once that she knew him well, but also that she barely knew him at all. Her heart thudded in her chest.

He took her hand, gazing into her eyes. Beside her, Belinda heard Estelle draw in a breath, and she knew her sister was staring at them.

"Thank you, Lord Grayleigh," Benedict said, turning to Papa. He turned to Mama, and then to herself and Estelle, his lips lifting. "I would like to invite you all to Norendale Manor, if I may, to join us for an afternoon picnic."

"Today?" Belinda gaped. He nodded.

"Whyever not?" he asked.

"Indeed! Whyever not?" Papa echoed, and Belinda smiled at him.

"That sounds very pleasant, Your Grace," Estelle murmured, looking up at him shyly and then looking down again. Belinda smiled, seeing her sister so evidently nervous of him, but yet trying

143

so valiantly to overcome it.

"I will be pleased to see you there," the Duke said warmly. "Now, I must return home, but I look forward to seeing you all at luncheon."

Belinda gazed up at him and he smiled back, and she felt her heart fill with warmth. She could barely wait to see him in just a few hours' time.

Chapter 25

Benedict stood in the hallway at Norendale Manor, his heart thudding in his chest. His cravat felt impossibly tight, his breathing slow and nervous. In a few minutes, Lady Belinda and her family would arrive.

Beside him, Rowan panted and made small whining sounds of anticipation. Benedict ruffled his ears, the gesture as calming to himself as it was to Rowan. Nancy grinned up at Benedict.

"It's all right, brother!" she said warmly. "You look splendid," she added, her dark eyes gazing up at him.

"Thank you, Nancy," he answered. "I don't know if I feel splendid."

"You'll have a grand time," Nancy assured him. She walked to the window and looked out to the drive. Her long white muslin dress swayed in the slight breeze, her hair styled simply and decorated with little white flowers.

"I hope so," Benedict answered. Rowan whined and ran to the door, clearly wondering why they were not going for a walk. Mama came down the stairs, her voice brisk.

"Come on! Nancy, come upstairs. Benedict? Why is your dog down here?"

Benedict glared at his mother. "Rowan is here with me," he said firmly.

His mother glared at him, as if she was about to argue the matter, but she let out a sigh as if she had decided to accept his choice.

"Well, then. Nancy, come upstairs," she said firmly. "It is not seemly for a young lady to wait in the hallway."

"But Mama..." Nancy began, and their mother interrupted her.

"Come upstairs. The guests will arrive soon enough."

Benedict was about to object—Nancy's presence eased his nerves—but before he could say anything, Nancy went obediently to the stairs. A knock sounded on the door and the butler stepped briskly forward. Benedict stood back to give him space to do his job.

"Lord and Lady Grayleigh, and the ladies Belinda and

Estelle," the butler announced gravely.

Benedict's eyes moved at once to Lady Belinda. She was wearing a long white muslin day-dress, the light fabric patterned with a pattern of little flowers in blue. Her hair was styled simply, decorated with a ribbon in the same shade of blue. Her green eyes moved to his face, and he forgot where he was for a moment—all that he could see was her green gaze. He looked down at the rose he held in his hands. He had picked it that morning from the garden, a deep red rose. He bowed.

"Welcome to my home."

Lady Belinda's eyes widened, and she dropped a low curtsey.

"Thank you, Your Grace."

Benedict handed her the rose and she took it in her pale hands, her fingers brushing his. He felt his heart leap. He tried to recall what he wanted to say but no words came. Lady Estelle grinned at him.

"Good afternoon, Your Grace," she murmured, curtseying. She wore a plain white dress, her hair in ringlets about her face.

"Good afternoon," he replied, bowing formally. He greeted her parents in turn and gestured to them to follow him to the stairs.

"My mother and sister are awaiting us in the drawing room, with tea. Rowan! Easy, boy," he added, as Rowan, who could contain himself no longer, burst forward, tail wagging, eyes shining, and ran straight to Lady Belinda, who held out her hand to the big dog so he could sniff it, then ruffled his head, smiling at him.

"He's so beautiful," she murmured. "Who's a big fellow?" she added to the dog, who panted happily, gazing up at her with wide eyes.

"He likes you," Benedict commented, feeling his own heart fill with warmth. Lady Belinda was a delight—so warm, friendly and understanding. He stood back for her, Estelle, and Lady Grayleigh to ascend the stairs, and then he and Lord Grayleigh walked behind. Rowan bounded up the stairs, chasing after Lady Belinda.

They all reached the drawing room.

"Good afternoon," Mama greeted them coolly, and offered them a formal curtsey.

Nancy was effusive, grinning at Belinda as though she

already considered her a friend.

"Good afternoon, Lady Belinda. So pleased to have you here."

"Thank you," Lady Belinda murmured softly, and offered Nancy a shy smile. Lady Estelle curtseyed politely, and Benedict smiled to himself, seeing the two young ladies smile shyly at each other. Nancy's gaze was warm, and Benedict guessed that the two would get along famously.

They all settled down at the tea-table. Rowan lay down on the mat by the fire, fortunately not too far from Lady Belinda for his liking.

As they sat down, the butler appeared in the doorway. Benedict frowned, but Mama nodded to him to come forward.

"Another party of guests has arrived, my lady. And a rider."

"Tell them to step up," Mama said at once, her tone hard. Benedict glanced at her, but she shot him a warning glare. He said nothing, but looked down at his tea, struggling to rein in his anger. He had asked in particular that Lady Belinda and her family be invited for a picnic. He had meant only them, not a party for many guests.

His head whipped around to the door as his mother stood up.

"Lady Kearney! Lord Kearney. Lady Penelope!" she said warmly, going forward to greet the new guests. "Lord Rathgate!"

Benedict felt his rage grow uncontrollable as Darrow, Lord Rathgate, stepped in. He met Benedict's gaze, his own brown eyes lit with triumph, an unpleasant smirk twisting his lips.

Benedict's gaze flew to Nancy, who was standing automatically as his mother beckoned to her to greet the guests. As Nancy walked over, his horrified gaze moved to Lady Belinda. Her green eyes were soft with concern. He felt himself relax.

"Well!" His mother said, turning to beam at the rest of the guests. Benedict and Lord Grayleigh had both stood, as was proper when women entered the room, and Benedict glared at Darrow, who smirked back. "Now that our whole party has arrived, perhaps we should commence with the picnic?"

Benedict felt his hands ball into fists, and he took a deep breath. She had put him in an impossible position. He could not confront Darrow and throw him out of the house in front of the other guests, who would expect that he knew of their attendance. He glanced at Lady Belinda, who was standing to go to the door. The gaze she threw him was compassionate. He let out a long breath.

She seemed to understand his feelings.

He was left in the drawing room with Lord Grayleigh, Lord Kearney and Lord Darrow while the ladies went down ahead of them. He glanced from Lord Grayleigh to Lord Kearney, trying pointedly to ignore Darrow, who seemed to exude a triumphant arrogance as he stood there.

"Well, this is a fine day for a picnic," Lord Grayleigh said with a cheery voice. Benedict smiled at him.

"It is," he agreed softly. Lord Grayleigh was a pleasant man, he thought, with a narrow face and a thin frame, his eyes bracketed with deep wrinkles and his face lined in a way that showed he smiled often. He had an easygoing, friendly nature and Benedict gravitated towards him immediately.

"Well, then," Lord Grayleigh continued. "Shall we go down?"

"Yes," Benedict replied, striding to the door before Darrow could get there. Rowan bounded beside Benedict.

Darrow almost collided with him at the door. Benedict glared at him and had the satisfaction of seeing a brief glimmer of alarm deep in his eyes. Rowan growled and Darrow stepped back nervously.

"Your Grace," he said mockingly, standing back for Benedict. Benedict glared, pushing past him.

The two older men conversed a little stiltedly as they all went downstairs and through the front door.

"This is very commodious," his mother commented as they all sat down on the rather-elaborate picnic rug that the butler had laid out for them under the trees. Benedict had settled beside Lady Belinda's family—on Lady Grayleigh's right. Lady Belinda sat on Lady Grayleigh's left. His mother insisted on Lady Kearney and Lady Penelope sitting on his left-hand side. Nancy was seated opposite, next to Mama. Darrow sat on her left. He regarded Benedict with a glimmer of challenge in his eye. Rowan came padding over. Benedict saw Lady Penelope flinch and he smiled grimly to himself.

"Come, Rowan," he called him, gesturing for him to settle behind him. Lady Grayleigh turned and smiled at Rowan.

"Such a pretty fellow," she murmured to Benedict warmly.

"Thank you."

His mother opened the picnic basket, and Nancy handed out plates. Benedict accepted one from Lady Kearney.

"What a fine garden!" Lady Kearney declared. "Is it not fine, Penelope?" she asked her daughter. Lady Penelope turned to Benedict.

"Most fine," she said softly. Benedict felt his insides tense. Lady Belinda was here watching all this. He glared at his mother. How could she put him in such an awful position? He tried to ignore Lady Kearney, but she persisted.

"Penelope went for a fine walk yesterday. Did you not, Penelope? All the way to Rowanhill village."

"Yes, Mama," Lady Penelope murmured. Benedict took a deep breath.

"You must tell the Duke about the market there. Such fine things!"

Benedict thought that even Lady Penelope looked uncomfortable, and he cleared his throat.

"We have a fine market here in Norendale village, do we not, Mother?" he asked his mother. She blinked at him in surprise.

"Beg your pardon?" she asked, as if she had not expected him to address her.

"I said, we have a fine market in Norendale village. I am sure Lady Kearney would be very interested to hear of it."

His mother shot him a look, but he smiled thinly and reached for the bottle of cordial. If she could put him in a difficult position, then he could make her a bit uncomfortable, just for once.

He selected a sandwich and bit into it, leaning back with his eyes closed. He enjoyed picnics, mostly. If it was just himself and Rowan, maybe Nancy too. He smiled to himself.

And Belinda, he thought warmly. If she was there, I would be happy.

He was intensely private and trusted only very few people. It was unusual for him to accept someone so readily—but then, she was very easy to like, he thought fondly.

He glanced over at her. She was eating a cucumber sandwich, a little blob of butter somehow stuck to her nose. It looked adorable, and he ached to wipe it off with his handkerchief, but it would be a scandalous thing to do and so he resisted the urge.

"Your Grace?" Lady Penelope spoke up from his left, making him jump. "Do you care for peaches?" She was holding one out to him and he flinched, not sure whether to take it or refuse. He did not want to upset her, but he also did not want to convey a false impression.

"Thank you," he said swiftly. "But I have an allergy to peaches. They upset my stomach. I shall not delve into the details in this polite company."

She withdrew her hand, gazing at him with round blue eyes and a vaguely disgusted expression.

Benedict reached for another sandwich and chewed contentedly.

He looked up to see Lady Belinda watching him. Her green gaze was warm, and his soul soared. He forgot the awkwardness for a moment, and even forgot Darrow sitting across from him, his dark eyes narrowed as he watched him. All that mattered to him was Lady Belinda and he longed to speak with her.

Rowan, sitting beside him, whined impatiently and Benedict smiled as an idea occurred to him.

"I trust you can excuse me for a moment," he said, addressing the guests at large. "Rowan wishes to stretch his legs, and I would like to do likewise. Lady Belinda?" he asked, turning to her. "Would you care to accompany me?"

He tensed, thinking that perhaps he had put her in a bad position, but she smiled graciously and stood up.

"Thank you, I would like to. Excuse me," she added, turning to her family, and her mother patted her hand.

"Of course, Belinda. I'm sure we can spare you for a minute or two."

Belinda smiled at her family and walked over to join Benedict. His soul soared as she came to walk beside him, and they wandered away from the picnic rug. Rowan was delighted, running around them, barking, gazing up at Benedict with big loving eyes. He looked around and spotted a stick and threw it for Rowan. He bounded after it.

"Thank you for joining me," Benedict murmured, feeling shy. Lady Belinda was a few inches from him, close enough to be able to smell the scent of her. He breathed in the sweet lavender and rose smell, which made his senses swim.

She smiled at him. "Of course," she said lightly.

"I am sorry," he added after they had walked a little further. They were heading towards the ornamental lake at the back of the grounds. "I did not know that Mother had taken it on herself to include other guests."

"I understand," she said softly.

"I had to walk," he said at once. "It was so damnably uncomfortable there. Sorry," he added, going red. "I didn't mean to swear."

"It's quite all right," Lady Belinda said with a smile. "You have never heard my papa at a cricket match, evidently."

"Really?" Benedict roared with laughter. Rowan, hearing his laugh, bounded towards them, delighted by the sound. Benedict took the stick and threw it for Rowan, who ran off after it. "He seems so mild mannered and quiet."

"He is," Lady Belinda agreed softly. "But it's the one thing he gets truly angry about."

"Really?" Benedict repeated in surprise.

"Truly."

He laughed, and their gazes met and held. They had reached the lake and the water shimmered under the afternoon sun, ripples like silver filigree painted on its expanse. The light shone full on Lady Belinda's face, and she gazed up at him, her eyes drawing him in so that he could look nowhere else.

"My lady," he murmured, his throat tight. "I am...so glad to have you here."

"And I am glad to be here," she said softly.

Benedict swallowed hard. He was standing so close to her, the sweet scent of her hair filling his senses, and he suddenly longed to bend forward and press his lips to hers. He tensed, forcing himself to ignore the urge, and cleared his throat.

"You...I am glad to show you my home," he managed to say. "Your presence brings light to it."

Lady Belinda gazed up at him, her lips parting in a small expression of astonishment, and Benedict thought for a frightened moment that he had gone too far, that he had upset her, but then she sighed, and her lips lifted in a smile.

"Your Grace," she murmured. "That is such a lovely thing to say. Thank you."

"Benedict," he said softly. "Please. Call me Benedict."

She stared up at him. "Benedict," she said gently. His senses screamed with longing. "And you must, then, call me Belinda."

"Belinda."

She beamed and he bowed low, taking her hand in his own. He gazed into her eyes, and she gazed back, and he fought the urge to kiss her. He would have, but he did not want to scare her. He stared at her, and she smiled, and he felt his heart melting in the sweetness of her gentle stare.

At that moment, Rowan chose to burst out of the bushes, barking in delight, his fur damp, and with a big canine grin on his face.

"Rowan!" Benedict greeted the dog happily. "What have you been doing?"

Rowan barked excitedly and Belinda laughed.

"Does he want to play?" she suggested. Benedict nodded, laughing at the big dog's joyous barks.

"He assuredly does," he agreed, and looked around for a stick, then threw it for the big dog. He raced off.

They smiled at each other a little shyly. Benedict glanced up the path towards where the picnic was taking place.

"I suppose we ought to go back," he murmured. He did not wish to. "This path is long," he added, gesturing to the one that led up a winding way past the stables. They had arrived on it too, but it had seemed short when they walked to the lake. She nodded.

"I suppose we should go back," she agreed.

They walked back up the path. Rowan appeared, bounding up, his stick held firmly in his mouth, and Belinda, laughing, took it and threw it for him. Benedict watched joyfully. The big dog brought the stick back, and Benedict threw it. Belinda smiled at him warmly.

They walked back towards the picnic rug at a slow pace together, and Benedict was surprised that Darrow's presence had slipped his memory. He didn't really care about him being in attendance, as all that mattered was Belinda and her big, beautiful smile.

Rowan ran up to the rug with them and they settled beside

each other, and nothing mattered to him just then but the fact that she was sitting next to him, and his heart soared happily.

Chapter 26

The scent of lavender hung in the drawing room air; the result of Miss Lucas having just washed the floor. Belinda sat on the chaise longue and breathed in the smell, her thoughts drifting in a peaceful haze. She reached for the book she had chosen to read for the morning—a light novel, something entertaining rather than thought-provoking. It was a quiet, still day and she looked forward to a morning of easy, pleasant distraction.

Her thoughts drifted back to the previous afternoon. Walking with Benedict had been so beautiful. She recalled standing beside him at the lake, the way he took her hand and the dark-eyed stare that had drawn her in, so warm and compelling that she felt spellbound.

"I wonder when he'll visit next," she said to herself. Mama had invited Nancy and him to call on them in two days' time, for afternoon tea. She felt her stomach knot with anticipation.

"My lady?" The butler was in the doorway, and she looked up from her book.

"Yes?" she asked softly.

"Her ladyship your mother required me to say that she has left some copies of the *Ladies' Gazette* in the anteroom for you to look at."

"Thank you," Belinda said politely. Mama would mean her to go through the periodicals and choose ideas for new gowns from the illustrations in them. She smiled to herself. She would do that later. Mama and Estelle had gone to the modiste to choose a ballgown, and Belinda had elected to stay behind at home. Papa was meeting with his solicitor in town, and that meant that she was alone in the house, aside from the household staff.

"Bliss," she murmured to herself as the butler withdrew. Of course, she loved her family dearly, but having time and space to do exactly as she pleased for a few hours felt good.

She leaned back on the velvet-covered chaise longue, shutting her eyes. Her entire body seemed to relax, from her toes to her head, and she smiled to herself as thoughts of the Duke of Norendale drifted into her head. She could spend an entire morning thinking if she wished.

"I'll do some work on my flowers," she told herself, glancing at the clock, "and then send for a dish of hot chocolate and read my book."

Bliss.

She sat down at the table and reached for the big map-book she'd used to press some of the small flowers. As she opened it, the butler appeared in the doorway again.

"Begging your pardon for disturbing you, my lady," he murmured. "But there is a visitor downstairs. What ought I to do?"

"I think you should not show him in," Belinda said hesitantly. If it was Mr. Holford, who had suggested he might come to speak to Papa about investing in Chinese vases, then it would be improper for him to call on her alone, but Papa had left no instruction as to what to do.

"The visitor is a lady, my lady," the butler demurred at once.

"Oh! Then please show her in," Belinda said instantly. The awkwardness of having to turn away a business associate of Papa's would have been horrid.

"Yes, my lady."

Belinda sat where she was at the tea table, a frown creasing her brow as she tried to guess who it might be. She glanced down at her dress. She was wearing a simple white muslin day-dress. It was a new one, plain, but of a good cut, and she was glad she'd chosen it despite not having planned to have visitors.

"Good morning," a tight, hard voice announced. Belinda tensed immediately. In the doorway, wearing a black gown, her dark hair covered with the briefest of black lace widow's caps, was the Duchess of Norendale.

She stood up at once, dropping a curtsey. The butler waited in the doorway. "Good morning," Belinda said quickly, then turned to the butler. "Please bring tea for..."

"No, thank you," the Duchess said at once. "I do not intend to stay."

"But..." Belinda trailed off, her heart thudding. If she was not there for tea, she wondered, then why had she called on her?

"Should I fetch tea, my lady?" the butler asked, clearly confused.

"No. Thank you," Belinda said swiftly.

The butler lingered in the door for a second or two longer,

155

but the Duchess turned and glared at him, and he bowed and withdrew. Belinda stood with her back to the window. The expression on the face of her visitor was anything but friendly. She stiffened her back, reminding herself she had faced far worse things than the Duchess.

"I have come to tell you in no uncertain terms what I think of your dalliance with my son," the Duchess said tightly.

"I beg your pardon?" Belinda demanded, gaping at her. "Dalliance? What dalliance? We are courting."

"I know," the Duchess said tightly. "And it is to that which I refer. I have not consented to that, and nor would I have, had my son asked my opinion on the matter."

"He is a grown man," Belinda began angrily, but the Duchess shouted her to silence.

"He is a Duke! And he is my son! And he cannot simply choose idly because he wishes it. The future of the family line depends on it."

"I am the daughter of an earl," Belinda said, her cheeks flushing red with anger. "I see no reason why I should not be courted by a Duke."

"Silence!" The Duchess shouted. Belinda took a step back. In her rage she seemed like a dark specter, not a person, and she shivered a little, her resolve crumbling under the onslaught. "The Duke of Norendale comes from a respectable family! Your family is far from respectable."

"My family are good people," Belinda whispered, but the Duchess sneered.

"You have the worst reputation in the city."

Belinda felt a tear run down her cheek. That was her objection, then. Those terrible lies. They were still following her, still alive after all those years despite the author of them still living in India without return.

"It's not true," Belinda whispered, her voice wavering with a sob. "It's not..." She gasped to draw breath, but the Duchess interrupted again.

"I don't care if it's true or not!" she raged. "It is talked of from the one end of the respectable half of London to the other and that is all I care about. My son will not be associated with a woman who is a constant subject of gossips in tea-houses."

"Is that my fault?" Belinda whispered.

"You will be quiet," she demanded, dark eyes flashing. "You will let my son be unencumbered so that he can wed a suitable duchess. I have already found one for him. I will not let you get in my way."

Belinda gaped at her. "You have already found one..."

"Of course!" the duchess hissed. "I have known for months who I would choose. Someone with a meek disposition, biddable and with a good reputation. That is what I wish for the next Duchess of Norendale. I will not have someone dragging the scent of scandal into my halls."

Belinda sobbed. She had intended to stand up to the duchess, but she could not find strength. Being reduced to a bad smell in the nostrils of society was too much to withstand. She sobbed again, looking around the room, wanting only to escape.

"I cannot..." she began, but she interrupted her again.

"You will do as I say."

"No," Belinda whispered, finding deep inside a spark of courage. She straightened her back, glaring at the Duchess. Let the shame go—it belongs to those who would shame you, she reminded herself. She cleared her throat, still feeling frightened. "No, I will not do as you wish. I will make up my own mind about my own future. There is nothing stopping me from doing so."

the Duchess gaped at her for a moment, but then her eyes narrowed, and Belinda flinched.

"You are a little upstart wretch," she hissed. "You are a dark stain on society, and I will not have you smirch my family with your scandalous ways."

Belinda gasped. Nobody—not even the malicious gossips—had ever called her such horrid names before. She felt tears start and she turned away.

"You will at least have the courtesy to get out of my house," she whispered at the Duchess, who was turning in the doorway.

"I am going," the woman said stiffly. "I would not choose to stay a second more than I have to."

Belinda felt as though she had been slapped and tears ran down her cheeks. She could not stay indoors a second longer—not in the room that still echoed with the cruel words the Duchess shouted—and she ran down the stairs towards the garden.

"My lady!" the butler shouted, but she ran down the garden steps, heedless of the fact that they had just been washed and were soaking. She screamed as she lost her footing and then she hit the ground with a thud and the world went black.

Chapter 27

Benedict hummed to himself as he walked up the hallway to his study. He had just returned from a ride to London, and he felt exhausted, but also contented. He and Clinton had called on a goldsmith, with the intention of commissioning a work for Belinda as a gift. He smiled to himself, thinking of the piece he had finally chosen. He was sure Belinda would love it.

"Brother! Brother," Nancy hissed from the drawing room. Benedict frowned.

"What is it, Nancy?" he asked softly. His sister's dark eyes were distressed.

"Hush," Nancy whispered back. "Mama is in the antechamber, and I don't want her to hear me. I need to talk to you."

Benedict gazed at her, concern making his brow lower worriedly. "What is it?" he asked her gently. "What has upset you, Nancy?"

"Shh," she said. "Please, Benedict. We must be quiet. Can we talk in there?" she asked, gesturing down the hallway to where the stairs led down to the library.

"Of course."

They hurried downstairs to the library, and when they reached it, Nancy hastily shut the door behind them, looking around nervously.

"What is it?" he asked softly. Nancy let out a sigh.

"I was in town today, Benedict," she said hastily. "I was calling on Amelia. We went with Amelia's mother to the tea-house, and then to the modiste to fetch Amelia's new gown. When we were walking back from the modiste, who should I see but Mama?"

"Mother was in town?" Benedict asked with a frown. He vaguely recalled that she had said she would call on a friend there.

"Yes! She was talking to Lady Haddon, who is a good friend of Lady Kearney, Penelope's mama. She was confiding in Lady Haddon that she had called in at Payton House just a few hours before."

"Payton House?" Benedict spluttered. Whatever motive

would his mother have to visit Belinda? As far as he could tell, she disliked her and her family immensely. Not that it was easy to tell with his mother—she was distant with most people.

"Yes! She said she had gone to put that scandalous little wretch—those were her words—in no doubt about her place. That was what she said," Nancy whispered. She looked frightened. "I don't know..."

"What has she done?" Benedict hissed.

"I don't know," Nancy repeated.

"Sorry. Sorry, Nancy," Benedict said instantly, seeing his sister take a step back. He must have had a terrifying look on his face. He took a deep breath and tried to feel calm, but he was desperate to call on Belinda. If his mother had upset her, he would...he did not know what he would do, but she would wish she had not. "I didn't mean to affright you. Thank you. Thank you so much for telling me," he told Nancy firmly. He took her hand in his, looking into her eyes. "I can't thank you enough."

He took another breath in, trying to decide what to do. If his mother had gone all the way to London to insult and wound a woman who had already been insulted and wounded for most of her adult life, his anger would be unstoppable. But, a quiet part of his brain reminded him, would her family not have protected her?

He pushed the thought aside. It did not matter. He had to ride there at once to set matters to rights. He turned to Nancy.

"Thank you," he said again. "Could I ask you to tell Mother I am going for a ride? I might return late."

"It's almost five o' clock," Nancy pointed out. "It'll be dark in a few hours."

"I know," Benedict said swiftly. "But I have to do this, Nancy."

"What will you do?" Nancy asked him softly.

He sighed. "I don't know yet," he admitted. "But I have to apologise to Belinda. I cannot let Mother insult her, as I am sure she did."

"Yes," Nancy whispered. "You are right. Mama can be so cruel." She had tears in her eyes and Benedict frowned.

"What is it, Nancy?" He asked her gently. "You're crying. What happened?"

"Oh...oh, brother..." she was sobbing, and Benedict reached

for her and wrapped his arms around her, holding her tight to his chest as he had done when she was just five or six and she was crying about some hurt or other. He rocked her gently, stroking her hair and she slowly stopped crying and sniffed, taking a breath. "It's...it's Mama. She's so cruel. I can't do this anymore. I cannot pretend to like Lord Rathgate anymore. I cannot!"

Benedict stepped back and looked down at her in disbelief. She was still crying, tears running down her cheeks, her eyes reddening at the edges with her sobbing. Her statement was almost unbelievable; utterly unexpected.

"You mean, you truly do not like him?" he asked, feeling silly. She had said so, and yet somehow it didn't make sense to him. He had been convinced Darrow had fooled her completely, like he had managed to hide his true nature from his mother.

"No!" Nancy sobbed. "No. I can't bear him. All he cares for is himself. All he wants is to be thought clever and admirable, and if one expresses any opinion at all besides to echo how wonderful he is, he flies into a petty rage."

"The fool," Benedict whispered. He felt anger filling him at the thought.

"Please," Nancy whispered. "I just don't want to have to see him again."

"I can arrange that," Benedict said firmly.

"You can?"

"Yes," Benedict said at once. "I can arrange that right away. I will go up to the anteroom now. If you could wait here, Nancy? Don't come up. I don't want you to be there if Mama and I have words. I don't want to distress you."

"Benedict..." Nancy whispered, but he just smiled at her, seeing she was worried for him.

"I'll be quite all right," he said gently. "You wait here. I'll be back in a moment."

"Yes, brother."

Benedict smiled at her, then went through the door and out into the hallway. He marched grimly up the stairs. As he reached the middle section of the stairway, he heard footsteps coming down. He looked up and his fist clenched as he saw Darrow, walking lightly down, his long, slim legs fast.

"Darrow," he growled.

Darrow blinked in surprise, then turned a disinterested gaze on Benedict. "That's Lord Rathgate now," he said in a bored tone. "Or Rathgate, for those who know me well."

Benedict didn't move out of his path, but remained blocking the stairwell, his big, muscled form taking up a lot of the room.

"I know you well," Benedict said lightly. "I know precisely what a petty coward you are."

Darrow went pale, his brow raised, his lips compressing into a line.

"Did you just call me a coward?" he demanded. "I say! That is a smirch on my honour. I shall not have my honour questioned. I should challenge you to a duel."

"You want to fight me?" Benedict inquired; one brow raised. "Go ahead."

Darrow drew himself up to his full height, which was considerable, but he still lacked half an inch to reach the same height as his foe. His expression was astonished, but also frightened, his hazel eyes round and wide, his skin white. Benedict, still blocking his path, just stared.

"I..." Darrow murmured, and Benedict pressed his own lips together to hide his wry smile. He could practically smell the fear. "Do not think you could stand against me!" He blustered. "I have a quick draw with a pistol. I..."

"It would be my choice what weapon we used, Darrow," Benedict reminded him. "You challenged me, remember? So, I'm the challenged party. And I would not choose pistols."

"Then...Damn you!" Darrow hissed. "Damn you, Benedict Chesterton, as a coward and a liar. I never had to face such treatment in my life. I...I..." His face was white, two angry spots of red appearing on his cheeks.

"You don't want to fight me, do you?" Benedict said grimly. "Not without four or five cronies to back you. Not so appealing then, is it?"

"This...this is not to be borne!" Darrow declared loudly. "I will not stand here and be so insulted. Get out of my way!" He tried to push past Benedict on the stairs, but all Benedict had to do was stand still and Darrow could not budge him. He bit his lip, grimly amused by how little effort it had been to hold him off.

"It's my house, Darrow," Benedict said tightly. He pushed his face close to Darrow's, narrowing his eyes. "It's my house. And I am telling you to get out of it. Get out of this building now, and if I ever catch you in here again, I will give you the whipping you've been begging for since you were ten."

"You...you beast!" Darrow exclaimed.

Benedict just raised a brow. "Get out of here, Darrow," he said tiredly. "Or you'll wish you had sooner. On your way."

He stood back and Darrow pushed past him and scrambled down the stairs, scuttling for the door. Benedict watched him go. The fellow moved at a run and Benedict heard the front door slam and he stood where he was until he was sure he'd disappeared and then walked slowly up the stairs.

He'd been afraid of Darrow for years. And now he saw that Darrow was nothing but a coward. He blinked in amazement and shook his head, then walked on up the stairway.

As he reached the top, his mother came out of the drawing room.

"Benedict!" she declared loudly, her gaze narrow and angry. "What was all that noise? What has been going on here?"

Benedict sighed. "I threw Darrow out. He's not welcome."

He held her gaze. She looked at him in astonishment.

"You threw him out? Benedict! How dare you! After how hard I've worked. After all my effort. What will Nancy say?"

"She will be glad not to have to see the odious little fool here a second longer," Benedict said tightly. "She disliked him too. You probably knew that, but you didn't care. Did you?"

"She'd get used to him," Mama countered, her tone defensive. "She didn't know him. That's all."

"She'd get used to him?" Benedict said softly. "Like I was supposed to get used to being beaten by five boys at school. You really care nothing, don't you?"

His mother stared at him. For a moment—just a moment—he could see her shock, as if she realized something. Then the anger descended, and the defensive shouting began.

"How dare you?" she yelled. "Of course I care! I put hours of work into arranging a match for you both. Hours, and hours! And then, at the last minute, when my work is almost done, you come in and ruin it! How dare you!"

Benedict stood there tiredly. He was exhausted after

confronting Darrow, but he still had to ride to London, which would take three hours. He did not argue, but when she had stopped shouting, he fixed her with a firm gaze.

"I know that you called on Belinda today," he said quietly. "I heard about it in town," he added, not wanting to suggest that Nancy had told him. "I am going to ride to London now to put whatever you did to rights."

His mother went pale for a moment, then her eyes narrowed.

"Benedict...You will do no such thing! She's scandalous. You're a Duke, and you need a suitable duchess. You do not need someone with a terrible reputation, someone who cannot be seen in public without rumours flying."

"She is kind and warmhearted," Benedict said quietly. "And funny and wise. And that is what I want."

"You're a fool!" his mother yelled as he turned his back and walked down the stairs. "You'll be ridiculed throughout London. What will people say about you? What will the gossips whisper?"

Benedict turned around and looked at her. "They can say what they like," he said quietly. "I am the one living this life. Not them."

He turned around and walked down the stairs.

His mother said nothing, but when he reached the hallway and walked swiftly across the tiled floor to the door, he heard her voice yelling as she hurried after.

"Benedict! Benedict! Wait! Don't ride to London. It's late. Go tomorrow. Stay here."

"I'm going to London," Benedict said firmly, turning around so she could see his face. "I will stay at the townhouse overnight if I have to. I will speak to you tomorrow morning."

"Benedict!"

He turned and walked through the door and hurried to the stables. It was half an hour past five and he still had three hours to ride. He called for the stable-hand and waited while his horse was saddled and then stepped up swiftly. He had a long way to ride and a lot to do before he rested.

Chapter 28

"Move!" Benedict whispered under his breath as he rode around the corner of Park Lane in Kensington. To reach Payton House, he needed to ride through London and then a mile or two outside, and the traffic in London was—predictably—almost standing still. It was eight o' clock in the evening and it seemed that everyone in the city was on the street—going to and from their homes to theaters, tea-houses and opera houses. He swore under his breath and sat still on his horse, waiting as a member of the city Watch rode up to a man with a handcart who was obstructing the traffic.

"Move along, please, sir," he said.

The man with the handcart spat in the dirt, but pushed his cart off the road and Benedict breathed a sigh of relief as the traffic began to flow again. His forehead was wet with perspiration and his legs and back were aching. He'd ridden as fast as he could from Norendale Manor to London, and he still had a few miles to go before reaching Payton House.

"Easy, boy," he said quietly to his horse, patting his neck to calm him as a big coach rattled along past them. He drew in a breath and rode forward at a trot, guiding his horse through the traffic.

He rode along at a trot, keeping his eyes on the road as they hurried through town.

The road to Payton House left London and kept going into the countryside. His thoughts were full of Belinda and what he would say to her when he saw her.

Payton house came into sight after half an hours' riding.

"Thank Goodness," he murmured, and rode briskly down the drive, dismounting at the stairs. "Take my horse to the stables, please," he addressed a gardener who wandered up confusedly. "And please make sure he gets some water and bran mash."

"Yes, my lord."

Benedict tapped on the door, his heart racing. He had wanted to get some flowers to bring with him as an apology, but all the florist's shops in London were closed. He swallowed hard, shifting his weight from foot to foot as he waited.

"Good evening?" the butler said a little suspiciously as he opened the door.

Benedict bowed low. "Apologies for the disturbance," he said swiftly. "I am here to call on Lady Belinda and her family. Please convey my apologies for the lateness of the hour," he added, reddening slightly.

"Of course, Your Grace." The butler paused. A strange expression crossed his face; almost accusatory. It was gone almost as swiftly as it appeared. "Lady Belinda is indisposed," he added coolly.

"What?" Benedict demanded. "I beg your pardon?"

The butler took a breath. "She is indisposed, your grace. She is injured. She..."

"Oh! Your Grace!" A woman's voice cried out, and Benedict looked up to see Lady Grayleigh and Lady Estelle coming down the stairs. When they saw him in the doorway, they ran to him. Lady Grayleigh held out her hands to him. Her face was white.

"Your Grace. It's Belinda. She...she..." She sobbed and Benedict pressed his hand to his heart. He gaped at her in horror, but Lady Estelle, seeing his horror, began talking too.

"She's alive, Your Grace." She explained swiftly. "Just badly hurt. We don't know when she will recover," she added, and then she was crying too. Benedict stared, shocked.

"Whatever has happened?" he whispered.

"I am sorry, Your Grace," Lady Grayleigh said softly. Her brown eyes were wet, huge seeming in her pale face. "She fell, and the physician says she has a bad concussion." She paused, sniffing. "I am overcome with emotion. I'm just so grateful you're here! Perhaps your presence will help her. The physician says she may awaken soon."

"Fell?" Benedict echoed, confusedly. "How?"

"She was running down the stairs," Estelle said in explanation. Her voice was small, her hazel eyes big and round. Benedict rested his hand on her shoulder as he might with Nancy, trying to give her strength. She took a breath. "She was running into the garden, the butler said, and she fell on the step that had just been washed. She must have hit her head terribly hard," Estelle added softly. "What do you think will happen?"

Benedict took a deep breath, seeing the two women staring

up at him. He could think of nothing to say. He was in shock too. He wanted to see Belinda and that was all he could think of.

"I do not know," he said quietly. "I cannot imagine that she will not wake up," he whispered. "I want to see her," he added, his voice rough with feeling. "Please. May I?"

"Of course," Lady Grayleigh said at once. "I hope that your presence will soothe her." Lady Estelle nodded.

"Indeed, your presence may prove most efficacious in the matter!" she said, looking hopeful.

Benedict swallowed hard. "Let us go and see her."

The two women walked with him upstairs. The two ladies reached a door and went in ahead of him. He paused in the doorway. This was obviously Belinda's bedchamber: The scent of lavender was everywhere, mixed with rosewater. He could not breathe in without thinking of her and his heart twisted painfully.

"Come in," Lady Grayleigh called.

Benedict stepped in and his heart ached as he caught sight of Belinda's pale form. She was asleep, it seemed, her eyes shut, her long lashes resting on her cheeks. He went to her bed and sat down on the chair beside it, taking her hand. It was warm.

"Belinda," he whispered softly. "I'm here."

He said nothing else, just stared at her as she slept there. She did not move, but he could detect the slight sigh of breath through her lips. He gazed at her, his eyes wandering from her pale hair to her petal-soft skin to her nose and soft pink lips. He wished she would open her eyes. He longed to see her staring up at him, those soft lips curving into a big smile.

"Talk to her," Lady Estelle suggested. "Maybe she'll hear you."

"Estelle..." Lady Grayleigh said hesitatingly. Benedict nodded.

"I would be happy to talk to her," he said softly. He turned to Belinda, focusing only on her. He soon forgot that Lady Estelle and her mother were in the room and talked to her freely as if they were alone.

"Belinda," he said softly. "I love you. I have wanted to tell you this for days now. When I met you, I admired your courage, and that admiration grew into fondness and friendship. That friendship is now also love. You are so beautiful, so strong. You make me laugh and you make me think. I miss you. Please. Please, come back."

He could feel tears in his eyes as he spoke, and his voice cracked as he said it. He sniffed but felt no shame in crying. Lady Belinda was right—what reason was there to feel shame? He gripped her hand, wishing he could imbue her with some of his own life, some of his own strength and warmth. He just wanted her to wake up.

"Come with us, Your Grace," Lady Grayleigh said gently. "Have some dinner with us. You must be exhausted after your ride."

"No," Benedict murmured, turning to face her where she stood behind him. "I am not tired. I want to stay with Belinda. I know it's improper," he added quickly, but Lady Grayleigh inclined her head.

"If her maid is here to chaperone you, I think we might make an exception." She glanced at Estelle. "Come, dear. Let us go down to find your Papa and eat some dinner."

"Yes, Mama," Estelle said softly. She looked at Belinda, her eyes soft with care. "What about Belinda having dinner?"

Benedict's heart twisted. Lady Grayleigh replied.

"She cannot eat, my dear. When she wakes, we will have some gruel sent up for her."

The two ladies went through the door and closed it softly. A second or two later, a gentle knock sounded and a young woman with dark hair and a thin face came into the room. She looked up at Benedict, her brown eyes huge in her face.

"What do you think will happen to her ladyship, Your Grace?" she asked softly, her eyes moving to Belinda.

"I think she will wake up," Benedict said firmly.

"You do? Good. Good."

Benedict gazed down at Belinda, ignoring the chaperone, who went to tidy Belinda's things on her dressing-table. He held Belinda's hand, stroking it gently, saying her name softly, over and over again.

His eyelids drooped and he leaned back in the chair. He really was exhausted, the exertion catching up with him as he sat in the silent room. He held Belinda's hand between his own and let his eyes close.

A noise woke him. He blinked in confusion for a moment, and then his eyes widened. The noise that had woken him was Belinda, coughing.

"Belinda!" he whispered. She turned and saw him, and her eyes widened and then a smile lit her face. She gazed up at him, then frowned.

"Benedict?" she said softly. "What are you doing here? Where am I?"

Benedict smiled, squeezing her hand fondly. It was natural that she would be confused—she'd slept for hours and woken to find him in her chamber.

"I came to see you. You're in your bedchamber. In Payton House. You fell. You slept until now. It is now..." He reached for his pocket watch and blinked in surprise. "Ten o' clock at night."

"Ten o' clock?" She frowned deeply. "But I..." her gaze went cloudy. "I remember...I was running down the steps. I fell..." Her voice trailed off and she looked up at him confusedly. "How are you here?"

He laughed. "I had to come," he said swiftly. He frowned. "I heard that my mother came to see you. I wanted to apologise," he added quickly as her eyes grew round and fearful.

"Yes. Yes! She was here. That was why I was running. I was so sad. She said..." She started sobbing and Benedict reached for her, ignoring the gasp of the chaperone who stood somewhere behind him. He held Belinda close, rocking her in his arms as she sobbed, and he stroked her hair.

"Shh. Shh, sweetling," he murmured, then blushed as he realized he had called her by a term of endearment for the first time. "Hush. It's all right. Don't strain yourself," he added as she loosened her grip, staring up at him.

"She said that I was a terrible future Duchess. That I should let you have a proper duchess. Like that woman...the one she chose." she sobbed again, and Benedict looked at her steadily.

"I have found my duchess," he said softly. "She is right here, in reach of my arms. I have found the woman I love, and nothing—*nothing*—will ever cleave her from me. She is the light on my horizon, the stars that guide me. I love you, Belinda," he said, his voice hoarse with unshed tears. "I love you so, so much. You must know that."

Belinda blinked at him, and her eyes were suddenly filled with tears too.

"I love you, Benedict," she whispered softly, smiling even as her eyes grew damp. "I love you so much. You are the one I want. You are my strength and my courage, my light in the dark."

He reached for her and held her and blinked back his own tears as she cried. When she looked up at him again, he smiled.

"I am honoured, my dear. But I don't think I am your courage. Your courage is much too big."

She giggled. "You're not small, Your Grace."

He roared with laughter, for once, feeling nothing but delight for his own strong height and build.

"No," he agreed softly. "No, I suppose I am not."

He held her gaze and he knew that he had never felt so happy in his life—that he had found the woman that he loved, and she returned that love. He bent forward and pressed his lips to hers and they kissed.

Behind him, he heard the indrawn gasp of the chaperone, and he ignored her, but Belinda, when she had moved back from his arms, looked up at her fondly.

"It's all right, Gertie," she said gently. "If you like, I'll ring the bell and summon somebody to fetch Mama and Estelle, and then you don't need to worry anymore. Is that better?"

"Yes. Yes, milady." She sounded relieved.

Benedict smiled as Belinda tried to sit up in bed but then shook his head as she tried to slip out from under the covers.

"It's all right," he said gently. "I will go and fetch your mama and sister. And then nobody can say anything improper happened."

"Come straight back," Belinda asked as he went to the door. He grinned and nodded.

"Of course," he agreed.

He walked down the hallway, his head still reeling from the kiss. He followed the staircase down to the dining room, and when he put his head around the door, Lady Grayleigh gasped, clearly thinking something bad had happened.

"What is..."

"I came to inform you," Benedict said swiftly, "that Belinda has awoken."

"What?" Lady Grayleigh beamed at him; her face transformed into a picture of joy. "Heaven be praised! That's wonderful!"

"Belinda!" Estelle yelled, and was already running to the door as Benedict, grinning, stood back for her.

"Not too fast," Lady Grayleigh called, already hurrying to catch up. "We don't know how tired she is. She could still be in a bad state."

"She seems tired," Benedict agreed. "But well enough. She'll be delighted to see you," he added. Estelle was already at the top of the stairs, running to her sister's room.

Lord Grayleigh followed the group more slowly and Benedict stood in the doorway while the three women embraced. Belinda was crying again as she held her mother and her sister close. Estelle was kneeling by the bed, her arms tight around her sister. Lady Grayleigh sat where he had been sitting, by the bed. All of them had wet faces, tears streaking down.

"How wonderful," Lord Grayleigh murmured warmly from the door. "It's a miracle."

"It is," Benedict said softly, and he felt his lips lift in a smile as he recalled the kiss. "It certainly is."

Lord and Lady Grayleigh insisted that he stay the night in their guest-suite. He agreed to take some supper on a tray in the drawing room, and Belinda, who insisted that she felt well enough to stand and walk to the drawing room, came to sit with him as he ate.

"I'm so pleased you're here," she said softly, sitting across from him at the table.

"As am I, my dear," he answered smilingly, his gaze holding hers. "As am I."

The supper was a light one of sandwiches and a slice of cold pie, and he gobbled it down as fast as he reasonably could, so that he could reach for Belinda and hold her again.

"I love you, Belinda," he murmured, bending to kiss her tenderly on the top of her head.

"I love you, too."

She smiled up at him and he smiled back, and he knew his world was complete and that life was beautiful indeed.

172

Epilogue

"Is the coach here?" Estelle asked with a bright voice, gazing out of the bedroom window. "I can't see to the door from here."

Belinda, standing by her dressing-table opposite the window, smiled a slow smile.

"I am almost ready," she assured Estelle, who was leaning out of the window, trying to crane her neck around the corner. Her beautiful pink silk dress was being a little crushed on the windowsill, but it would survive a few seconds of being leaned on.

"Good! I can hear the coach now!" Estelle exclaimed excitedly. "Oh! I must fetch the flowers." Her silk-clad feet hurried soundlessly to the door and up the hallway to the drawing room.

Belinda smiled to herself, then grinned at Gertie, who was helping to arrange her hair. Gertie looked worried, but a brief grin crossed over her stern features before a small frown of focus appeared again.

"Almost done, milady," she told Belinda in a clipped, firm voice. "I just need one more pin to hold the veil in place."

"Of course, Gertie," Belinda said gently. "Take your time."

Gertie cast a worried glance in her direction, but then continued with the task. Belinda smiled to herself, a bubble of joy rising in her stomach, so bright and warm that she could not help grinning. In a few hours, she would be wed to Benedict, and her world was full of excitement and joy.

Gertie was not used to having to create such elaborate hairstyles—particularly not ones that sported flowers and veils together—but she was on her way to creating something lovely.

"There!" Gertie exclaimed, standing back. She beamed at Belinda. "There, milady. My! But you look pretty."

"Thank you." Belinda glanced at the looking glass.

The thin gauze veil fell back from her hair, which was arranged in a chignon decorated with summer roses. The dress she wore was white brocaded silk, decorated with white patterns worked into the fabric. The long skirt fell from a high waistband, also of white silk, and the neckline was a low oval, a necklace with a single pearl on it around her neck.

She glanced at her face, and she smiled at herself, seeing

radiant joy in her own eyes. She took a breath.

"I'm ready," she told Gertie.

"Belinda! Belinda!" Estelle appeared in the doorway; her arms full of roses. "Here they are! The flowers!"

Belinda grinned at her sister, whose excitement was like fireworks. She held out her arms for one of the big bouquets, and Estelle passed it to her. Belinda had chosen the flowers herself from their gardens. Pale pink roses were mixed with gypsophila and pale gladioli. She breathed the scent of the flowers and felt herself calm slightly. She was still bubbling with excitement, but it was a quieter joy than Estelle, who was running about making sure everything was ready.

"This is the one I am supposed to hold?" she asked Belinda, gesturing to her own bunch of flowers, which also featured pale pink and apricot blooms. Belinda nodded.

"Yes. Now I think we are ready. Gertie?"

"Oh? Oh, yes, milady," Gertie replied, nodding.

"Good. Let's all go down, then," Belinda suggested lightly.

"Yes. Yes. I have my flowers and my shawl, and you have your flowers. Let's go." Estelle went swiftly out of the door, standing back in the hallway so that Belinda could go ahead of her down the stairs. Gertie followed after her. She was going to attend the wedding too, which would be held in a small private chapel on their estate.

Mama and Papa were waiting at the bottom of the stairs, along with the rest of the household. Belinda held her breath as she walked down, seeing their smiling faces filled with love as they looked up at her. Her heart filled with love, and she looked at the window opposite, trying to keep her head up so that the tears would not spill over to her cheeks.

"You look beautiful, my dear," Mama whispered. Her eyes were damp.

"Thank you, Mama," Belinda murmured.

"This is a hard day for me," Papa said, his tears unashamedly glinting. "But I am so happy too."

Belinda squeezed his hand, her own heart filling with love.

They went down the stairs and Papa helped her into the coach. Mama and Estelle clambered in too, and then they set off the brief distance to the chapel, which lay at the far eastern reach of the estate. They could have walked there, but their dresses would have been ruined on the muddy earth of the path, and Mama and Papa had insisted they ride in the coach.

Belinda jumped down as Papa held out his hand for her and together, they walked to the chapel. She took a deep breath, her eyes damp as she gazed at the flowers around the doorway. The staff and Estelle had assembled the arch about the chapel door, and it was a work of much love.

"I love you, daughter," Papa whispered as he pressed her hand. Belinda swallowed hard.

"I love you, too, Papa," she whispered.

Then they were walking down the aisle, and she could see nothing except the man who stood there. His back had been to the door, but when they arrived, Benedict turned to face them, and she grinned as he gazed at them.

Benedict was wearing a black jacket and black trousers—she had never seen him wearing anything else—his tall, broad form strong and muscled, his black hair bright in the soft light of the candles. His smile lit up the room, and his eyes, so full of love, made a lump form in her throat. She swallowed hard; her own heart so full of love she thought it might burst. The veil was down over her face, but it was thin enough that she could see through it quite well, the light in the church bright with the candles.

She walked up to stand beside him and the priest, Father Lucas, beamed at them both.

Clearing his throat, the priest intoned the opening lines of the ceremony.

Belinda stood beside Benedict, gazing up at him at intervals through the thin veil. She smiled as his eyes met hers; impossible to hide the joy that was in her heart.

The priest was talking, and she realized she hadn't been listening to a word he said. Her gaze had been lost in Benedict's, and she blinked and focused on the words of the ceremony.

Behind them in the pews, Mama, Papa and Estelle sat, along with Lila and her parents, Nancy, Lord Clinton, Rowan—who was sitting at Nancy's feet and watching them intently—and Gertie. The rest of the household staff from Payton House were there too. Benedict's mother had declined to come, marking the ceremony with her disapproval. Benedict had grinned, saying they weren't alive for her approval or disapproval, and Belinda had been relieved by his wise words.

Her attention came back to the priest as he reached the part where they had to say their vows.

"...And do you, Belinda Eliza Payton, take thee Benedict Nicholas Chesterton to be your lawful wedded husband?"

"I do." She spoke the words firmly, every part of her heart in them.

The priest, who had given all the church services she had ever attended, turned to Benedict.

"And do you, Benedict Nicholas Chesterton, take thee Belinda Eliza Payton to be your lawful wedded wife?"

"I do."

Belinda gazed up at him, her heart melting with love, and then the priest was reaching the last part of the ceremony and her heart raced as she knew what must come next. She gazed up at Benedict through the veil and the priest—joyously, to her ears—said the words.

"You may kiss the bride."

Benedict smiled down at her through the veil and then, very tenderly, lifted it and bent down.

His lips pressed against hers and his arms moved around her, and Belinda shut her eyes as his kiss, soft and tender, filled her soul with love.

He stepped back and then they turned to face their friends, who were all grinning and smiling, some crying and some laughing with joy.

They walked down the aisle to the coach, that awaited them, and Benedict reached into his pocket to find the purse of coins, which he would throw for the children of the cottagers, who—along with all the tenants and farmers who lived on the Payton properties—would be attending an informal banquet outdoors at trestles arranged beneath the shelter of the trees.

Mama, Papa and Estelle were waiting to embrace her, and Belinda hugged them and then she was clambering into the coach, Benedict's hand helping her up. He stood outside the coach and threw the coins and the cottagers' children scrambled for them, laughing in delight.

Then Benedict was clambering up into the coach and

shutting the door, and they were rolling the few hundred yards back towards Payton House.

Belinda gazed up at Benedict and he looked into her eyes. His own eyes were full of love, shining bright.

She smiled at him, and he smiled at her and bent close, pressing his lips to her cheek.

She shut her eyes, then opened them as he kissed her again.

"I love you," he said softly.

"And I love you, too, Benedict," she said with sincerity and delight in her voice. "I love you too. So very much."

He wrapped his arm around her and held her close and the coach rattled onward towards the estate.

The garden was bright with sunshine and filled with late summer flowers and Belinda, staring up at Benedict and then out at the beautiful scene, knew that she was as happy as she could ever have imagined and that the course that will bring greatest happiness is written in the words of one's own heart, waiting to be followed.

Extended Epilogue

Belinda gazed out over the lawn, the border of white daisies and gypsophila nodding in the breeze. The garden staff had done an excellent job laying out the plants in a way she had planned with them in winter, so that in midsummer the borders and ornamental gardens were a riot of beautiful blooms.

The picnic rugs that had been laid out in the shelter of the trees were just visible from where she stood in the garden. She frowned lightly—there were certainly enough rugs, but then they were expecting a lot of guests.

"Sweetheart," a voice called behind her, from the front drive. "I'm sure it's all ready. Don't you want to come and take some lemonade? It's hot out there in the sunshine."

Belinda turned and smiled as Benedict came closer. He was walking slowly, but then that was necessitated by the small boy who held onto his finger, his own chubby fingers closed firmly around Benedict's. Behind Benedict and the little boy, Rowan walked slowly; his gaze on the child watchful and caring.

"Alexander," Belinda called softly, gazing lovingly down at the child. "Isn't it too hot out here for you?" He was wearing a little velvet jacket in pale blue, a miniature version of his father's, though Benedict's was predictably dark in color.

"Hot!" Alexander, now three years old, declared cheerily. "I like hot."

Belinda laughed and bent down to kiss him. His hair was soft brown. She wondered on occasion if it would darken to the black of his father's hair or stay the light colour of Mama's hair. Alexander beamed up at her, his brown eyes wide. His eyes were like Nancy's —not the black of Benedict's, and not green, though Benedict said they were almost hazel and so might become greener as he grew up. They both agreed his mouth was hers, and his nose. His eyes and chin were all Benedict's. He beamed at them, showing a dimple in his chin that neither of them had.

"Come on, young fellow," she said to him warmly. "We'd better go inside. We'll be spending long enough outdoors today."

"Outdoors! Playtime," Alexander insisted happily. Benedict bent down and lifted him up, making him whoop with delight.

"We'll have plenty of time to play, young man," Benedict told him, setting him down on his feet and then lifting him up again, holding him up overhead. "But now, we have to go inside and get some lemonade. You must be thirsty."

"Want to play!" Alexander told him, but he was laughing as his father held him in his arms and ran towards the house.

"It's a horse-race!" Benedict yelled. "We're winning!"

"Faster!" the boy yelled, and Belinda, laughing, walked briskly after them, feeling perspiration bead on her forehead in the hot sunshine. Rowan was bounding after them. He was always so gentle with the little boy that it moved Belinda greatly. He clearly understood the small human was not as robust as he himself was and needed caring for.

They walked up through the vast front doors. Payton House was much less imposing than her current home, but Belinda had become reconciled to living at the manor after four years—especially since Benedict had allowed her to have free rein with the gardens. She had enjoyed every second, and each year she spent weeks in the kitchen with the housekeeper and the head gardener, dreaming up new displays of blooms for each part of the garden.

Norendale Manor was always cool inside in summer—the windows faced mostly east, rather than directly south, and so they received cool morning sun and were shielded from the worst of the afternoon glare. She walked lightly across the front hallway and into the dining-room.

"Here, my dearest," Benedict said lightly, passing her a glass of cool lemonade. Belinda sipped it, appreciating its crisp sweetness and feeling cooler instantly.

"Me too!" Alexander insisted, and Belinda laughed.

"Here, young man," Benedict said, sitting Alexander—who had been supported by his left arm—in one of the dining room chairs. "This is for you." He poured a generous measure of lemonade into one of the small liqueur glasses. "But you have to drink all of it, mind you."

"Lots!" Alexander said excitedly, and lifted the little glass, holding it to his lips and drinking it back in one go.

Belinda chuckled to herself, seeing how thirsty the little boy had been. Benedict shared a warm smile. Rowan lay down on the mat, occasionally glancing at Alexander if the child giggled or

179

squealed; guarding him from all harm.

"The guests will arrive soon," Belinda commented, looking over at the big doors.

"They will," Benedict agreed.

"We'll wait here," Belinda suggested, and he nodded.

"It seems a fine idea," he added with a lift of the shoulders. "Nice and cool in here."

"Quite so," Belinda agreed, relieved to be in the cool space, which was tiled with marble and was beautifully cool in summertime.

They sat in the dining room for a few minutes, and then the butler appeared in the doorway.

"Your Graces?" he greeted them. "I apologise for the disturbance, but a carriage has arrived."

"Who is it?" Benedict asked, a small smile lifting the corner of his lips.

"It bears the insignia of House Eldridge."

Benedict grinned and Belinda felt a bubble of excitement rise inside her.

"Send them into the dining room, please," Benedict said at once and Belinda smiled over at him, seeing how his eyes sparkled.

A second later, the sound of feet in the hallway made Alexander look up from his contemplation of the tablecloth. He beamed a big grin as two tall people walked into the dining room, one red-haired and one black-haired.

"Nancy!" Benedict greeted his sister, wrapping her in a crushing hug. "Clinton."

Rowan ran to the two people, barking with delight, jumping at Nancy, who giggled and knelt to ruffle his ears.

"Rowan!" she said lovingly, hugging the huge dog firmly round his neck. "So good to see you, old chap."

"Benedict, old fellow," Clinton greeted Benedict warmly, cuffing him playfully on the shoulder. "It seems like an age."

"It's been a few months," Benedict said with a smile. "How do you fare?" He turned to Nancy, who smiled at him fondly.

"Well, brother," she said softly. "Very well."

Belinda smiled from Clinton to Nancy, inclining her head politely. "Welcome to you both," she said softly.

180

"Belinda! So good to see you." Nancy wrapped her in a hug and Belinda held her close. Nancy had become almost like a sister—though nobody could be anything like as close to her as Estelle was, of course. Still, she had grown to be very close to Benedict's younger sister. She smiled up at Clinton, who raised a brow.

"And I shan't be playing whist, Your Grace, before you ask," he said with a chuckle. "I am sure I would lose terribly, all the more so after two hours in the coach."

Belinda laughed. "Look, Alexander," she commented to her son, who was gazing up at Clinton, his pale brown eyes wide with interest. "It's your uncle, Clinton."

"Uncle! Uncle!" Alexander greeted him cheerily. "Pick me up."

Clinton—who was almost as tall as Benedict—laughed and, putting his hands around the small child's waist, lifted him up high over his head.

"Eek!" Alexander squealed, though it was a delighted yell as well as a little fearful. "Papa! Papa!"

Benedict—who had been talking to Nancy—turned and saw the little boy and went to Clinton, holding out his hands for Alexander.

"Where's my little fellow? Eh? Are you a little eagle, then, that you fly so?"

"Put me down!" Alexander squealed, and Benedict reached for the little boy and lifted him up, then set him down carefully on his feet on the floor again.

"There. Maybe Uncle Clinton will play with you with your new horse," he suggested.

"Horse!" Alexander was excited. He ran over to the fireplace, where, fortunately, the housekeeper had left his things lying in a small pile from where he'd been playing the previous day.

Clinton followed him to the fireplace and Belinda drifted over to watch Alexander play. Rowan had followed the child to the fireplace, and he settled down to watch him. Benedict and Nancy soon followed him. The four adults looked down fondly as the little boy made his wooden horse run around the marble tiles by the fireplace. Rowan gazed at the child for a moment, then shut his eyes to sleep.

"He needs someone to race," Clinton suggested, looking around. Belinda thought he might mean the Chinese figurine on the mantel, which depicted a man carrying two water-buckets and which was extremely costly, but fortunately he didn't, as he bent down to grab a toy coach from the pile. "He can race the coach-horses."

"I trust you had a pleasant journey?" Benedict asked Nancy. She nodded.

"Very pleasant, brother," she assured him. Belinda watched the two of them as they spoke. In the last four years, Nancy had blossomed from a shy seventeen-year-old girl to a beautiful young woman. Her face had softened a little, a delicate blush on her cheeks, her long black hair arranged in a soft chignon and covered with the briefest lace cap to indicate her married status.

Belinda glanced over at the fireplace, where Clinton and Alexander were still intent on their game. She smiled at Clinton.

"Shall we go outside?" she asked Nancy and Benedict. Clinton looked up at her with a smile.

"Outside! A capital notion. Eh? What do you say, you ambitious racer, you?"

"Outside!" Alexander declared excitedly. Belinda smiled to herself. She knew that the little boy liked nothing more than playing outdoors. He squealed as Clinton lifted him up, running with him to the door to the terrace.

"Let's go outside! I bet you a penny you won't find an acorn."

"Acorns!" Alexander yelled. Rowan bounded after them.

Benedict grinned at Belinda, and they all walked towards the doors. As they went through to the terrace, the butler appeared in the doorway.

"Your Graces? My lord? My lady? I apologise for the intrusion. But another coach has arrived in the drive."

"Oh?" Belinda beamed. She knew who that would be. "Please, show them in at once Mr. Holburne."

"Of course, my lady."

Belinda felt her stomach twist with excitement as the butler went off to invite in the guests. A minute or two later, walking slowly between the pillars around the outside door, Estelle and Jeremy appeared. Estelle was leading her little daughter, just a little over one year old, by the hand.

"Estelle!" Belinda declared, standing up from the chair and running over. "Lily!"

She bent down to her niece and smiled into her pale blue eyes. Lily beamed at her, and Belinda felt her heart fill with warmth. The little girl reminded her—for some strange reason—of their mother. Estelle bent down and lifted Lily up into her arms.

"Look, little one. Look who it is."

"Beenah." Lily greeted Belinda. She couldn't quite manage to pronounce Belinda's name yet, but Beenah was the name she had settled on and Belinda grinned at her. "Good day, Lily," she greeted her warmly. "How do you fare today?"

"Oof," Lily told her with a big smile.

"How are you? Are you hot after being in the coach?" Estelle asked the little child, who had Estelle's blue eyes and blonde hair, and Jeremy's mouth and chin.

"Hot!" Lily told Belinda and Estelle loudly, grinning.

"Oh, dear!" Belinda exclaimed theatrically. "You must have some lemonade, then. Does she need some lemonade?" she asked Estelle, who nodded.

"That would be very welcome, please," she agreed. She smiled at Belinda. "It's so wonderful to see you, sister."

"It's so wonderful to see you," Belinda told her warmly.

"Delighted," Jeremy said, bowing low.

Belinda smiled at him. She had always liked him, and he seemed exactly as he had when she first met him—kind, gentle and easy to like. He smiled at Estelle; his pale brown eyes full of tender love.

"Come, my dear," he said to Estelle gently. "You must need to sit down after such a long trip."

"I would like to take a seat out on the terrace," Estelle agreed. "It really was hot in the coach," she added to Belinda, who nodded.

"I can well believe it would be. It's a very hot day today."

"Quite so. Quite so," Jeremy agreed.

The picnic blankets were all laid out in the shade, but they settled on the terrace for a moment or two longer. Belinda gazed out over the garden, listening to the rise and fall of conversation and waiting for the next coach to arrive.

"Your Grace?" The butler made her jump as he spoke from close beside her. She had not noticed his arrival. "I apologise for the interruption," he said quickly. "But a coach has arrived."

"Please show the guests out to the terrace," she told him at once. She glanced at Benedict, who was seated opposite her, laughing at some amusing story Clinton told. He saw her looking and nodded as if he guessed what she was thinking. She could not wait to see the next guests.

She heard footsteps and looked up in delight as Mama and Papa appeared. She had not been sure they would be able to come—they had been busy in London, but she was delighted that they could be there. "Mama!" she exclaimed. "Papa!"

She stood to greet them, then frowned as two more people appeared in the hallway. Her heart leapt as she saw who it was.

"Lila!" She gasped, and she beamed at her friend, who arrived with Captain Pearson, a handsome guardsman she had recently married, by her side.

"Belinda." Lila reached for her and hugged her swiftly, then the tall captain was bowing low, and Belinda dropped a curtsey.

"Delighted, Your Grace," he murmured.

"I am so pleased you're here," Belinda said, gazing in bewilderment at Lila. "How is it that you are here?"

"Your parents," Lila said simply, and Belinda beamed at her mother, stepping forward to give her an embrace.

"Mama!" She welcomed her, feeling warmth flood her heart as she held her mother close and smelled the familiar floral perfume she wore. "It's grand to see you."

"And you, my dear," Mama said, her gaze soft. She glanced over at Benedict, who was holding Alexander on his knee and her eyes brightened as she gazed at the little boy. "And where is my dear grandson?"

"Grandma!" Alexander yelled, and wriggled off his father's knee, running to his grandmother. Rowan padded after him. Mama bent to hug him, holding him close.

"Good afternoon, young fellow," she murmured into his ear. "So grand to see you."

"Grandmama. Grandmama," Alexander said excitedly. "And Grandpa?"

"Here he is!" Belinda's father greeted the little boy, bending down and lifting him up, hugging him close. Belinda smiled, watching her parents with the little boy. He loved their visits to Payton House—especially the garden, where he played for hours on end, watched lovingly by Mama and Papa.

"We were going to visit your parents," Lila explained as they went to sit on the picnic rugs in the shade on the big lawn together. "But when we arrived, they explained they were going to call on you the next day, so they were busy arranging everything. Your mother instantly thought of the idea of me accompanying her. I thought it was a lovely idea," she added, smiling warmly at Lady Grayleigh.

"I'm glad that she thought of it," Belinda replied. She beamed at Mama. Mama inclined her head.

"It is pleasant to see old friends, and you are so rarely in London," she added, and Belinda inclined her head.

"I love it here in the countryside," she admitted.

Norendale Manor was situated further from London than Payton House was—a good three hours' ride at least. It felt as though they were deep in the countryside, and she loved it. She glanced over at Alexander, who was walking uncertainly towards Lily, who was in Estelle's arms.

"Look!" Estelle said to Lily warmly. "Look who it is. Your cousin. Alexander."

"Leksanda," Lily greeted him, using the closest version of the name she could pronounce. She grinned shyly at the older boy, who smiled at her warmly.

"Here. Do you want to go and greet him?" Estelle asked. "Or do you want to play?" Lily chuckled.

"Play!" Lily declared. It was one of the few words she never tired of using. Belinda grinned to herself. Lily had a small vocabulary, but one which was tailored to her needs. She watched as Estelle set Lily carefully down on her feet and Lily took a few halting steps towards Alexander.

"Lily?" Alexander greeted her inquiringly. "Do you want to play with Horsie?"

"Play!"

Belinda grinned to herself. The two children had played together ever since Lily could walk, and she trusted Alexander to be careful with his small cousin. He was a big child for his age, but he seemed to understand instinctually that Lily was smaller than him and he was always gentle and protective. She smiled to herself. He was like his father.

She gazed lovingly across the rug.

Benedict was sitting opposite her, in between Mama and Clinton. He had opened the picnic-basket and taken out a sandwich for Alexander—a small, neat one with no crusts—but the little boy was running on the lawn, holding out his hand for Lily, who was toddling with remarkable speed.

"Leksanda!" she yelled, running as fast as she could. Alexander waited for her to catch up, holding out his hand for her. They headed a few paces towards where Alexander's wooden horse lay on another picnic blanket. Clinton must have fetched it, Belinda thought absently, as the little boy showed his cousin the horse.

"Shall we begin the picnic?" Benedict asked their guests. Mama, sitting beside him, nodded appreciatively.

"We certainly should," she told Benedict, who laughed.

"Well, Lady Grayleigh, since it meets with your approval, we shall start."

Mama flapped a playful hand at Benedict, and he grinned. Belinda caught his eye, and they shared a smile. Benedict had been in the middle of opening the basket, but Belinda had distracted him for a moment. He blinked, seeming to recall what he had intended to do.

"Lemonade?" he asked, producing a bottle of their cook's special lemonade. It was, Belinda admitted to herself, not quite as good as the one the cook at Payton House produced, but then the lemonade at Payton House was particularly good.

"Please," Estelle murmured, accepting a glass from Benedict.

Belinda watched as Benedict poured lemonade for all their guests and held out her glass to him. He filled it up, his dark gaze holding hers.

She smiled at him and thanked him warmly.

"Lemonade!" Alexander yelled as Benedict was about to put the bottle away. "Thirsty."

Belinda grinned. "You drank a big cup of it just twenty minutes ago," she reminded him.

"Thirsty again," he insisted.

Belinda watched as Benedict poured Alexander another cup of the sugary beverage, and then poured another measure into a child-size glass for Lily.

"Thank you, Benedict," Estelle murmured, coming over to join them and holding the cup for Lily to drink.

Belinda leaned back where she sat on the rug, her head tipped back so that the warm sunshine shone full on her face. She kept her eyes shut and then shrieked in delight as a big wet canine tongue slathered over her face.

"Rowan!" she yelled. "You big, daft dear!"

"Woof!" Rowan said loudly, making her wince, since he barked just a few inches away from her ear. She drew him into her arms, burying her face in his soft, dusty-smelling fur.

"You dear creature," she said softly. She sat up again and ruffled his ears and he came to sit down beside her. When he and she were both sitting, he was taller than she was, his fluffy head an inch higher than hers. She put an arm around him, and he panted, making his big canine grin.

Alexander, who had been intent on a discussion with Clinton about the horse, saw Rowan and came running.

"Rowan! Rowan!" he yelled, throwing his arms around the big dog. Rowan flattened his ears at the sound but sat stoically and received the crushing hug from the three-year-old. Belinda smiled, her heart filled with love, as Rowan licked Alexander's face.

"Rowan!" Alexander shouted joyously. He laughed, and Belinda could have sworn Rowan was grinning back as the little child sat down beside him, just half the height of the graceful dog. Rowan had white in his muzzle here and there, though he was still very much in his prime. Belinda was grateful to him every day for his tireless care of Alexander—it was possible to leave the little boy unattended on the lawn with Rowan to guard him, as if anyone had approached the child and shown any sort of malicious intent, Rowan would certainly attack.

"Here, dearest," Benedict said from across the rug, passing Belinda a plate of cold pie. She smiled at him gratefully.

"Thank you, dear," she murmured, and reached over to the basket for a fork with which to eat it. Alexander received a slice of cold pie from his grandfather, who was managing remarkably well to help the little boy master the use of a knife and fork. Benedict had commissioned a silversmith to make a miniature knife and fork set for Alexander to learn with, and he was already managing remarkably well.

"There!" Papa declared as he watched over the small boy. "You're grand at this."

Alexander looked up lovingly at his grandfather and Belinda felt her heart twist with love so strong it was almost painful. She looked around the group of people—Estelle, Lily, Jeremy, Mama, Papa, Alexander, Lila and the captain, Nancy, Clinton, Rowan and of course Benedict—and she felt so much love for all of them that a lump formed in her throat.

This was her family—her dear, beloved, wonderful family. All of them meant the world to her and having them all at Norendale Manor at the same time was a blessing.

She leaned back and shut her eyes, feeling the sunshine pour warmly onto her face and a grin lifted her lips.

"Horses!" Lily declared and Belinda opened her eyes. She thought that the little girl meant the toy that Alexander and Clinton had been playing with, but then she saw that their groom was exercising two of the horses—Nightshadow and a mare, Firelight. The two beautiful creatures were trotting on the section of lawn by the stables, perhaps thirty or forty paces away behind a screen of trees. Every so often they would appear in view as the groom led them around the lawn.

"Yes. Horses!" Estelle exclaimed, smiling at Lily. "Do you want to go and see the horses?" She glanced at Benedict and then at Belinda. Belinda nodded.

"Of course, she can go and see the horses. Alexander would likely like to come with her," she noted, and glanced over at the little boy, who was staring at the horses, his eyes round and wide.

"Horses, Papa!" he declared, gazing at them. He turned his gaze to Benedict. "I want to ride."

Benedict glanced at Belinda. They had discussed a pony for Alexander so that he could learn, and they had already decided he would receive one for his birthday when he turned four.

"You will, young fellow," Benedict declared, reaching out to ruffle the boy's hair fondly. "But for the moment, you have to go up on Nightshadow with Papa holding you. Soon you'll be able to ride by yourself."

"When?" Alexander insisted, but Benedict just smiled.

"Soon," he informed him. "Now, do you want to go and see?"

"Yes!" Alexander declared, a big grin on his face.

Belinda glanced at their guests, who had mostly eaten their fill of pie and sandwiches and were sipping lemonade or sampling the sweet tarts that the cook had baked as a dessert course.

"If everyone would like to, we could all walk over to the stables," she suggested. "And then perhaps we could sit in the arbor, where there is shade."

"That sounds like a lovely idea," Mama said with a warm smile.

Belinda smiled at her appreciatively, and gradually people got off the rug and walked over to the stables. She walked beside Benedict, who was holding Alexander by the hand. Jeremy had lifted Lily onto his shoulders. They walked towards the stables.

"I received a letter," Benedict told her as they walked between the trees. "I will give it to you to read later."

"Thank you," Belinda said, frowning. Benedict was usually not cautious about what he said, and she guessed it was from his mother. She had retired to one of the Norendale country estates as soon as Belinda moved in and tended to stay aloof from family gatherings. Benedict had said that, in many respects, it was a good thing, since he and she had never been particularly close. Belinda accepted his words—in many respects, he did seem much happier now that his mother had settled in the countryside and was a good distance from them. Still, it troubled her now and again that Alexander did not know his paternal grandmother.

They reached the stable, where Alexander insisted on being held in Benedict's arms so that he could reach up and pat the horses, gently touching their velvet-soft noses. Benedict carried him through the stable, telling him the name of each horse, and Belinda walked slowly beside them, her heart filled with love as her son gravely listened and touched each horse with gentle respect. It had been important to both Benedict and her that he learned to appreciate and respect all living creatures.

When they settled in the arbor together, where Alexander contented himself by chasing grasshoppers on the lawn with Lily

189

under Estelle and Jeremy's loving gaze, Benedict handed her the letter.

Son, she read. I am writing to you to inform you that I will be sending a gift to Norendale Manor. The gift in question is rather large and has four legs and a considerable appetite. I will not be accompanying him—he is a pony from Highgate Estate, where Lord Gracefield has his home. I trust that my grandson, who I believe from accounts, in both your and Nancy's letters, to love horses, will find joy in the gift. I am still ensconced at Highgate, where Lord Gracefield and I spend the summer months. I will call on Nancy and Clinton briefly and mayhap we might meet in London for tea, if you would be amenable. Yours sincerely, Mother.

Belinda glanced over at Benedict. His face was very still but his eyes showed real warmth. Belinda swallowed hard. She had not realized how his mother's choice to vacate the manor hurt him. But she thought with a grin, it seemed to have had some unexpected results.

"Highgate Estate?"

Benedict grinned. "Mama met Lord Gracefield in London when he was there for the Season. They seem to be very well matched."

"That's wonderful." Belinda smiled warmly. She felt no animosity in her heart his mother, despite the woman's antagonism and cruelty towards herself. She was merely glad that the situation had resolved and that she could live peacefully here.

"It is," Benedict said softly. "I might call on her in London for coffee—especially if Nancy and Clinton will be there."

"Of course," Belinda agreed. She hesitated to offer to come—much as his mother had warmed, she still preferred to avoid her. Benedict smiled.

"Good," he said. "I'm glad."

"Of course," Belinda repeated warmly. She gazed down at the pond.

The arbor had been neglected when she had arrived, but she had arranged for the pond to be cleaned and pink lilies to be planted in it, the banks of the pond planted with ferns and irises. She gazed out over the water now, watching butterflies reflected in it as they flitted here and there about the roses that grew in the rest of the arbor.

"It's so beautiful," Benedict murmured. His gaze was on her and she felt her cheeks flush with warmth.

"It is beautiful," she agreed softly. Her heart filled with love as he reached out and took her hand. His large hands were warm, and she loved the feel of them—callused from riding—where they rested on her own.

"It is beautiful, and you are beautiful, my dear," he said softly, and kissed her on the lips, a quick kiss that nevertheless made her heart race with joy and longing.

"You're also rather pleasing," she teased, smiling up at him. He grinned.

"Thank you," he said with some irony. She leaned back on the bench, her heart flooded with love.

"Is it very hot out here?" Belinda asked, frowning at him.

"In the arbor? No. It's cool," Benedict said, his gaze narrowing with care. "Are you all right, dearest?"

"Yes. Yes, I'm quite all right," Belinda said, and a shy grin moved to her lips. "I suppose it must be my...my condition."

"Condition?" Benedict inquired, then his eyes widened as he began to understand. "You mean you...you..."

"I am expecting a child," Belinda said softly. "Another child."

"You are?" Benedict's grin was huge, lighting up his face. "Why, that's wonderful!" He beamed at her, his dark eyes sparkling, and rested his hand on her shoulder, staring into her eyes. "That's so wonderful."

"It is," Belinda said gently. "I wonder what Alexander will say?"

Benedict chuckled. "He'll be delighted. Look at him with Lily. If he had a brother or a sister to play with, he couldn't be happier."

"I think so too."

Benedict gazed into her eyes and then bent to kiss her, pressing his lips to hers. She wrapped her arms around him and held him close, shutting her eyes, losing herself in the warm leather-and-musk scent of him, the strength of his arms, the feel of his breath and heartbeat as she held him.

He sat back and smiled at her.

"Of course, I'm going to ask you if you need anything. A shawl, perhaps? Or to sit in the shade?" He smiled. "You'll need to accept me fussing about you a great deal."

Belinda chuckled. "I'm quite all right, dearest. Though a little fussing is welcome," she added, smiling up at him fondly.

He laughed.

They sat side by side and watched the butterflies flit across the pond and the bees buzzing drowsily from flower to flower and Belinda felt complete contentment fill her.

Benedict's hand tightened on hers and he smiled lovingly at her.

"I am so excited," he said softly. "And so happy. So very happy."

"Me too," Belinda replied. "I am so very happy."

"I love you," Benedict said in a quiet, intense tone.

"I love you too," Belinda murmured, gazing up at him. "So very much."

She wrapped her arm around him, and they sat and gazed out over the pond and Rowan came running up to find them. Estelle and Jeremy followed, with Alexander and Lily, and Belinda held out her arms to the big dog and then to the two children who ran at her.

"Auntie! Auntie!" Lily yelled. Belinda chuckled. That was a new word.

"Yes," she said, ruffling Lily's hair fondly. "I am your auntie."

"Woof!" said Rowan, who lay down beside her on the grass and rested his head on her knee.

Alexander clung to her, and she hugged him tight, smelling the soft newly washed scent of his hair. Benedict rested his hand on her shoulder, and she shut her eyes for a moment, her heart filled with happiness.

The End

Made in United States
Troutdale, OR
07/08/2024

21099507R00110